MRS. Claus and the VERY VICIOUS VALENTINE

LiZ IRELand

Kensington Publishing Corp.

kensingtonbooks.com

KENSINGTON BOOKS are published by
Kensington Publishing Corp.
900 Third Avenue
New York, NY 10022

All Kensington titles, imprints, and distributed lines are available at special quantity discounts for bulk purchases for sales promotion, premiums, fund-raising, educational, or institutional use.

This book is a work of fiction. Names, characters, businesses, organizations, places, events, and incidents either are the product of the author's imagination or are used fictitiously. Any resemblance to actual persons, living or dead, events, or locales is entirely coincidental.

To the extent that the image or images on the cover of this book depict a person or persons, such person or persons are merely models, and are not intended to portray any character or characters featured in the book.

Special book excerpts or customized printings can also be created to fit specific needs. For details, write or phone the office of the Kensington Sales Manager: Kensington Publishing Corp., 900 Third Avenue, New York, NY 10022. Attn. Sales Department. Phone: 1-800-221-2647.

Kensington and the Kensington cozies teapot logo Reg. U.S. Pat. & TM Off.

ISBN: 978-1-4967-4896-6 (ebook)

ISBN: 978-1-4967-4895-9

First Kensington Trade Paperback Printing: October 2025

10 9 8 7 6 5 4 3 2 1

Printed in the United States of America

The authorized representative in the EU for product safety and compliance is eucomply OU, Parnu mnt 139b-14, Apt 123 Tallinn, Berlin 11317, hello@eucompliancepartner.com

Praise for Liz Ireland and her Mrs. Claus mysteries!

Mrs. Claus and the Santaland Slayings

"An exceptional series launch. . . . This fun, well–plotted mystery is the perfect holiday entertainment."
—*Publishers Weekly* (Starred Review)

Mrs. Claus and the Halloween Homicide

"Brings the Christmas cozy to dizzying new heights of cuteness."
—*Kirkus Reviews*

"This is a wacky story with a bit of *Elf* meets *Nightmare Before Christmas* meets *Murder She Wrote*. It will definitely entertain readers during the HalloThankMas holiday season."
—*The Parkersburg News & Sentinel*

Mrs. Claus and the Evil Elves

"A fresh take on a Christmas cozy. It's a delightful mix of humor, technology, and murder in an unconventional mystery."
—*Library Journal*

"*Mrs. Claus and the Evil Elves* is the coziest of cozy mystery series, and well-worth a read for anyone wanting an extra touch of whimsy, seasonal or otherwise, with their whodunnits."
—*Criminal Element*

Mrs. Claus and the Trouble with Turkeys

"Readers of cozy mysteries will gobble up this seasonal novel with a fun plot and featuring naughty and nice humans, elves and reindeer." —*Toronto.com*

Mrs. Claus and the Nightmare Before New Year's

"April's efforts to protect Santaland's secret by pretending the magic place is actually part of Canada—for example, camouflaging the elves' pointy ears with a variety of scarves and hats and playing Anne Murray and Celine Dion songs instead of the usual Christmas tunes—have a certain zany charm." —*Kirkus Reviews*

Books by Liz Ireland

Mrs. Claus Mysteries

MRS. CLAUS AND THE SANTALAND SLAYINGS

MRS. CLAUS AND THE HALLOWEEN HOMICIDE

MRS. CLAUS AND THE EVIL ELVES

MRS. CLAUS AND THE TROUBLE WITH TURKEYS

MRS. CLAUS AND THE NIGHTMARE BEFORE
NEW YEAR'S

MRS. CLAUS AND THE VERY VICIOUS VALENTINE

Anthologies Featuring Mrs. Claus

HALLOWEEN CUPCAKE MURDER
(with Carlene O'Connor and Carol J. Perry)

IRISH MILKSHAKE MURDER
(with Carlene O'Connor and Peggy Ehrhart)

IRISH SODA BREAD MURDER
(with Carlene O'Connor and Peggy Ehrhart)

HALLOWEEN NIGHT MURDER
(with Leslie Meier and Lee Hollis)

Published by Kensington Publishing Corp.

Mrs. Claus and the Very Vicious Valentine

Chapter 1

"Ruffles suit mademoiselle."

Madame Neige made the declaration in her usual French cadence. How the North Pole's doyenne of dressmaking had acquired this exotic accent was a mystery to everyone in Santaland, but no one would dare question the no-nonsense elf in her black, immaculately tailored clothes. The formidable elf's austere gaze could shrivel a person's ego faster than a clothes dryer could shrink a wool sweater.

Her perfectly plucked, black eyebrows arched as she took in my friend Claire Emerson modeling her wedding dress. "But perhaps its effect would be better without zee cone of snow?"

Claire barely seemed to hear her. When Snappy's Snow Cones and Slushies opened as a food cart in Christmastown three months ago, Claire had been incensed to find a competitor to her ice cream business, the Santaland Scoop. Lately, however, the two proprietors seemed to have reached a rapprochement. Now Claire rarely seemed to go anywhere without a paper snow cone dripping in her hand, or slurping on a slushy.

Madame Neige eyed today's cherry red cone with disdain bordering on panic, as if the creamy white of Claire's wedding dress was in imminent peril.

As I took in my friend Claire in the wedding dress that Madame Neige and her harried assistants at the Order of Elven Seamstresses had created, I couldn't see that a few streaks of color would do too much damage. The explosion of ruffles on the otherwise slinky dress were . . . odd. Chiffon ruffles curled up the bias-cut, form-fitting white dress, culminating in a full ruff at her neck. The overall impression was half velvet negligee, half circus clown.

I glanced over at my fellow bridesmaids: our friend Juniper Greenleaf, and Dolly Frost, the groom's cousin. Both had glazed, blissful looks on their faces as they gazed upon the bride-to-be. Wedding fever had taken hold of their senses.

"Claire, you're so beautiful," Juniper gushed. For Valentine's Week, her curly locks had been newly styled into an updo piled on top of her head. "This is going to be the most gorgeous ceremony. And you know what they say: weddings beget more weddings."

It was clear Juniper hoped that would be the case. According to her, her current beau, Sterling Redwinkle, a fireman with the Santaland Fire Brigade, was *the one*.

There had been other *the ones* before, so I was trying to be supportive while maintaining my silent skepticism.

"Do you think Sterling will pop the question?" Dolly asked Juniper.

Juniper's cheeks reddened. "We'll see. I'm going to dinner at his mother's house tonight."

That answer threw me. "Would he propose in front of his mother?"

Juniper looked thoughtful. "I don't know. Her opinion means a lot to him. He's devoted to her."

"Sounds like he's having you over to see if you'll pass muster." Claire tipped her snow cone to slurp some of the icy sugar water from the tip, sending Madame Neige into a panic.

Madame snapped her fingers and an elf flitted in to drape a snowy white napkin around Claire's neck like a bib. Just in time, too. A blob of red blossomed on the white cloth. Claire didn't seem to notice.

The whole fitting had me flummoxed. Was I the only one who

thought Claire's dress was like something you'd see on the runway at Milan fashion week? The kind of dress you'd look at and think, *No one would ever wear that in real life.*

Yes, real life in Santaland still seemed surreal sometimes. In this magical realm, snowmen talked, reindeer flew, and elves . . . well, they were elves. But I couldn't imagine any reality in which Claire would think that dress was okay. We'd logged a lot of hours in dressing rooms during a decade of friendship that had taken us both from Cloudberry Bay, Oregon, to Christmastown, and never once had she expressed a desire to wear exploding clown ruffles. Yet here she was, staring at her reflection like someone hypnotized.

Actually, she didn't seem pleased so much as dazed. Like a body-snatched bride. Maybe Snappy was lacing those snow cones with something.

Come to think of it, maybe *I* needed one of those snow cones. Between bridesmaid duties and my job as judge of the first rounds of the Valentine's Tournament of Chocolate, an icy narcotic might be just what this week called for. The tournament was a four-night event—Night 1 was Nougats and Creams; Night 2, Nuts and Caramels; Night 3, Fudge; and Night 4, Brittles and Truffles—that culminated in a final competition the morning of Valentine's Day, to be judged by my husband, Nick.

Madame Neige turned to me. "What do you think of zee dress, madame?"

Why ask me? Because I was Mrs. Claus? Because I was Claire's maid of honor? Because Madame Neige's client, the actual bride-to-be, seemed hypnotized by an icy dessert?

I hitched my throat. "It's certainly different."

Okay, I know what you're thinking. *Mrs. Claus, you're a coward.* I'm not completely spineless, but until Claire weighed in, I couldn't be sure if criticism would be a friendship ender. Brides could get spiky about their dresses. Not to mention ruffled—literally, in this case.

Juniper sighed. "Exactly. It's so unique!"

"Dreamy," Dolly chimed in. "And marrying Jake would be a dream, so it's perfect."

Dolly had just moved to Christmastown from the Frost family home in the Farthest Frozen Reaches. Jake was one of the few social connections Dolly had in Christmastown, so Claire had felt obligated to ask her to be a member of the wedding party. The trouble was Dolly's weird fixation on Jake. She never failed to look dewy-eyed when she talked about him. And she was so over-the-top eager for this wedding, you'd be excused for thinking she herself was the bride.

At the moment, she seemed *more* enthusiastic than the bride.

Claire pivoted nonchalantly to eye the dress from a side angle, ignoring the red-stained bib. "I guess it works."

I couldn't stifle myself any longer. "Even with that ruff thing?"

Dolly gasped in shock. "I *love* the collar! And if anyone in Santaland can pull it off, Claire, it's you."

Madame Neige eyed me disdainfully over her round, black-rimmed glasses, before pivoting back to the bride. "Of course, if you've changed your mind and you want a typical, frothy wedding cake kind of dress, I'll send Blanchette to the office to bring some more traditional designs. *Those* we can have made in no time at all."

Blanchette, Madame Neige's second-in-command, tensed to dash off to do her mistress's bidding.

Claire waved a dismissive hand. "No, this is fine."

Since when was *fine* the standard for bridal gowns? The bar for saying yes to the dress was supposed to be a little higher than "meh, okay." In our younger days, I'd seen Claire spend longer picking out socks at Target.

"But do you love it?" I asked her.

"It's original." She frowned toward a little cooler sitting outside her dressing room. "Can somebody bring me the slushy I brought with me?"

Dolly was happy to oblige.

Satisfied that the main fitting was done, Madame Neige clapped her hands, and without further instruction, two assistant elf seamstresses grabbed the dress's slinky train and steered Claire back toward the dressing room.

"Now for our bridesmaids," Madame Neige announced. She turned to her assistant. "Blanchette, I leave them to you."

She turned and marched away. The founder of the Order of Elven Seamstresses, a fortress of the fabric arts, instilled a strange devotion in her apprentice elves. Some of them had joined her as teenagers and planned to spend their lifetimes here in this place that was equal parts house of haute couture, craft-centric convent, and sewing boot camp.

I felt a twinge of foreboding about my bridesmaid dress. I'd seen sketches, so I knew the design was perfect for a Valentine's wedding—red raw silk with velvet trim to complement the bridal gown's fabric. The question was whether I'd be able to fit into it.

My anxiety increased when the considerable muscle power of both Blanchette and another assistant, Snowbell, were required to zip up my back. I had to suck in my breath, my gut, and practically every corpuscle I possessed. Even so, I heard the poor elves grunting.

"I hope this dress has reinforced seams," I said.

Blanchette's Cupid's bow lips formed a moue as she stared at me in the mirror. "Those seams will have to be let out. Give me your tape measure, Snowbell."

Snowbell scrambled to unloop her tape measure, a common accessory around the necks of the assistants of the Order of Elven Seamstresses.

Before the underling could hand over the tape measure, however, Blanchette hopped back in horror. "Snowbell, you're bleeding!"

Snowbell looked down at her little hands and gasped. "I'm so sorry, Miss Blanchette—it must be from the roses. I was working on them all morning."

Because hothouse roses were difficult to come by at the North Pole, the seamstresses made an annual February ritual of fashioning artificial ones to supply florists for Valentine's Day. These roses appeared realistic right down to the dyed, dried rose stems that were used. Madame Neige even scented the buds with rose oil. It was time-consuming, painstaking work. And apparently could lead to thorn cuts.

Blanchette didn't show a lot of pity for the assistant's injury. "What if you had bled on the bride's dress?"

I didn't particularly want anyone bleeding on *my* dress, either. I dug in my bag for a moist towelette—essential for those of us prone to clumsiness. I offered it to Snowbell, who quickly wrapped it around her finger.

"Go find a real bandage," Blanchette ordered, her lips curling in disgust. "And be more careful."

"Yes, Miss Blanchette." Snowbell sent me an apologetic glance and scurried away.

Blanchette turned her attention back to me and my dress. Her lips didn't uncurl.

"The dress shouldn't be *this* tight," I said with the hiccup of air I'd managed to wheeze into my lungs.

"It was made exactly to the measurements we took in November."

November was one Christmas and several million calories ago.

"I usually lose a little weight after the holidays," I said, "but this year I'm judging the Valentine's Tournament of Chocolate."

Blanchette's perfectly plucked brows arched. "So you've been practicing?"

Ouch. The humor in her eyes made me laugh, though—as much as my bridesmaid sausage casing would allow. "When you know you're going to be consuming chocolate for a solid week, dietary fatalism sets in, you know?"

She nodded.

"If you just let it out an inch all over, it should work, right?"

Her lips twisted. "Madame has worked miracles before."

"Great." I backed toward the dressing room. "I'll just change back into my clothes."

"Not yet, Mrs. Claus. We must have a viewing." Blanchette had mastered her boss's brook-no-argument stare. Small wonder that it was rumored that Santaland's foremost couturier was grooming Blanchette to be Madame Neige's successor. Not that Madame Neige looked as if she was in danger of kicking off anytime soon.

I wheezed in more air and returned to the viewing room.

Juniper was pirouetting before the three-way mirror, admiring her dress. It was identical to mine, but she didn't resemble a plump mouse being strangled by a boa constrictor.

Her eyes shone in the mirror. "Don't you just love, love, love it?"

"Mmm," I responded thinly.

"I *love* it!" Dolly bounded out of her dressing room like a silk-and-velvet-clad golden retriever puppy. "We are going to make an awesome trio at Jake's wedding." She hurried over to stand between Juniper and me before the mirrors. "I think you both look fantastic! You *should* show off those curvy figures. You're not too old yet."

It was impossible to miss the flash in Juniper's eye—it was the same as mine. Between the two of us and the multiple mirrors, we created a funhouse exhibit of irritation.

Dolly blinked. "Did I say something wrong?"

Before I could answer, Snowbell rushed back in a flutter, holding a long, thin white box tied up with creamy pink ribbons. A white bandage was wound around her trigger finger. "Look what was left at the door," she said, breathless. "There was no name on it. It must be for one of our guests. A sticky note on it just had the words 'Wedding Party.'"

The box bore the green foil label of Flock and Ivy's, the biggest florist in Christmastown. From the expression on her face, Juniper noticed the green sticker at the same time I did. Looking as if she'd bitten into a raw cranberry, she poured herself a tall glass of sparkling wine that Madame Neige had left out for us.

Ivy, the co-owner of Flock and Ivy's, was currently going out with Juniper's ex, Smudge Candymint. Juniper and Smudge's on-again, off-again relationship had baffled me for years. It was currently off, and Juniper swore she'd found true love with Sterling Redwinkle. Judging from her reaction, though, maybe the past wasn't as deeply buried as she wanted us to believe.

Dolly snatched the slender box from Snowbell. "I bet it's a single rose. I've always read about those in books, though of course I've never received anything romantic like that myself. We don't even have roses where I come from."

Claire emerged from the dressing room, back in her own clothes, which today was her uniform of black jeans and a red turtleneck sweater with the Santaland Scoop logo on the front. Though she owned the Scoop, she was also there every day serving ice cream. Business was the only reason she would appear in public with a grinning ice cream cone across her chest.

She'd heard what Dolly said, and looked understandably bemused as she sipped her slushy through a candy-cane striped straw.

"I don't think that's for me," she said. "Jake's not a single-red-rose type."

A private detective, Jake Frost was the kind of guy who showed his affection by making sure his lady love's deadbolts functioned properly.

Juniper colored to the roots of her hair. "Maybe Sterling sent it to me. I told him we had a fitting today."

"I know it's not for me," Dolly said with an exaggerated pout. "I'm new here." She turned to me with bright eyes. "But maybe Santa sent it to April."

Every gaze in the room turned toward me. I'd also informed Nick that we were having a fitting today, but I didn't think for a moment that he would send me a rose—at least not until Valentine's Day itself. We'd been married for four years and loved each other as much now as we did the day we said "I do"—more, maybe—but spontaneous romantic gestures were already fewer and farther between.

When *was* the last time we'd done something fun, romantic, and spontaneous?

Juniper snapped her fingers to get my attention. "April, you've zoned out."

I shook my head. "Let's just open it and see if there's a card inside."

Dolly reached for the box, but Blanchette jerked it out of her grasp. "It was delivered to the Order, so I should open it."

Not *"Madame Neige should open it,"* I noticed.

She carried the box to a table and carefully untied the bow. Then she removed the lid and pulled the tissue paper aside, revealing the expected, perfect, fragrant rose—probably created right here before it was sold to Flock and Ivy's. But on top of the rose lay a piece of white paper with a message written in red marker, made to look like dripping blood.

Violets are blue,
Roses are red,
Surprise, surprise,
Someone wants you dead.

Chapter 2

Surprise didn't begin to describe it. We all gaped at the message in full-blown shock.

Taking in the expressions around me, I discerned the same silent calculation in each face: *Could someone want* me *dead?*

Dolly was the first to speak. "It can't be me. I'm new here. I barely know anyone except Jake—and you three."

"I sell ice cream," Claire said, as if that fact exempted her from being a target.

I sort of agreed with her. Surely no one would want to kill the sole ice cream maker in Santaland. Who didn't like ice cream? Snappy, the sno-cone and slushy maker, was a rival—but presumably that tension had been resolved now that Claire was his best customer.

"Maybe someone wants to kill April," Dolly suggested.

Juniper shook her head. "Golly doodle, that makes no sense. She's Mrs. Claus. April is very popular here."

Juniper was a loyal friend and tended to wear rose-colored glasses with people she loved. I'd probably made an enemy or two during my years in Santaland. For one thing, I'd helped Constable Crinkles collar a few naughty elves. And some of my own in-laws were none too fond of me. The arctic chill between my mother-in-law, Pamela, and me had never completely thawed. But we weren't at a poison-pen level of conflict.

"I know," Dolly continued. "Someone's probably jealous of Claire. I bet all sorts of elves were in love with Jake before she came along."

"I can't think of anybody," I said.

Juniper agreed. "Jake was always a loner."

"He never mentioned any ex-girlfriends or unrequited crushes to me," Claire confirmed.

Dolly's complexion turned a little redder. "Jake never mentioned anybody close to him back in the Farthest Frozen Reaches?"

Juniper, Claire, and I shook our heads.

While we were talking, Blanchette had been investigating the handiwork of the artificial rose. "This rose is *not* one of ours," she said. "The handiwork is shoddy. The petals are already becoming unstuck from the stem."

I picked up the box and investigated it. "Snowbell said that there was a sticky note attached to the box," I said. "Where is it?"

Snowbell scurried forward and pulled the note out of her uniform smock's pocket. The yellow note did indeed have the words *Wedding Party* written on it, but the deep blue, almost purple ink was smeared—almost as drippy looking as the red words in that poem.

"What smeared the writing?" I asked.

"It's snowing outside, ma'am," Snowbell said, still breathless. She wasn't used to being the center of attention. "Button, the elf minding the door, said that it must have been put there after you all arrived, or else she would have seen it when she let you in. But no one rang the bell."

I considered the blurred words again. The two words had been fashioned to look like the letters in a first-grade handwriting primer, with perfect round printing. No one wrote like that. "The handwriting won't be much use to us."

"Use as what?" Blanchette asked.

"As a clue to who left it," I said. "But the blue ink might be helpful."

Snowbell frowned at the note.

"Is something wrong?" I asked.

She shook her head. "No, ma'am."

"The box is from Flock and Ivy's florist." Blanchette nodded at the label.

Juniper paled, no doubt thinking of Smudge's new love interest. Would Ivy have done such an unhinged thing? "That could be just a coincidence, couldn't it? There aren't many florists in Christmastown. The person who sent this probably just had one of their boxes around . . ."

I chewed my lip in thought. "Even so, I think we need to have a word with Ivy."

"Yes, I think you should," Blanchette said with a nod. "And I need to let Madame know that this terrible thing has happened here. She will not be pleased."

I was ready to dash right over to Flock and Ivy's. Unfortunately, my transportation wasn't. When we all trooped out to where I'd parked outside the Order of Elven Seamstresses, my sleigh was sitting where I'd left it, but Cannonball, the reindeer who'd pulled us here, had slipped his harness. For a reindeer of Cannonball's roly-poly size, wriggling out of a harness was no small feat.

The Order of Elven Seamstresses was housed in a mansion a half mile up Sugarplum Mountain's winding snow path, just below where Kringle Heights began. The Christmas Tree Forest, which threaded through Santaland like a giant green ribbon, skirted the edge of the property. The evergreen branches were almost disguised by new snow, a little of which was falling now. It was bitter cold. Not a good day for sleigh trouble.

Claire gave the empty harness in the snow a deadpan stare. "Looks as if your reindeer's been raptured."

"Cannonball's been acting flaky lately," I said. "I don't know what's going on."

"It's Valentine's Week," Juniper said. "The reindeer have their big All-Herd Muzzle Nuzzle coming up."

"Love is in the air for everybody," Dolly said wistfully. "Except for me, of course."

"I don't see why a reindeer social that's four days away means we have to walk today," Claire grumbled. "It's cold."

Said the woman who'd been sucking on ice all morning.

Not that I didn't feel a little annoyance, too. Cannonball was susceptible to crushes, but he'd never abandoned me because of one before. Luckily, my sleigh was a hybrid that worked on both battery and reindeer power.

"Hold on," I told my companions. "I just need to put the harness away and fire up the motor."

Hopefully it was juiced up enough to get us downtown.

At that moment, though, the jangling harness of the Sugarplum Mountain sleigh bus reached our ears. Claire was already backing away. "Actually, April, I *really* need to get back to the Scoop. I'm going to hop on the bus."

We'd run out of power on a trip to Tinkertown recently. Clearly I hadn't yet earned back her trust.

"And I need to hurry back to the library," Juniper said, joining her.

I suspected Juniper didn't want to be with me when I talked to Ivy. I could see how it might be awkward for her.

That left Dolly and me.

"Good thing *I* don't have a job to go to," Dolly said brightly. "I'll be able to tag along with you."

"Great." I tried to inject a little enthusiasm into my voice. Dolly wasn't my favorite elf in the world, although I couldn't put my finger on why. She was perfectly nice. And chipper. Almost too chipper—while at the same time devotedly self-centered.

That was an ungenerous thought. Dolly was a newcomer to Christmastown. Of course she was focused on her own life and making friends. I took in her sunny smile and the bright new red coat she was wearing. She'd been quickly replacing the dark colors and homespun fabrics of the Farthest Frozen Reaches with the eye-popping color palette of Santalanders.

My sleigh's battery was at fifty percent, which would get us back into town, no problem. Claire was such a coward.

"Do you really think Ivy the florist could have sent the rose?" Dolly asked when we were gliding down the snow path into town.

I gave it a little thought. "It seems too obvious."

Her forehead wrinkled below the knit brim of her heavy winter cap. Say what you will about the icy climate of the Farthest Frozen Reaches, it gave the elves up there the impetus to learn how to triple knit.

"But what if that's why she thought she could get away with it?" Dolly said. "Because we would naturally think it would be *too* obvious for someone to send something like that with her store logo on it. The old double fake."

"We'll know more after we've talked to her."

"Unless she's a liar," Dolly said. "Lots of criminals can lie to your face as easily as they breathe."

I looked away from the snow path for a moment to glance at her. "You have experience with criminals?"

"There are *lots* of dodgy elves where I come from."

True enough. The vast, inhospitable Farthest Frozen Reaches was Santaland's repository for elves who committed crimes—everything from candy cane theft to elficide.

"Detective expertise is probably in my blood," Dolly continued. "I'm a Frost, after all. When I was younger, I dreamed that Jake would take me on as his partner." She sighed. "I used to have the biggest crush on him."

Used to?

"Jake's a lot older than you," I said.

Truth be told, I had no idea how old he actually was. I wasn't sure Claire did, either. Jake Frost was an enigma. A smidge of that personality seemed to be rubbing off on Claire. Something seemed to be going on with my friend, but she wasn't telling me what it was.

Sleepwalking through dress fittings wasn't the only clue that something was wrong. Claire was ceding important decisions about her wedding not only to Madame Neige, but also to my mother-in-law, Pamela. Nick's mother wanted the wedding to take place at Castle Kringle, which I'd thought was a nice gesture to my friend.

But once Claire had said yes, Pamela had taken the bit between her teeth with bridezilla zeal.

And so far, Claire had been going along with each suggestion as if none of it mattered to her. I'd seen her nodding along to Pamela's every idea, from cake flavors I knew she didn't actually like for the wedding cake, to over-the-top decorations, to a harp septet for the day's entertainment. Who even knew Santaland had seven harpists?

I wasn't used to seeing Claire be passive. Here was a woman who'd taken it upon herself to close her successful ice cream shop in Oregon and resettle at the North Pole on the basis of getting to know Jake during a single two-week vacation. She wasn't someone who just let life—or large weddings—just happen to her.

Something was distracting her, but so far she hadn't opened up to me about it.

"To me, Jake is ageless," Dolly rhapsodized on. "If I were about to marry Jake, I'd be on Cloud Nine."

She was giving off such crazy vibes, I was starting to worry that *she* was the poison-pen writer. It was a relief when we reached Flock and Ivy's.

After parking the sleigh, I decided to lay down some ground rules. "When we go inside, let me do the talking," I said. "We're not trying to be confrontational."

"Of course—you don't want to tip off the lunatic that you're on to her."

"Ivy might have nothing to do with this."

Her face set in a frown as she hopped off the sleigh. "Juniper obviously thinks it was her. I could tell by the look on her face when she spotted that florist box label."

"We don't know what Juniper thinks. There's no reason why there should be any animosity between Ivy and Juniper."

"Ivy is involved with Juniper's ex-beau," Dolly said.

"I know, but both Juniper and Smudge have moved on. Jealousy shouldn't be a factor."

"If you say so . . ."

"Hello, Mrs. Claus." At first I didn't see where the friendly if slightly lugubrious greeting had come from. Then I noticed a familiar bowler-wearing snowman positioned a few feet away from the entrance to the florist's.

"Hi, Bumble," I said.

He stood next to a sign reading *HAPPY VALENTINE'S DAY! GIVE A LITTLE—RECEIVE A SNOWMAN HUG!* A donation jar sat atop the stand the placard was leaning against.

"What's this for?" I asked.

The snowman eyed me eagerly, as if he knew he'd found an easy mark. "Donations benefit the Santaland Snowman Mobile Support Unit."

That was a worthy cause. Snowmen in Santaland usually had long lives, but sometimes they came to grief. They could get stuck in snowdrifts, buried in blizzards, and knocked over by branches, to name just a few problems. Most could be rescued if reached in time. Although rerolling a snowman was not without risks, the only certain snowman death was a complete meltdown.

I reached into my purse but realized I didn't have any change. "I left my coin purse at home."

"Oh well," he said in his sad, stuffy voice. "Next time . . ."

His voice reminded me of Eeyore, my favorite Pooh character. Somehow that made me feel worse for letting him down.

Dolly and I continued into the florist's. Flock and Ivy's wasn't doing anything by halves when it came to Valentine's Day. The place was deluged with hearts—hearts in satin, Ivy hearts, hearts fashioned from colorful ribbons. The store was a riot of red and pink, and the air was perfumed with the scent of cut flowers and potpourri.

"Mrs. Claus!"

An elf in bright green and red hurried toward us as soon as the bell above the door tinkled its greeting. Flock the florist smiled at me eagerly. Castle Kringle was one of the shop's best customers—especially this week. My mother-in-law was relying heavily on Flock and Ivy's to provide decorative arrangements for Claire's wedding at the castle.

"How can I help you today?" he asked.

"I was actually hoping to speak to Ivy." I didn't see her, but there was a workroom in the back.

A little of the eagerness slid from Flock's expression.

"But it doesn't matter, does it?" Dolly piped up. "We don't know who made the threat. It might have been Flock."

What happened to letting me do the talking?

"You *are* Flock, I assume?" she persisted.

"Yes . . ." He cocked his head in confusion. "Threat?"

I lifted a hand to intervene. "We aren't sure—"

"What else would you call a venomous poem inside a box sent from *this store*?" Dolly crossed her arms. "It was supposed to be anonymous, but it's as obvious as an avalanche that it must have come from either you or Ivy. The only question I have left is, who do you want dead?"

Flock stared at us, dumbfounded. And defensive.

Way to go, Dolly. I shot her a look.

Dolly feigned innocence. Or maybe she actually didn't understand how ham-fisted her approach was.

A rustling in the workroom doorway heralded Ivy's arrival. The elf's delicate features were a stark contrast to her personal style— black hair cut in a blunt, angled bob. She wore sturdy coveralls with a Flock and Ivy smock apron over them. Her only makeup was a slash of dark red lipstick. There was an unthinking stylishness about her I couldn't help admiring.

"What's going on, Flock?" she asked.

The store's coproprietor sputtered in confusion. "Mrs. Claus says I threatened to murder someone."

"Wait—no." I shook my head. "That's *not* what I said. We just need to ask you some questions."

Before Dolly could interrupt and do more damage, I told the florists about the package that had been delivered anonymously at the Order of Elven Seamstresses in a box from their business.

They traded looks I couldn't read.

"*Nothing* was sent from the store to the Order of Elven Seamstresses today," Ivy said flatly. "I would remember a single rose with a threatening poem. That's weird."

"And frightening," Flock added.

"Maybe the threat was put in *after* it left the store," Dolly said. "Who's your delivery elf?"

"His name is Flit," Flock said. "He runs Flit's Messenger and Delivery service."

"But Flit's a good elf, very conscientious," Ivy insisted. "He wouldn't have had anything to do with the threat you're describing."

"Just like *you* wouldn't pack a threatening flower and seal it in a box with a sticker from this store?" Dolly turned to me and added in a stagey aside, "*So* many elves have reasons why they couldn't have done this thing, but where's the proof of their innocence?"

Good grief. She made it sound as if we'd talked to half the town.

"Usually you're supposed to find proof of guilt," I told her.

Dolly grumbled, "Well, if you're going to get nitpicky, we'll never track down this evildoer."

"Evildoer?" Ivy repeated in disgust.

Flock tapped his fingers together nervously.

I cleared my throat and turned my attention back to the proprietors. "I just wanted to know if a package like the one I described went out today."

"You heard Ivy—the answer is no," Flock said. "Not to Madame Neige and the Order."

"What about to your other customers?"

"What our customers order is confidential," Ivy said, growing more defensive now. "None of them have asked us to include a threat—we would never agree to that, anyway. It's ridiculous that I even need to state that."

"Hmph," Dolly said.

The sound brought an exasperated response from Ivy and Flock. I thanked them and tugged Dolly out of there. She'd done enough damage for one day.

Back at the sleigh, my frustration bubbled over. "You were supposed to leave the conversation to me," I reminded her.

"*Someone* had to take charge. You were just standing there like a bump on a pickle."

"I was trying to use finesse, because I know these elves. You're new here, remember?"

She lifted her pointy chin. "Maybe that gives me a fresh perspective. In my opinion, those two"—she tossed a disdainful glance back at the florist shop—"are definitely up to something."

"Yes—trying to run a business during one of their busiest weeks," I said.

"I wouldn't trust them any farther than I could throw a walrus," she said dismissively as she climbed onto the sleigh. Then she turned a bright smile on me. "Can you give me a ride to Jake's?"

Dolly was staying in Jake's spare room until she found a permanent place of her own.

Reluctantly, I steered the sleigh into the street.

"I can't wait to tell Jake all about this," she said. "I really think I might be a very clever detective." She leaned back and gushed out a satisfied sigh. "I wonder if he wants a new partner."

I glanced sharply at her.

She blinked at me, all innocence. "In his detective business, I mean."

Chapter 3

After dropping off Dolly, I headed home. On my drive back up the mountain to Castle Kringle, I overtook Cannonball on the snow-path.

He stopped in surprise as I pulled alongside him. "Oh, Mrs. Claus—there you are!"

As if *I* was the one who'd disappeared.

"What happened to you?" I asked.

"I saw a reindeer in distress and decided to help her."

Her, I noted. "That was good of you. What was the problem?"

Cannonball dipped his head. "Er, well . . . she was walking down the mountain alone."

"Uh-huh." Walking down Sugarplum Mountain didn't exactly make her a doe in distress.

"I thought she was lost," he added quickly, "so I escorted her back to her herd."

I decided to drop it. He'd obviously taken a fancy to this reindeer, and my transportation situation had worked out fine. "No harm done. I had plenty of battery power—there's even enough to spare to get me back up the mountain."

He brightened. "Really? Then you won't mind if I go check up on Flouncy."

"Flouncy?"

"The reindeer I helped today."

Hadn't he just left her? "You said she was back with her herd."

"She is—I just want to double-check that she's not lame from her long walk. I could swear she was limping slightly."

It was hard to imagine that a simple walk down Sugarplum Mountain could make a healthy reindeer go lame. But what could I say? I'd just admitted that my sleigh still had plenty of juice left to get me up to Castle Kringle. I didn't want to stand in the way of true love.

"Okay," I said. "I probably won't need you for the rest of the day."

"And if you do need a reindeer, there's always Wobbler. He's been goofing off lately, if you ask me," Cannonball grumbled.

"I hadn't noticed." For instance, I hadn't noticed Wobbler ditching *his* harness and taking off without a word.

But it turned out that I was talking to air. Cannonball was already fast-trotting away.

The ways of reindeer were still hard for me to fathom.

Salty, the groundskeeper of Castle Kringle, met my sleigh when I pulled up to the castle's portico.

"What happened to Cannonball?" he asked.

"He wanted to check on a reindeer he met today."

His mouth turned down. "Flouncy?"

Okay, maybe he *hadn't* just met her today.

"He and Wobbler have both gone cuckoo for that reindeer," Salty said. "She's stringing them along as surely as she had them in double harness."

"Both of them?" That didn't sound good. "She must be some reindeer."

Salty lowered his voice. "One of the Vixen herd. They have a reputation."

I swear, Christmastown could be as judgy as *Peyton Place*. "Apparently love is in the air, even for reindeer."

"It's that Muzzle Nuzzle. There's always trouble. Some years it turns into a Muzzle Melee."

I tried to look on the bright side. "Maybe this mania for Flouncy is just a Valentine's Week fancy."

The elf's lips turned down. "Let's hope that fancy doesn't turn fatal."

I found my mother-in-law, Pamela, in the castle's large family salon, studying her seating chart for Claire's wedding. Her round glasses were perched on the edge of her nose as she hovered over the poster-board diagram of the castle's great dining room. For some reason, a second poster board had appeared since I'd left the castle just after breakfast. There was barely enough room on the low coffee table for the tea service, which contained a pot, several cups, and a small tiered tray of goodies. Those scrumptious offerings were a welcome sight.

"What's this?" I asked, pointing to the second poster board.

"It's the overflow dining room. I thought we could set up several long tables in the Old Keep."

"How many guests are you expecting?" I confess I hadn't been paying attention to too many wedding details. From the grumblings of Jingles, the castle's head steward, I'd figured the guest list had ballooned a lot, but I hadn't realized it was going to require an extra banquet room.

Paula squinted through her bifocals at a notepad at her elbow, then flipped the page. "We've had five hundred and forty-three yes RSVPs."

"Five hundred and forty-three!"

She clucked. "I know. Uneven numbers are such a problem."

That wasn't what shocked me. "Did Claire invite all these people and elves?"

She pursed her lips. "Naturally, as hosts, the castle has some latitude in the guest list."

Translation: Pamela had commandeered the guest list.

"Did Claire agree to having so many?"

"What's there to agree to?" Pamela responded blithely. "Every bride loves a big wedding. I don't like to bother her with every little detail."

Five hundred forty-three guests were a little detail? Maybe this was why Claire seemed so quietly freaked out. When she and Jake decided to get married, I doubt she imagined half of Santaland in attendance.

I didn't know what to say. "You didn't invite that many people and elves when Nick and I got married."

She looked back down at her chart. "Well, no. *That* wasn't an occasion to get carried away over."

I tried not to take offense. The year Nick and I got married, his elder brother Chris—the former Santa—had recently died, and the family had been mourning his sudden passing. No one had been in the mood for merriment.

Still . . . 543. How would they all fit?

"Doesn't shunting half the guest list into another wing pose a bit of a problem? The Old Keep's not in the best shape. The ceiling collapsed in there once."

She dismissed this worry with a wave of her hand. "That was over fifty years ago. I've got some elves in there now shoring up the diciest-looking support beams."

I made a mental note to ask Nick about the advisability of this—and to make sure we got a seat in the main hall. I eyed those charts with more interest now.

"I thought we could swag bunting around the Old Keep in this color." With a flourish, Pamela unraveled some ribbon from a plate-sized spool. "What do you think?"

The color gave me a start. It was creamy beige with more than a hint of pink.

"What's the matter?" Pamela eyed it more critically. "Too pink?"

"Did you get that ribbon from Flood and Ivy?"

"Of course. I've hired them to do all the floral arrangements and decorative swags."

"I saw that ribbon earlier today on a package containing a poison-pen letter."

"You mean a threat?" Nick asked from behind us.

I turned. Even though we'd been married four years now, my

heart still skipped a blub-dub when I caught sight of Nick. He was tall, with a dark beard just starting to show flecks of gray. His broad shoulders topped a physique that was more fit than the Santa ideal. Not that I was complaining.

Beneath his furrowed brow, Nick's brown eyes appeared troubled. He'd entered the room just in time to hear the last of our conversation about poison-pen letters.

Pamela immediately started preparing a plate for him from the tea tray. It was testament to my distracted mental state that I hadn't grabbed any food yet.

Nick settled on the couch next to me. I eased closer and filled him and Pamela in on what had happened at the Order of Elven Seamstresses. From his plate, I grabbed a Linzer cookie in the shape of a heart. Hearts were ubiquitous now.

"How could such a thing happen right here at the North Pole?" Pamela asked.

"The package was left on the doorstep." A thought suddenly occurred to me. "I wonder if Madame Neige has security cams."

Nick and his mother blinked at me.

"Security what?" Nick asked.

Come to think of it, I'd never seen a security cam in Santaland. The closest thing we had to official surveillance were snowmen. They didn't move much, which made them natural spies.

Unfortunately, I hadn't spotted any snowmen positioned outside the Order of Elven Seamstresses that morning.

He looked over the goodie plate and chose a white-chocolate scone. No heart-shaped cookie for him, I couldn't help noting. "That letter is very disturbing."

The castle steward, Jingles, glided silently into the room. His sudden appearance startled me. Part elf, part human, he was taller than most of the staff at Castle Kringle, but some of his stature also came from his assumption of authority. Even now, his gloved hands folded calmly over the slight paunch of his middle, Jingles seemed to look at us all as if we were his slightly exasperating charges.

"Excuse me, Mrs. Claus," he said—to Pamela, not me. Technically, she was the Dowager Mrs. Claus, but he couldn't very well use that title when addressing her directly.

"Yes, Jingles?" She was still absorbed in her charts.

"I hesitate to bring these little problems to you when I know you're so busy, but with the wedding just days away . . ."

At the mention of the wedding in conjunction with "problems," Pamela was all ears. "What's the matter?"

"The Angelica Harp Septet is a harp short."

"Oh dear." She turned to the rest of us. "That's the group that's going to play during the ceremony and the wedding supper." She made a fretful noise. "What happened to the seventh harp?"

"It fell off a truck and broke. The group is trying to source another concert grand pedal harp, but they aren't easy to come by."

"Could they extemporize and become a sextet?" She sighed. "Although I did so have my heart set on the larger group. 'The Wedding March' played on seven harps is something you never forget."

"I can imagine," Nick said, exchanging a smile with me.

Jingles made a note on a clipboard he carried. "I'll suggest shaving off a harpist as an alternative if they can't get their hands on another instrument."

"You mentioned other problems," Pamela said. "What's happened?"

"The crystal situation is reaching a crisis," Jingles replied. "We're fifty-seven goblets short."

She hopped to her feet, tutting. "Goodness gracious! It slipped my mind. We'll have to see if Mildred Claus has any to spare—she inherited some really fine crystal, which you'd never guess because she always uses her ticky-tacky glassware."

When they were gone, I looked over at Nick. He was wearing his everyday Santa wear—a red jacket and red wool pants tucked into black boots. His familiar piney aftershave made me scooch a little closer to him on the couch.

"Do you think the poison-pen message was for Claire?" he asked.

I'd been wondering about that. "It was her fitting. Who else could it have been for?"

"The bridesmaids."

I remembered the words "Wedding Party" written on the note accompanying the long rose box.

"No one's ever jealous of bridesmaids," I said. "No one in their right mind, at least."

"Anyone sending poison-pen letters has a screw loose," Nick pointed out.

I thought about Ivy. She certainly hadn't seemed deranged today. And why should *she* be jealous of Juniper? Ivy was dating Smudge, Juniper's ex, but if Juniper didn't feel any jealousy about that, why should Ivy?

"Who knows?" I said. "Maybe the letter was directed at me."

Nick drew back. "Why?"

I took his arm playfully. "You never considered that there might be someone out there with a hopeless Santa fetish who would like to get me out of the way?"

"No, and if it did cross my mind I wouldn't find anything amusing about it."

"You're right." I drew back, assuming a sober expression to match his. "Just because something's ridiculous doesn't mean it's a laughing matter."

He angled a skeptical look at me. "Is that supposed to be funny?"

"Absolutely not."

We looked at each other and then both broke up at the same time.

When I was done laughing, I reached for another cookie. As long as the seams were being let out . . .

"Hopefully whoever it was got the venom out of their system with that letter," Nick said.

I pondered the situation as I chewed my cookie. How would I feel if a crazed elf was after my husband?

"Why bother to send a poison-pen letter and not make it obvious who the target is?" he wondered aloud.

"Maybe when they planned it, they thought it would be obvious."

He nodded. "Because it was Claire's wedding, Claire's fitting. Claire had to be the target."

But who would hate Claire? I remembered how subdued she'd appeared today. Did she know more than she was saying? We'd been friends for over a decade. I couldn't imagine her not telling me if someone was trying to kill her.

Or maybe it wasn't a crazed bridal stalker she'd been thinking about. Maybe it was those 543 guests.

"Do you ever wish we'd had a bigger wedding?" I asked Nick.

The change of subject surprised him. "The thought's never crossed my mind. Wasn't our wedding enough?"

I shrugged. "Your mom really seems to enjoy planning Claire's big day. It reminded me that ours was very low-key."

"Our wedding was fine," he said. "Got the job done."

My lips twisted. Nick had never been a lover of pomp. It had taken a couple of years after his brother died for him to grow comfortable with assuming the mantle of Santa and being the figurehead of Santaland. Now the ceremonial role seemed so second nature to him, I sometimes forgot that it was a constant stretch for him. Naturally he wouldn't have relished a huge wedding.

Calling our marriage "the job" wasn't exactly flattering, though.

"I'm going to ask Constable Crinkles to get to the bottom of that letter," Nick said.

Constable Crinkles and his deputy, Ollie, were the law enforcement in Santaland. I didn't rate their investigative prowess up there with Eliot Ness's or Matt Dillon's. Their success rate at catching criminals was roughly the same as Wile E. Coyote's at catching the Road Runner.

"The only thing I would depend on Crinkles getting to the bottom of would be a bag of gumdrops," I said.

Nick laughed, then stood up, wrapping a scone in a napkin. "I need to get back to work," he announced.

I nodded, resigned now to the fact that I was married to a workaholic Santa.

That evening progressed like every other. Jingles and I worked on the gift boxes for the winners of the Tournament of Chocolate. Then we had dinner with the family, and afterward I read an Agatha Christie while Nick finished his work for the day. Before I slid sleepily under the bedcovers, I received a text from Madame Neige.

Your alterations, they are done. Please be here for a final fitting at your earliest convenience. I will expect you tomorrow morning.

My lips turned into a frown. "Your earliest convenience" was evidently something Madame Neige decided for people. I didn't relish the discomfort of staring at myself in those unforgiving three-way mirrors again, especially under Blanchette's critical gaze.

In retrospect, though, how nice it would have been if a little discomfort had been the worst outcome of that unfortunate fitting.

Chapter 4

"Here we are again," Dolly said, practically dancing with enthusiasm. "Isn't this fun?"

We were back at the Order of Elven Seamstresses under the hawk-sharp eyes of Madame Neige and Blanchette, her mini-me.

"What are you doing here?" I asked Dolly. "They didn't make any alterations to your dress, did they?"

"No, but Claire told me she was coming in to try on her veil. I didn't want to miss out."

As if on cue, Claire emerged from a dressing room. Her veil was unlike any I'd ever seen. The great piece of tulle draped over her head like a semitransparent tablecloth that dipped down to her waist in front and down to her knees in the back. The fabric was lined with the same ruffle as her dress.

Dolly exclaimed, "That is *stunning*!"

"What do you think, Madame Claus?" Madame Neige asked me.

I was stunned, all right. The veil looked like a shroud. Claire was giving off ghost vibes. "It's   ."

Thankfully, I was saved from making any pronouncement when Juniper emerged from the adjacent dressing room. "Merciful muffins, Claire!" she exclaimed. "Is that your wedding veil?"

She and I exchanged glances. *Ghost vibes.*

Dolly obviously saw nothing wrong with the specter-like appearance of the bride-to-be. She gushed, "Makes me wish *I* were getting married."

Juniper bit her lip. She was definitely less effusive than she'd been yesterday.

In fact, a lot about her had changed overnight.

Dolly noticed, too. "Your hair looks different today," she said.

"I got it styled yesterday because I was going out last night," Juniper said. "I don't know why I bothered. This morning I just brushed it out."

Uh-oh. It sounded as if Mother Redwinkle hadn't bestowed her seal of approval.

Who in the world would object to Juniper as a potential daughter-in-law? She was adorable.

"I'm so new here, I haven't even had time to find a hairdresser," Dolly said.

"My cousin Sparkle has a chair at the Three French Hens Beauty Salon on Licorice Lane," Juniper told her.

"Three French Hens . . . I need to write that down." Dolly looked around for her little handbag. "Oh, I must have left my purse in the sleigh! I'm such a puffin brain!"

After she dashed off, I turned to Claire. "What do *you* think?" I asked her.

She eyed her reflection in the three-way mirror, then did a quarter turn to check the way it draped in the back. "I like it, I guess. Don't you?"

"I'm not the one getting married."

"Could you hand me my slushy?" Claire asked.

Juniper hurried to the side table to retrieve it and carefully passed it under the edge of the veil. Claire sucked on the straw.

"I'll have to try Snappy's Slushies," I said. "They seem to have a soothing effect."

Claire nodded. "Snappy made this one especially for me. Lemon-ginger."

Blanchette bustled into the room, giving the slushy cup the hairy eyeball. Then she turned her attention to me. "Your dress looks better today."

"I can breathe, at least."

"Madame Neige works miracles!" Blanchette gushed.

It hadn't been *that* tight.

Okay, maybe it had.

"But I might need to adjust that strap just a little." Blanchette pivoted. "Where is Snowbell when I need her?" She steamed toward the door in search of her underling.

"Sparkle promised to come to the castle the morning of the wedding and style everyone's hair," Juniper said.

Returning to the room with her bag, Dolly skidded to a stop. "Even me?"

Juniper laughed. "Of course. You're part of the wedding party."

Dolly looked thrilled, then shot me a nervous glance. "I thought maybe up at Castle Kringle they have their own hairdresser."

The idea of an in-house coiffeuse at the castle made me laugh. "My mother-in-law's been winding her hair into the same ballet bun for decades, and my sister-in-law puts more thought into reindeer grooming than her own." Before I got too carried away criticizing my in-laws, I caught my reflection. My hair had a serious case of the frizzies. "Then again, I'm not exactly persnickety about my hair myself."

Dolly nodded as she looked at my loose locks. "I guess once you're part of an old married couple you don't worry about your looks so much."

Old?

"Nick and April have only been married for four years," Juniper said.

"That's long enough to feel settled, though," Dolly said. "You don't have to worry about romance."

Especially when Nick spoke of our wedding in terms of *getting the job done.*

"You can afford to let yourself go," Dolly added.

Did Claire really need three bridesmaids? Because I was ready to strangle Dolly.

I glanced over at Claire and through the scrim of her veil caught a humorous glint in her eye. "Everything fits," she declared. "There's no point to hanging around here."

"I have an idea," Juniper said. "Let's go have lunch at the Midnight Clear diner."

Claire and I seconded that idea.

"Can I come, too?" Dolly asked. "I've never been there."

The slightest hint of disappointment ricocheted between Juniper, Claire, and me.

"Of course," I said and gritted out the words with what I hoped passed for enthusiasm.

We were all turning to go back to our respective dressing cubicles when Blanchette appeared in the doorway. I hadn't noticed that she'd left the room.

"You have a visitor, ladies." With a flourish worthy of a game show hostess revealing what was behind Curtain Number Three, she stepped aside and beckoned the visitor into the room.

I wouldn't call myself an elf fancier, but Sterling Redwinkle was quite a specimen, especially when he was in his dress fireman's uniform as he was today. The braid-trimmed red tunic fit snugly against his broad shoulders and highlighted chest and arm muscles bulging beneath the wool. His dark wool pants were tucked into black boots buffed to an onyx shine.

He doffed his official cap, which he held in one hand as he approached Juniper. The other hand held a square package about half the size of a shoebox. As with yesterday, the white box had a metallic green sticker affixed to it, and was wrapped up in ivory-pink ribbon.

Juniper's cheeks bloomed with red. It took me a moment to register that this was not a flush of pleasure. More like annoyance. Her mouth set in a firm line—not quite the reaction I would have expected from someone whose heartthrob was surprising her with a gift.

"You shouldn't be here," she said. "It's bad luck to see me in my dress."

Sterling stopped, frowning. "Doesn't that only go for the bride?"

Flustered, Juniper pointed at Claire. "Claire's here, too—you probably shouldn't see any of us."

Despite the fact that Claire was conspicuous in her bridal finery, Sterling was laser-focused on Juniper.

Claire and I exchanged a significant look.

"I'd better change," she said under her breath.

"Me too," I agreed. We backed toward the dressing rooms, wanting to give the couple privacy, but still burning with curiosity to find out what he was doing here.

"Don't go," Juniper called out to us.

"Yes, please stay," Sterling said to us. "You're Juniper's best friends, so it's only right that you should be witnesses."

"What about me?" Dolly piped up. "I want to be a witness, too."

Sterling looked over at her. He clearly had no idea who she was. Nor did he seem to care. He sank to one knee.

"Oh!"

The exclamation came from Juniper, but she could have been speaking for all of us. Was this what I thought it was?

Sterling grasped Juniper's hand like a cavalier of old. "Juniper, meeting you has been the biggest happening of my life so far."

Her lips parted. Her face was flaming—but it seemed more from embarrassment than delight. "Aren't you uncomfortable?" she said, looking as if she wanted to back away. "That stone floor doesn't hurt when you're kneeling?"

"Sugarplum, I wouldn't mind if the floor was made of broken glass. I only have eyes for you."

"It's not your eyes I'm worried about. It's your knees."

"Forget my knees." He held out the box. "I brought you this."

Juniper gaped at it warily. "What is it?"

"Open it."

"It looks like a corsage box from Flock and Ivy's . . ." She tilted her head. "You're dropping to your knee to give me a corsage?"

Annoyed by her lack of enthusiasm for his grand gesture, he hauled himself to his feet again and impatiently yanked the ribbon off the box. "I had this made for you special." He opened the box himself, revealing a compact spray of small pink rosebuds.

"For you," he said, softening again. "My little rosebud."

"Aww . . ." Dolly said. "That's so sweet."

But Juniper stood frozen as he removed the corsage from the box and pinned it to her dress, just under her collarbone. "It's very nice, Sterling."

The corsage was better than nice. It was gorgeous.

Juniper eyed it dully.

I exchanged a concerned glance with Claire. What the heck was going on? From hearing Juniper go on about Sterling Redwinkle these last few weeks, I would have expected a gesture like this to make her ecstatic.

What had happened at that dinner last night?

Then again, maybe it was just that Juniper was flustered by his popping up out of the blue. Love was full of surprises, but surprises weren't always loved.

"I'm not going to be wearing this dress today," Juniper said. "We're going to the diner. Maybe I should take it off." She reached to unpin it.

"No!" Sterling blocked her hand, grabbing the base of the corsage as if to prevent her from putting it back in the box. Just as quickly, he jumped back, flapping his hand. "Ouch!"

"What's the matter?" Dolly asked.

"One of those thorns pricked my skin," he said on an uptake of breath.

It was like what happened to Snowbell the day before.

Blanchette hurried forward. "Would you like me to help, Mr. Redwinkle?"

"No, I'm fine," he said quickly, then winced in spite of himself. "Son of a nutcracker!" He brought the cut finger to his lips again. "Excuse my language. I've never been stung by a rose before." He gulped in a breath and tried to recover his equilibrium. "But believe me, Juniper, that thorn wasn't nearly as strong as being pierced by Cupid's arrow."

"You ought to get a bandage," Juniper said, frowning.

"Nothing could make me leave your side right now," he said through a cough. "Just as nothing will cleave us for . . . for years . . . to come."

He sank to his knees again. This time it seemed less like a gallant gesture and more like a partial collapse. A sheen of sweat had broken out across his forehead.

Juniper bent over him. "Are you all right?"

"Do you understand"—he gasped—"what I'm asking you?"

Her brows drew together. "Sterling, you really don't seem well."

He wheezed in a rattly breath. "I . . ." His skin had turned grayish-blue, like his uniform tunic.

"Sterling!" Juniper's voice sounded really alarmed.

Fear ricocheted around the room, yet we all stood rooted to the spot.

"I . . . can't . . ." He cratered to the floor.

Juniper dropped down next to him, and I thought I heard something metallic roll along the tiles. "Call Doc Honeytree!" she called out.

Blanchette whipped out her phone.

I was distracted by an object that had dislodged from Juniper's clothing as she started to do CPR on Sterling. I walked over to the corner where the little shiny object had come to a stop and picked it up.

It was a small diamond solitaire.

An engagement ring.

Chapter 5

"I don't know what happened," Juniper whispered in shock as she emerged from the dressing room in her own clothes. The ambulance sleigh had taken Sterling away nearly a half hour before, and we hadn't yet received word on his condition from the Infirmary.

His chances for survival hadn't looked good even before the elf paramedics had hauled him away on the stretcher. His skin had grown more ashen, and his pulse ever fainter, in the minutes it took the ambulance to arrive. My hope was that they had whisked him to Doc Honeytree's skilled care fast enough.

Claire sucked on her slushy. "It all happened so fast. One minute he seemed fine, but then . . ."

"It was like he was choking," I said.

But he hadn't been eating anything, or even chewing gum. And before he'd collapsed, he was talking. Choke victims couldn't talk—their windpipes were completely blocked.

"I thought he was having a heart attack," Juniper said. "That's why I tried CPR."

Madame Neige, who in her layers of black now seemed the most appropriately dressed for the occasion, wandered in to look at the place where Sterling had collapsed. "Perhaps he had some kind of shock."

Yes, the shock of feeling his life seeping away. I'd seen fear in his eyes. I shuddered inwardly at the memory. My heart constricted in my chest in sympathy with poor Juniper, who was obviously remembering that moment, too.

"Don't give up hope," I said.

Please let him be okay . . .

"But he looked so ghastly," Dolly said.

I tried not to glare at her. Claire wasn't so successful.

Juniper shook her head. "What was he doing here?" Her voice was barely above a whisper. "I didn't need a corsage. It didn't make sense."

The ring I'd picked up suddenly felt like a boulder. I didn't want to compound her anguish by showing the engagement ring to her now, with an audience looking on. In the past few minutes, the doorways had filled up with other elves who worked for Madame Neige.

"I'm so sorry, Junie," Dolly said, looping her arms around Juniper in an unsolicited hug. "I hope he'll survive. It would be too awful for him to collapse just as he was going to ask you to marry him."

"I don't know that he was going to ask me," Juniper said. "I worried, of course."

Worried? Yesterday, becoming Mrs. Redwinkle had seemed like her deepest wish.

"Of course he was going to propose," Dolly said. "That's why he brought the ring."

Juniper untangled herself from her. "What ring?"

"The one that fell out of your corsage when you bent over him," Dolly said. "April picked it up."

Juniper turned to me, confused.

Heat filled my face. "I wasn't sure what to do with it." I dug into my pocket for the ring and held it out to her. "Sterling clearly meant to give this to you."

She raised up her hands in the schoolyard "no backs" gesture. "But he *didn't* give it to me. You should return it to him the next time you see him."

If I ever saw him.

"The ring was in the corsage," I told her. "He probably intended it as a surprise."

Juniper's eyes narrowed on the single diamond solitaire. "You'd need to ask him that. That ring's not mine."

Maybe this weird reaction was her way of dealing with shock. I glanced uneasily at Claire, who seemed as perplexed as I was. Not knowing what else to do, I slipped the little ring onto my pinky and went to the door to wait outside for Constable Crinkles. I'd called to let him know what had happened, just in case. What happened to Sterling was setting off alarm bells inside me.

Surprise, surprise,
Someone wants you dead.

That was yesterday. And then today Sterling collapsed.

As always, there was an elf stationed just inside the door. She took one look at me and took off the long crimson wool cloak wrapped around her shoulders. Unlike the others, I hadn't changed out of my bridesmaid dress yet. In addition to calling the constabulary, I'd been on the phone with Doc, and then Nick, to let him know what had happened.

"Please put on this cloak, ma'am. It's nippy outside today."

Was she kidding? This was the North Pole. Every day was like stepping into a deep freeze. It was a sign of how much Sterling's collapse had discombobulated me that I'd even approached an outside door without my puffer coat.

I took the cloak gratefully. "Thank you . . ." I smiled down at her. "It's Button, isn't it?"

"Yes, ma'am."

I wrapped the thick wool tightly around myself.

Wobbler, my reindeer, was waiting out front, shifting impatiently on his gangly legs. "This is taking longer than you said."

"I'm sorry," I told him. "There's been an emergency. You must have seen the ambulance—someone collapsed."

"Trying on clothes?" His large brown eyes blinked. "I've always said elves and people would be better off with fur, and this proves it."

I shook my head. "It was nothing to do with clothes. He collapsed while giving Juniper a corsage."

"Oh. I'm sorry to hear that." He ducked his head. "Pardon me, ma'am, I didn't mean any disrespect about your lack of fur."

"I know." I was still puzzled, though, over why Wobbler would be so out of sorts. It wasn't like him to be so irritable about being left waiting. Waiting was part of his job.

"Are you feeling okay?" I asked.

"Fit as a fox." He added under his breath, "Unlike a certain chunky reindeer I could mention."

"I hope that's not a swipe at Cannonball."

Cannonball, a big-boned reindeer, was always trying to trim down.

He dipped his head guiltily. "I apologize. The words just slipped out. But honestly, he's been getting *a lot* of time off lately. Including yesterday, when evidently he just skipped out without a word. Is that fair to you *or* to me?"

I suspected that Flouncy was behind Wobbler's complaint more than any true grievance about uneven time off between him and Cannonball. Yet he had a point. It wasn't fair.

"I'll try to even things out," I said.

Just then, I saw Constable Crinkles coming up the drive. I started to walk to meet him as he parked.

"You mean it?" Wobbler asked.

"Yes, I do."

"Good!"

Crinkles hopped down from his ski mobile. Santaland's premier lawman was a round little elf in a blue wool uniform with a black belt and chest cross belt. His brass buttons, as always, were buffed to a sparkly shine, and his policeman's cap was strapped tightly under his several chins. No one in Santaland could complain that their constable didn't take his uniform seriously. His job, on the other hand . . .

"They drove Sterling to the Santaland Infirmary," I told him.

The approaching reindeer bells of another sleigh made us turn toward the drive and watch Doc Honeytree approach. He sat so stiffly upright on the bench seat that he resembled a figure carved from wood. Our town doctor dressed all in black with a top hat and a long coat over his tunic, like an undertaker elf.

As he stepped down, his more-than-usually grim expression sent a wave of cold through me that Button's woolen cloak couldn't keep at bay.

"I'm sorry," he said. "Sterling didn't make it."

Crinkles gasped. "You mean he's dead?"

The doctor joined us under the overhang near the building's entrance and knocked some snow off of his stovepipe hat. "I came to tell Juniper—and to ask her if she'd like to accompany me to Tinkertown to give Mrs. Redwinkle the news."

"Aw, noodles!" Crinkles turned to me. "After I spoke to your husband about that vicious letter that arrived here yesterday, I was worried something like this would happen."

"Letter?" Doc asked.

I told Doc about the poison-pen letter. "Maybe it was just a coincidence, but the letter definitely indicated that someone wanted one of us dead. And now Sterling is."

What were the chances that two such strange events would happen within a day of each other?

Surprise, surprise . . .

I looked around, suddenly realizing someone was missing. Crinkles usually came to crime scenes with his nephew, who was his deputy constable. "Where's Ollie?"

Ollie wasn't much more efficient, law-enforcement-wise, than Crinkles, but he usually liked to be around during major incidents in Santaland.

The lawman's jaw dropped at my even asking the question. "Back at the constabulary, of course." When I didn't follow his meaning, he gave me a hint. "The Nougats and Creams category?"

My brain had to switch gears. The Valentine's Tournament of Chocolate began tonight, and Ollie would be participating.

"Ollie's entering his milk chocolate cherry creams," Crinkles said. "We call them Constable Creams. I have two boxes in my snowmobile, if you're feeling peckish."

"I'd better not," I said. "Wouldn't be ethical, since I'll be judging them tonight." It was very tempting, though.

His mouth formed a startled O. "That's right—ethics! Lucky you remembered."

"We should go inside," I said, shivering. Cloak or no cloak, my bridesmaid dress wasn't designed to stand up to subzero temps.

"Sad day," Doc said as we went through the cathedral-arched front doors of the Order of Elven Seamstresses. "I was at the Redwinkle home when Sterling was born."

As one of the few physicians in Santaland, Doc Honeytree had attended the births of most of the country's citizens under the age of fifty. He clearly felt keenly the loss of these elves he'd seen take their first breaths.

He repeated his sorrow to Juniper, who stood shell-shocked as he told her the bad news.

I gave her a hug. She looked pale, as if *she* could use wrapping in a woolen cloak. "I'm so sorry, Juniper."

"I don't know what happened, Doc," she said. "He just collapsed right at my feet all of a sudden."

"Several of us thought he looked like he was choking," I told the doctor. "But he could still speak."

Doc's mouth turned down. "I'm going to ask Algid to look into this."

Algid, his nephew, was Santaland's answer to Ducky in *NCIS*. Only stranger.

"Sterling was a fireman," I said. "He must have had physicals, and been deemed healthy enough to do his job."

"He *was* strong," Juniper said. "And stoic. I was shocked when he started making a big deal of a little cut on his hand."

Doc Honeytree frowned. "A cut?"

After he listened to our various remembered accounts of the minutes leading up to Sterling's attack, Doc eyed Juniper's corsage, which someone had put on a table next to her handbag. "Those are the flowers he gave you?"

She nodded. "Yes. He pinned them on me. I took them off because . . ."

She didn't finish.

"And he looked well up to that moment?"

We all nodded.

"Could have been an allergic reaction. Anaphylactic shock." Doc scratched his chin, talking to himself as much as to us. "Then again, given what April told me about that poison-pen letter, perhaps something more nefarious is going on."

That sounded reasonable, except for one small problem. "The flowers are fake. How could someone be allergic to fake flowers?"

"You'd be surprised," Doc said. "He could be allergic to something the flowers are scented with, or the material the flower petals are made from, or even the glue used on the corsage box."

"I knew someone who was allergic to chocolate," Constable Crinkles said. "Imagine being allergic to chocolate!"

Doc's eyes narrowed on the corsage lying on a nearby table. Then he looked again at Juniper. "Pardon me, but I think I'm going to have to take your flowers."

I'd never seen anyone comply with a request so swiftly. In almost one movement, she reached down, closed the florist box the corsage had come in, and handed it to Doc. "Take it."

"I can give it back to you once my nephew Algid finishes studying it," Doc assured her.

"I couldn't wear it now." She gathered up her things. "I really should go visit Mrs. Redwinkle."

Crinkles leaned back on his heels. "I should, too." From the set of his mouth, it was clearly not a task he was looking forward to. "I can give you a ride over there, Juniper."

"I can take you both on my sleigh," Doc Honeytree offered. "I'd like to express my condolences to Mrs. Redwinkle in person."

"Thank you." Juniper hooked her purse over her arm. "I'd like to go before word reaches Mrs. Redwinkle that her son is . . . dead." She said the word as if she still couldn't believe it.

I was having a hard time processing it myself.

"I've got some of Ollie's chocolates in the snowmobile," Crinkles said. "We can have them on the way over."

After they left, Dolly turned to Claire and me. "I've hardly ever had chocolate—it's not that common where I come from. The biggest treat we ever got was walrus blubber crackling."

"*Quel dommage*," Madame Neige said. At first it was difficult to tell whether she was referring to Sterling Redwinkle's untimely demise or Dolly's chocolate deprivation.

As it happened, she was referring to the skirt of my dress, where a little tear had appeared. It was also wrinkled and dirty—either from when I'd been outside talking to Wobbler or when I'd helped Juniper up from the floor after her attempt to give Sterling CPR.

"I'm sorry," I said, wincing under her disapproval. "The dress fits perfectly now," I added, as if that was some kind of consolation for the rip.

She looked me over with a more critical eye. "*Regardez*, Blanchette." Her two hands reached out like pincers to show where the dress was slightly loose under my armpits.

Frankly, after being squeezed into the dress yesterday like a sausage in a skin, I was happy to have a little give somewhere.

Madame Neige was having none of it, though. "Zee pucker, it must be fixed," she admonished her assistant.

As Blanchette curtsied obediently, red blotches appeared in both cheeks. "Yes, madame."

The proprietress eyed me. "You will be come back tomorrow, yes?"

I almost let out a petulant *Do I have to?* I'd hoped that this would be my last time here for a while. The last two trips here hadn't actually been great, peace-of-mind wise. First the poison-pen letter, now a sudden death.

A bad allergic reaction, Doc Honeytree had suggested first. Surely that made more sense than a psycho elf killing a firefighter whose girlfriend happened to be having a dress fitting.

Then again, there was the poison-pen letter. The sticky note on the box had read "Wedding Party." I'd assumed that meant Claire, or maybe the bridesmaids. I hadn't considered that escorts might be in peril.

I called Nick and felt a surge of relief to hear his voice answer. "You're okay?" I asked by way of greeting.

"As far as I know." He sounded amused, then asked, "What's going on?"

I updated him on the morning's events.

"I'll head over to Tinkertown and pay a condolence call on Mrs. Redwinkle," he said, his voice somber now. "Poor woman. And poor Juniper."

"She's gone to see Mrs. Redwinkle, too."

By the time I changed out of my bridesmaid's dress and back into my own clothes, Dolly and Claire were ready to go.

"I feel so bad for the Redwinkles," Claire said as we walked out. "And poor Juniper."

"And poor you!" Dolly added.

Claire frowned at her. "Why me?"

"You're probably thinking that you'll have to cancel your wedding now. I mean, there's been that crazy letter, and now the almost-fiancé of one of your bridesmaids has dropped dead. As we say back home, with luck like that, the next thing'll be a snow monster squashing your ice yurt."

"I hadn't thought of canceling my wedding over this," Claire said.

The words *over this* made me do a double take. It sounded as if she'd thought of canceling for other reasons.

"I bet Jake will think of it when he hears," Dolly said. "*He's* very sensitive."

It was hard to maintain my composure. "Something that apparently doesn't run in the Frost family."

As if to prove my point, she blundered on obliviously, "Are we still going to the Midnight Clear diner? I'm starving."

"No." Claire looked almost green at the thought. I could see why. Watching an elf die had killed my appetite. Hopefully it would return by the time I had to judge nougats and creams later this evening.

Right now it was hard to believe that Valentine's Week would continue as normal.

"I'm going back to the Scoop," Claire said.

I nodded. "I'll drive you."

Outside, my sleigh stood behind an empty harness. It was starting to feel like the movie *Groundhog Day*.

I bit back a sigh. I'd mentioned to Wobbler that I would even out the reindeers' free time. I didn't mean I would even it out *today*.

"Having your reindeer skedaddle is getting to be a regular thing," Dolly said.

"Reindeer in love are impulsive creatures." I stepped into the sleigh. It was fully juiced up, I noted with relief.

Dolly complained of hunger all the way down the mountain, so I dropped her off at the Christmastown Cornucopia grocery. Claire was still silent on the few blocks from there to the Scoop.

At the ice cream store, Butterbean, Claire's ebullient elf assistant, stood behind the counter in a sweater that matched hers. A motley cap in red and white, the Scoop's colors, perched atop his thick blond hair. His big smile and the ice cream parlor's colorful, retro decor seemed at odds with this morning's unhappy experience, and Claire's tense mood.

"May I get anything for you, Mrs. Claus?" he asked.

"No, thank you."

Never one to take no for an answer, the elf persisted, "How about a Sweetheart Shake?"

"What's that?"

"Strawberry ice cream with whipped cream and sprinkles, plus a special Valentine's heart-shaped butter cookie."

My resolve weakened, and my previously absent appetite returned. Sweets have that effect on me. "That sounds fantastic."

"One Sweetheart Shake, coming up!" He bounded right to work, while I joined Claire at a table by the front picture window. She gazed absently out onto the snowy street decorated in red swags with hearts dangling off them.

"Is something wrong?" I asked her.

She laughed mirthlessly. "An elf just died. I'd say *that* was something wrong."

I had to bite my lip to avoid asking, "Anything besides that?" That smacked of *apart from that, Mrs. Lincoln, how was the play?*

"And Juniper," Claire said. "What was going on there?"

I was as perplexed as she was. "She didn't seem as thrilled as you'd expect her to be this morning when Sterling came in."

"No kidding! It struck me as odd that she was so lukewarm about the whole surprising-her-with-flowers thing."

I was still trying to puzzle it out. "For weeks she's talked about what a paragon Sterling was, and speculating on where their relationship was headed. But the moment he decided to get serious, she looked as if she wished the floor would swallow her."

"She didn't even want to entertain the notion that he'd bought her a ring."

I leaned back, replaying the whole scene. "When he dropped to one knee, I could tell from the look on her face that his big romantic gesture was going to sink."

Claire mused, "It's like those women you used to see who got proposals via ballgame jumbotrons. I always wondered what they would do if they wanted to say no. Juniper's expression when Sterling went down on one knee gave me the answer."

Butterbean hurried over with my shake in an extra-tall fountain shop glass. As promised, it looked incredible. The sprinkles on the whipped cream were white and pink, and the cookie had a little message on it in letters meant to resemble a candy heart. *True love,* the cookie said.

My husband might be all business, but at least my cookie was effusive.

"You're the Michelangelo of frozen dairy treat artists," I told Butterbean.

He flushed at the compliment. "You're too kind."

The shake was tasty, too—perfect creamy strawberry flavor. I had to force myself to sip slowly to avoid the dreaded brain freeze.

Claire was back to staring out at the street.

"Are you sure you're okay?" I asked. "Even before Sterling died, you seemed low-key for someone getting married in a few days."

Her lips curled to hide a smile. "Were you doing high kicks down Celebration Boulevard before your wedding?"

"That was different. I was new to Santaland. I didn't have anyone to celebrate with except Nick."

Certainly not five hundred and forty-three elves and people.

Her expression turned thoughtful. "Maybe you two should have a second ceremony. Do it up right."

"A second wedding?"

"People renew their vows," she said.

"After four years?" How had she managed to steer this conversation away from herself and Jake and onto me? "I just wondered if you were having jitters. It's totally normal—it's such a big step."

She bit her lip. "That's what worries me."

"Everybody deals with nerves," I said, as if I were a matrimonial expert.

"Not everybody has a psycho stalking their wedding party, though," she pointed out.

"We don't know for sure if what happened to Sterling today had anything to do with the psycho who sent that letter yesterday."

She almost rolled her eyes. "How could they not be related? The poison-pen letter was just yesterday. Doc said he thought Sterling was in peak condition. And I know you noticed that box the corsage came in was from Flock and Ivy's."

"They're the biggest florist in town. Boxes with their sticker are all over the place." I tried to make sense of any connection between the letter and Sterling's death. "Why would anyone target the boy-friend of a wedding attendant?"

"Maybe someone wants my wedding to be a disaster."

"The only person who wants that is Dolly," I said.

She laughed. "I know she's annoying, but it's hard to hate some-one who loves Jake as much as I do."

"*More*," I said, which brought another laugh.

"Dolly's right about one thing, though," Claire said. "I probably *should* cancel the wedding."

"Absolutely not," I said.

"Is a ceremony worth someone dying for?"

"We don't know for certain that the letter and Sterling's death are connected." At her implacable expression, I added, "But I'll find out what I can."

The door opened and Jake Frost blew into the room. Jake wasn't entirely an elf—it was hard to pinpoint exactly what he was—and he never wore tunics, hose, and elf caps. The fedora on his head looked like something Humphrey Bogart might wear in a movie. A trench coat finished off the hardened private eye look. In his rush to talk to Claire, he didn't stop to take off any of his outside wear. He hurried over to her, then pulled her up into his arms.

"I just heard about what happened to Sterling Redwinkle," he said. "Are you okay?"

"I'm fine." She looked into his eyes, then gently pulled away. "It's Juniper that we should all feel sorry for."

"I do," he said.

Those two words brought a smile. "Trying to get your prac-tice in for the wedding?" Claire's smile faded just as abruptly as it had appeared. "If there actually *is* a wedding. I don't feel comfort-able celebrating when there's someone out there menacing my bridal party—and possibly killing them."

"We suspect the poison-pen letter yesterday was just a precursor to Sterling's death today," I explained.

A pained expression crossed his face. "You can't stop living your life because bad things happen," he told Claire.

"I'm not going to stop living my life," Claire said. "I'm going to postpone my wedding."

At her pronouncement, Jake looked as filled with dread as I was—with one difference. He was a disappointed bridegroom, whereas I was just disconcerted at the prospect of having to tell my mother-in-law that all her elaborate seating charts, place settings, and other preparations would be for naught. Call me craven, but that was a conversation I wanted to avoid.

I sucked down the rest of my milkshake and stood up. "There's no sense in speculating. Doc Honeytree and Algid are going to figure out what killed Sterling. If it's natural causes, all of this panicking will be for nothing."

"That elf didn't die of natural causes," Claire insisted. "And if there was foul play involved, I don't see how I can go ahead with a big wedding when there's a fiend on the loose targeting us."

"You can if the fiend is caught."

Her brows arched at me. "You're going to get to the bottom of this before the wedding?"

"Why not?" I replied. The wedding was still four days away.

Which gave me four days to catch a psycho-elf wedding killer.

Chapter 6

When I left the ice cream shop, I didn't expect Jake to follow me. "What are you doing?" I asked him.

"I'm a detective. I want to investigate."

"You're also a fiancé. You might want to stick around and convince Claire not to cancel the wedding."

"I can tell when Claire wants me around and when she doesn't."

What bride-to-be didn't want her groom with her during the lead-up to her wedding?

"Is everything okay?" I asked.

His gaze was stony, but I could tell from the twitch in the jaw that there was something going on. "To be honest, I worry Claire has cold feet. Maybe she's having regrets about moving here, or about me."

Coming from cool customer Jake, these two tersely spoken sentences amounted to an emotional outpouring.

I reached out and touched the sleeve of his trench coat. "I doubt she has regrets."

He bit his lip in thought. "Well, in any case, having threats and a suspicious death on her mind isn't helping. Last night I found her up in the middle of the night, staring out the window. She said she couldn't stop thinking about the poison-pen letter. She thinks it's a bad omen."

If Claire had been freaked out by the letter, small wonder she viewed a dead body as an even more evil portent.

"We'll get to the bottom of it," I said.

We didn't even need to discuss what our first stop would be. Our feet naturally turned in the direction of Doc Honeytree's house on the brow of a hill in a neighborhood just north of Christmastown's downtown. Normally I would have avoided trudging so far through February's snow and ice by taking my sleigh, but there was no telling if I'd see Wobbler again today, and I didn't want to waste power. Jake, of course, barely noticed the cold. He was a Frost.

The walk up the last hill on Bow Street to the deep red–painted house with white shutters that belonged to Doc Honeytree made me resolve to start an exercise program. And lay off the sweetheart milkshakes. Maybe after my work in judging the Tournament of Chocolate was finished . . .

Doc Honeytree opened the door, took one look at Jake, and guessed our purpose immediately. "Algid's working down in the basement. You know the way. I'm sorry I can't join you at the moment. An elf fell off a ladder putting up Valentine's Day bunting for the Tournament of Chocolate tonight. Dislocated his shoulder."

Valentine's Week was starting to seem hazardous in all sorts of ways.

Doc grabbed his old black medical bag off the counter and hurried out of the house as we entered it. He wasn't wrong about our knowing the way to Algid's laboratory. I'd been down there on several occasions and didn't bother taking my coat off as Jake and I descended the narrow steps to the basement. The temperature dipped with each step.

Algid was as much a natural at lab work as his uncle was at examining patients in person. He was such a lab rat, in fact, that his companion, Newton, was an actual rat. Both had pale skin and white hair, although Newton had red eyes instead of the pale gray orbs that stared out of Algid's thick, round glasses.

Algid and Newton heard us coming—or heard *me* coming, since Jake moved silently, as though he were floating. Both the elf and the rat twitched a greeting. Jake and I smiled, trying not to focus on the figure draped in a sheet in the corner of the frigid room.

Algid skipped pleasantries and preliminaries. "Poison," he announced.

"That's how Sterling Redwinkle died?" Even though I'd been halfway expecting foul play myself, the word *poison* still shocked me. "I don't want to believe it."

"No one wants to believe such things happen here in Santaland," Algid said, "but if we all refuse to accept it, more people might end up killed by the maniac who killed him." With his head, he indicated Sterling's shrouded figure.

I shot a look at Jake. This was precisely what Claire had been anxious about.

"How did it happen?" he asked.

Algid pushed his round glasses to the bridge of his nose, which twitched like Newton's. "The delivery system for the poison was the corsage." He held it up and pointed to one of the stems, which bore the thorn that had pricked Sterling's thumb. "That thorn delivered the fatal dose," Algid went on.

Jake looked as puzzled as I felt. "How?"

"Have you ever heard of thallium?" Algid asked.

I shook my head.

"It's a mineral that can be found in a lot of places—everything from trace amounts in cabbage to its raw form in minerals like volcanic rocks and meteors."

"I'm guessing the poison that killed Sterling didn't come from boiling down a cabbage," I said.

"Down where you're from," Algid explained, "thallium is used as a pest killer, typically on creatures we don't have here, like ants. A poison that can work through the chitin exoskeleton of an ant is very effective at penetrating the skin and getting into an elf's system." He eyed me. "As you know, elves are *very* susceptible to foreign toxins, especially heavy metals."

"Poison delivered through a thorn." I thought back to a news story I'd read once. "It seems so twisted, like spycraft. I remember that there was a man killed by a Russian assassin with an umbrella tip coated in ricin. But a poisoned rose?"

"It's the same principle," Algid said.

Jake's gaze was narrowed on the display of test tubes Algid had on the table in front of him. "So you've tested Sterling's blood and confirmed that the poison was actually the cause of death?"

"Of course," Algid said. "He was a very healthy elf otherwise."

A healthy elf who got his hands on a deadly corsage.

"He never had a chance once the poison hit his system," Algid said.

And to think I'd seen what happened to him, without knowing at the time that it was a fatal jab. A misbegotten marriage proposal had turned into an assassination. Who would have done that?

"So where would an elf in Santaland have gotten their hands on thallium?" I wondered aloud.

Algid rubbed his whiskerless chin. "I suppose someone very industrious could find and mine it in its raw form."

"Mine it?" I asked. "Like with picks?"

He nodded.

"That's right—you mentioned volcanic rocks."

"And also in rocks that contain other metals, or meteors . . ."

"Around here?"

"Oh, sure. In the mountains you could probably find a seam containing thallium. Especially up north."

The Farthest Frozen Reaches seemed to have an abundance of terrible things.

"But your garden-variety evil elf would probably just order some ant poison from somewhere," Algid continued. "You can mail-order anything."

That opened up *a lot* more possibilities for suspects.

Jake turned to me. "Where's Juniper?"

The deadly seriousness in his voice alarmed me. "What are you thinking?"

"That corsage was meant for Juniper."

The moment he said it, I could have kicked myself for not seeing the obvious. The corsage was intended for Juniper—and so, probably, was the murder. "Sterling was the conduit."

"We need to figure out where that corsage came from," Jake said.

"The box had a Flock and Ivy sticker on it." I was ready to charge to the florist shop then and there. "We should go there now."

Jake remained rooted to the spot, his face tense in thought. "Claire told me that the box with the poison-pen letter also bore Flock and Ivy's logo. What did they say when you asked them about that?"

"They said the box with the rose wasn't from their store."

"What would you expect them to say today?" he asked.

Algid snorted. "I doubt they'll say, 'Sure, we prepared that thallium corsage fresh this morning.'"

Newton's whiskers twitched in appreciation of this barb. It was hard to take scorn from a rodent.

I could see now why cool-headed Jake wasn't for dashing off there directly, though. My barging into the store yesterday just might have given them a heads-up to cover whatever tracks there were to find about a murder today.

"I see. We need to be more strategic." One possibility spurred me not to let the snow thaw beneath my boots, though. "If that corsage was meant for Juniper, then whatever psychopath wanted it delivered to her is probably frustrated that their poison killed the wrong elf."

"Where is Juniper now?" Jake asked me again.

"She went to give her condolences to Mrs. Redwinkle in Tinkertown."

"Good." He nodded curtly. "Go to the Redwinkles and have a word with her. She needs to be careful—and to try to think of anyone she knows who might have a vendetta against her."

"Vendetta?" That seemed an odd word to use in connection to Juniper. "She's a librarian."

She was also one of the nicest elves in all of Santaland.

"While you speak to Juniper," Jake continued, "I can go to the Tinkertown headquarters of the Santaland Fire Brigade and ask the firemen Sterling worked with if any of them know where he might have gotten that corsage. Maybe one of his coworkers was with him when he bought it."

At the moment I almost forgot to care who the culprit was. My main focus was warning Juniper before she became another Valentine's Week casualty.

The walkway to the Redwinkle cottage in Tinkertown showed evidence of a steady stream of condolence visitors. The pavement between the stone fence and the cottage's front door had scores of bootie prints in the snow.

Festa Redwinkle, a striking elf with blond curly hair and blue eyes similar to her late brother's, answered the door. I offered my condolences and asked to see her mother, adding that I was a friend of Juniper's. As Festa led me to the formal parlor, I couldn't help noticing the pile of condolence fruitcakes on the entry table and the many photographs of Sterling that lined the hallway. The corridor was almost a shrine to his every stage of development. The pictures couldn't all have appeared just today. This seemed to be a permanent, longstanding display.

In the middle of the sofa in the front parlor sat Mrs. Redwinkle, all in black. The lights were dimmed, giving the entire room, but especially her, a sallow appearance. Her eyes were red from weeping, and my heart went out to her. Juniper was seated next to her in the red tunic she'd worn this morning when she'd assumed she'd be returning to work at the library. The brightness of it was out of place in this house of mourning.

"Mrs. Claus, it's so kind of you to pay a condolence call in honor of my son," Mrs. Redwinkle said. "Santa was here earlier—he said such kind things about Sterling."

"I'm so sorry for your loss," I said. "It's a loss to all of Santaland. Sterling was a hero in the community."

She lifted a handkerchief to her eyes, and Juniper leaned toward her. "April was there this morning."

"So you saw . . ." The mother couldn't finish her sentence.

I sat next to her and took her hand. I had to hunch a bit and draw up my knees to fit on the elf-sized couch. I often felt like a giantess in elf cottages. "It happened so quickly. I know he didn't suffer." *Long*, I added silently.

It was the only consolation I could think to give her, but she seemed to draw some comfort from it. "And just when he was on the precipice of such happiness," she said. "Last night he asked me for my permission to marry Juniper, and I granted it. I thought I would be gaining another daughter. Now I've lost everything."

Juniper bit her lip.

Mrs. Redwinkle let go of my hand and reached over to grasp hers. "You must consider yourself a Redwinkle now. You're family. A living reminder of precious Sterling and the future he should have had."

Juniper shifted. I'd never seen her look so uneasy. "That's very kind."

The strain behind her eyes was unmistakable. And I was going to have to add to her worries.

"In fact, you could move into his room," Mrs. Redwinkle continued. "Sterling would have wanted that."

Juniper looked over at me, and it wasn't hard to guess that moving into her recently deceased boyfriend's childhood bedroom wasn't the most appealing idea. I'd heard that Sterling's mother had been very possessive. In her grief, apparently, she was ready to grasp onto Juniper as a substitute.

A living reminder . . .

Poor Mrs. Redwinkle. Suddenly I felt anguished over having to deliver the news that Sterling's death hadn't been from natural causes, and that he was the unintended victim of an assassination attempt against Juniper.

I cleared my throat. "I just came from Doc Honeytree's. I talked to Algid."

"The creepy nephew?" Festa asked. I'd forgotten that she was standing behind us. She frowned. "I thought it was just Doc who was there this morning."

Juniper obviously hadn't filled them in on details and speculation, but perhaps she hadn't found the appropriate moment to do so. Come to think of it, right now wasn't a great moment for that, either, but I blundered on.

"Algid ran tests on the corsage Sterling brought to Juniper. Doc thought that there might have been some sort of allergic reaction involved."

"Sterling *never* had allergies," Mrs. Redwinkle declared. "I just don't see how this could have happened to him. He was as healthy as a walrus!"

Walruses didn't strike me as a very flattering comparison, but maybe it was just one of those things that elves said. I nodded. "That's exactly what Algid said. Except he didn't mention walruses."

"So what did Algid conclude about the corsage?" Juniper asked.

I said in a low voice, "The stems of the roses in it contained something called thallium, which is a very potent poison."

Mrs. Redwinkle and Juniper blinked at me in shock. Festa, I couldn't help noting, narrowed her eyes as if she were already sifting through the implications.

"Poison!" Mrs. Redwinkle echoed. "Why would anyone put poison on a corsage?"

How could I state this delicately? "To cause someone harm."

The older elf's face darkened. "Mrs. Claus, are you telling me that my son was murdered?"

"The evidence indicates that, yes."

She bristled at the idea. "No one would have wanted to poison Sterling. You said it yourself—he's a hero in the community, beloved by everyone."

I nodded. "That's right. We—"

"He saved lives. Why would anyone want to take his?"

"We don't think they did," I explained. "It's all just speculation at this point, of course, but we think the killer had a different target in mind."

Festa was the first to say it aloud. "Juniper."

Juniper gasped. Or maybe the sound had come from Mrs. Redwinkle, or both of them at the same time. They gaped at me.

"Me?" Juniper squeaked.

"Of course," Festa said. "The corsage had the poison, and the corsage was meant for you."

Mrs. Redwinkle's jaw was working so hard it could have sawed through a century-old fruitcake. She seemed almost offended at the idea of Juniper being the intended victim. "*Sterling* was the one who was going to touch the corsage first, though."

"The killer might have assumed that Juniper would receive the box and handle the corsage herself," I said.

"*Might* have! Their assumption killed my son!"

Juniper had gone as white as snow. "Who would do such a thing?"

"We'll need to put our heads together and see if you can think of anyone," I told her.

"If what you say is true, they're still out there," Festa said. "And maybe frustrated that they hit the wrong target."

"Yes," I said, side-eyeing Juniper. She was still frozen in shock.

Mrs. Redwinkle drew back in outrage. "So you're telling me that my son's death was just a *mistake*?"

I swallowed. "It seems likely."

Shaking, Mrs. Redwinkle dropped Juniper's hand. "Get out."

Juniper blinked at her. Never in the history of Santaland had anyone lost honorary Redwinkle status so rapidly. "I beg your pardon?"

"My Sterling would be alive this minute if it weren't for you. What did you do to make someone hate you so much?"

"Nothing . . . that I know of."

Fresh tears flowed from the mother's eyes. "You brought death to my son—you might as well have poisoned him yourself."

Festa hurried to the back of the couch and touched her mother gently on the shoulder. "Mother, that's not fair. It's not Juniper's fault. Look at her—she's wrecked."

Juniper did look stung by the woman's words, but Mrs. Redwinkle certainly didn't consider her to be sufficiently devastated. She zeroed in on Juniper's bare ring finger. "Where is the ring?" she demanded.

"What ring?" Festa asked.

"Your grandmother Redwinkle's engagement ring. I gave it to Sterling last night to offer to Juniper."

"Oh!" I suddenly remembered the ring I'd slipped onto my finger earlier.

I held up my pinkie.

A horrified bleat burbled out of Mrs. Redwinkle. "What are *you* doing with the Redwinkle diamond?"

"I was just . . ." I suddenly realized that I couldn't say that I'd put it on my finger because Juniper didn't want it. ". . . just holding it."

Sterling's mother looked like she might blow a gasket. "Take it off."

"Of course." I immediately began tugging at it.

It was on tight. Stuck, in fact.

"It fell out of the corsage," I said nervously, trying to fill up the tense silence as I tried to work the ring loose. "I guess Sterling was trying to do one of those things where the guy hides the ring and waits for the woman he's asking to find it. You know, like putting it in the refrigerator or in a cake or something? I always think there's so much potential for it to go wrong, and—"

My words broke off, but the unspoken *and it certainly did in this case* seemed to ring in the air as clearly as the bells on Christmas morning.

"Get it off!" Mrs. Redwinkle growled.

To my relief, Festa swooped in to my rescue. She knelt down before me, holding a butter dish. She took a knife and slathered some on my finger. Then she held the ring and then I tugged my arm back with all my might.

The ring finally was released, sending us falling in opposite directions. Mrs. Redwinkle plucked the buttery solitaire from her daughter's hand.

"You both should leave," Mrs. Redwinkle said to Juniper and me.

"Mother . . ."

"You too, Festa. You just go back to your apartment or whatever you call that little room you moved into so that you could have your so-called independence. Sterling *never* left me." She lifted the handkerchief to her eyes again. "Not voluntarily."

Her mouth tight, Festa looked at Juniper and me and gave her head a quick nod toward a corridor that led to what I assumed was the little cottage's kitchen.

My goodbyes and a final "I'm so sorry" to Mrs. Redwinkle went unacknowledged. I felt terrible. Worst condolence call ever.

In the kitchen, Festa swung the door closed. "Would anyone like something to drink? I'm going to put a little something extra in my eggnog this evening."

She climbed on a stool to reach a shelf above the refrigeration cabinet where the family kept their liquor.

"Here, let me help." Being taller than 95 percent of the local population so rarely came in handy. I reached up, hesitating between several bottles. "Whiskey or rum?" I asked.

"Both," she said. "And you might as well get that vodka down, too. I have a feeling I'll need all the fortification I can get here in the coming days."

"You're staying?"

"At least for tonight," Festa said. "I can't leave her alone. She'll calm down."

Juniper wrung her hands. "Maybe I should stay, too."

"Oh, no," Festa said. "She really wants you to leave."

"I feel just awful," Juniper said.

Festa filled a glass halfway with rum and then opened the refrigerator cabinet to take out the eggnog. There was a little window to the outside inside the insulated cabinet, which served as the North Pole equivalent of a refrigerator.

"You *should* feel awful," Festa said. "Someone apparently wants to kill you."

Surprise, surprise,

Someone wants you dead.

Looking back now, I wanted to kick myself. Why hadn't we been more careful? We could have just stayed home. Some lunatic had sent us a handwritten warning that we were in mortal danger. Our cavalier attitude toward that note had cost Sterling his life.

Juniper's air of astonishment, horror, and dread had only intensified since we'd retreated to the kitchen. "I can't understand how this could have happened," she said. "I don't have any enemies."

"Everyone alive has enemies." Festa hipped the cabinet's door closed. "We just don't always realize it."

Juniper obviously had a hard time wrapping her mind around such a cynical thought. "Maybe Sterling picked up the wrong corsage. It might have all been a mistake."

That reminded me. "Do you know where Sterling bought flowers?" I asked Festa.

She shrugged. "Flock and Ivy's, I'd imagine."

"The box had their sticker on it," Juniper remembered. "Just like the box the single rose came in the day before."

"Single rose?" Festa repeated.

I explained about the rose, and the poison-pen poem.

Festa's brow crinkled in thought. "Why didn't they just say up front that they wanted *Juniper* dead?"

That had bothered me, too. "I don't know."

"This person had to be pretty sure of your schedules, and where Sterling would be taking that corsage," Festa continued.

"Not necessarily," I said. "It wouldn't have mattered if Juniper were poisoned at the Order of Elven Seamstresses or the library."

Juniper sank down in a chair by a little dinette set. "I still can't believe it. Poor Sterling." She looked up at his sister. "I really am sorry, Festa."

"You're not to blame—you certainly didn't *want* anyone to try to kill you." She tossed a glance at the closed kitchen door. "It's just that this has been the worst possible blow to Mother. If *I'd* dropped dead, she would have been sad, but not completely devastated. Sterling was her golden boy. Her whole world's just fallen down around her ears."

I remembered the entrance hallway, and all those pictures of Sterling. Had there been any of Festa? None that I could recall. That was some extreme favoritism.

Festa gulped down half a glass of her spiked eggnog. "Does anyone want some?"

Juniper and I shook our heads. Actually, I could have used a belt of something, but I was driving.

Festa flopped into a chair near Juniper. "Don't let this upend *your* life," she said, almost as if she were already tipsy. I got the feeling that this wasn't the first snort she'd partaken of since the news of her brother had reached her. "If you ask me, you've dodged a bullet. I loved my brother, but he was the biggest elf-child never to leave his mother's cottage."

Yet he'd been on the verge of independence. "He wanted to get married," I reminded her. "He wasn't going to be here forever."

Festa gave her head a firm shake. "He and Juniper would have been living here."

Juniper crossed her arms, but she didn't contradict Festa. Maybe this was part of the reason her attitude toward Sterling and their future had changed so radically between yesterday and today. During her dinner with Mrs. Redwinkle last night, Juniper must have twigged to the fact that Mother Redwinkle was never going to cut the apron strings.

"I still feel terrible," she said.

And part of that terrible feeling, I could see now, was guilt. The scales had fallen from Juniper's eyes just as Sterling had decided to take the plunge and have a married life. Married with wife *and* his mother. Now Juniper was in the unhappy position of mourning the elf she'd intended to reject.

"You're not the first elf to have this happen to her," Festa said. "Sterling was never short of females interested in him. He was so good-looking, and brave." She finished off her eggnog and sighed. "Brave enough to rescue elves from burning buildings, but not brave enough to break away from Mother."

Her mention of other elves interested in her brother sparked a thought. "Were there any elves whose hearts he'd broken recently?"

Festa shrugged. "I don't know if I would call it breaking any-one's heart. The girlfriends usually wised up before that could hap-pen." She bit her lip. "Although . . ."

I leaned forward. "Was there an exception?"

Her brow furrowed. "Yes, it's been a year since he brought this particular elf home for Mother's approval, which she didn't give."

"Who was it?"

"Well, if you must know, it was Ivy."

"The florist?" I asked.

Juniper and I tensed. Both the poem and the deadly corsage had arrived in a Flock and Ivy box. That couldn't be a coincidence.

Festa glanced between us. "I didn't meant to insinuate that Ivy killed my brother. Like I said, their breakup was a while ago."

"But she was definitely his last serious girlfriend before Juniper?"

Festa nodded. "I was sad when they called it quits. I liked her. It was just that Mother thought—"

"Thought what?" I asked when her words broke off.

"Well, the lack of family connection bothered Mother."

"Ivy has no family?" That was news to me.

Juniper nodded. "She's an orphan."

"You'd think that an orphan for a daughter-in-law would have suited Mother down to the heels of her booties—no in-law family to suck Sterling away from her orbit." Festa glanced at the kitchen door again and lowered her voice. "But no. Mother said she thought Ivy was *too* clingy." She huffed a gentle laugh. "Pot. Kettle. Black."

Juniper's frown lines deepened. "What made *me* different, I wonder?"

I tilted my head. "Different to whom?"

"Why did Mrs. Redwinkle decide that I was okay for her son, if she'd rejected Ivy?"

Festa stared into her empty glass. "Who knows?"

"You do," Juniper said. "You were here last night. Did your mother say anything to you? She must have, if she was handing over her grandmother's ring to Sterling."

"You might have expected that ring to be passed on to you someday," I added.

"I've learned to lower my expectations," Festa said. "I always knew that ring was destined for a daughter-in-law's finger."

"But why was *I* chosen to be the daughter-in-law?" Juniper asked again.

Festa looked down at her hands. "Well, if you must know, I did hear Mother's verdict. Not that Mother is the greatest judge."

"What did she say?" Juniper asked.

Festa took a deep breath. "She said a spinster librarian approaching middle age would be so desperate to keep a husband that you wouldn't make waves."

We didn't stick around very long after that.

Chapter 7

"Spinster librarian!" Juniper muttered. We'd barely climbed up on the sleigh before she began to vent. "I'm sorry, but Mrs. Redwinkle is a real picklepuss. I know she's devastated. But she called me a spinster librarian *last night*? After I sat through that awful dinner?"

"Grim, was it?"

She let out a long breath so heavy it seemed as if she'd been holding it for fifteen hours. "It was the stiffest meal I'd ever sat through. You would've thought I was meeting the queen mother. Sterling was a total jellyfish when it came to her. No backbone at all. It finally dawned on me that he would've thrown me under the sleigh-bus skids to appease Mrs. Redwinkle at the first sign of conflict. I hate to speak ill of the dead, but that elf had serious mommy issues."

"So you decided last night that you were going to dump him?"

"During the dinner?" She bit her lip. "Well, no. See, I went home and tabulated my responses on the compatibility quiz in *Elf World* magazine. It was called 'What's Your Sweetie Level?' I should have taken it before. According to the quiz, Sterling was just a Valentine Heart, leaning toward Cookie Bouquet." She shook her head. "Not great."

I frowned. "What would great be?"

"The Full Heart-Shaped Chocolate Box."

"This doesn't sound like a comprehensive relationship measurement," I said. "Besides, don't two people need to answer those questions? You can't take a compatibility quiz if it's just you."

"I'd sort of slipped some of the questions into my conversations with Sterling, I just hadn't sat down and looked at it scientifically."

I couldn't believe she would take a fluffy magazine quiz seriously. I was going to drop the subject, but I couldn't help asking, "What were the questions?"

"The first ones were about tastes you share and entertainment preferences. Trivial stuff. Then it pivoted to family life, and then the really philosophical issues."

"Like what?"

"Well, like say it's a gorgeous summer day. One of those rare warm ones where the mercury climbs up to thirty-five degrees. And you and your significant other are having a picnic when you spot a snowman in the distance in distress in the sunshine. Do you a) call the Society for the Protection of Snowmen, b) personally go yourself to take care of him and make sure he reaches shade, or c) keep eating and hope he won't melt before you've finished lunch."

"I'd call the Society. It's what they're there for."

Juniper tutted at me. "And then just leave that poor snowman to evaporate while you eat scones and clotted cream?"

Knowing that there were scones and clotted cream involved made me even less inclined to give up my hypothetical picnic, but I understood her point. "Surely Sterling wasn't for keeping eating?"

"Not in so many words, but his jaw twitched when I asked him about it."

It felt wrong judging the poor guy for an ill-timed twitch, especially since he wasn't here anymore to defend himself. "Maybe he was tired."

Juniper twisted when I blew past the turnoff to Christmastown. "Where are we going now?"

"Jake is at the firehouse, talking to Sterling's friends," I explained.

She turned back to me in alarm. "He doesn't think firemen are trying to kill me, does he?"

"No, he's just trying to gather info on Sterling. He speculated that Sterling might have shown off the corsage and mentioned where he got it."

"The box was from Flock and Ivy's," Juniper said.

"That's what we figured, but Jake wanted to nose around and maybe get some corroboration of our hunch. Flock and Ivy both denied that their store had any involvement in that poison-pen letter."

Juniper leaned back against the bench seat of the sleigh.

"It's weird that Sterling still used Ivy as his florist after they broke up," I said. "Do you think he was carrying a torch?"

As soon as the words were out of my mouth, I wanted to retract them. Sterling had died in the middle of giving Juniper the Red-winkle family ring. That would contradict his carrying a torch for another elf.

Juniper didn't take offense, though. "He never talked to me about her." She shrugged. "I'm beginning to wonder if I understand romance at all. Look at Jake and Claire. I used to think they were the Full Heart-Shaped Chocolate Box. But Claire's been acting so weird. Do you think this wedding's going to happen?"

"Of course." If I could find a murderer. "Claire's definitely acting strange about something, though."

"I asked her about it the other day," Juniper said. "She said she's worried Jake's making a mistake."

"*Jake?*" I asked. "Not her?"

"I know. It's strange," Juniper said. "Maybe *she* should take the sweetie quiz."

When we picked Jake up outside the firehouse, he didn't have any news for us. "No one remembered him saying anything about a corsage," he said, climbing onto the bench seat. "But every elf in there guessed where he would have picked one up. Guess who Sterling was involved with not too long ago?"

Juniper and I answered in unison. "Ivy."

Jake looked almost disappointed. We'd spoiled the one tidbit that he'd managed to glean.

"Festa Redwinkle, Sterling's sister, told us all about it," Juniper told him.

"We're going to talk to Ivy now."

Jake nodded. "Just what I was about to suggest."

As I turned on the sleigh path toward Christmastown, Juniper hitched her throat. "When we get back to town, I think you'd better drop me off at my apartment."

"You don't want to hear what Ivy has to say for herself?"

"It would be so awkward."

Maybe we could use the awkwardness to our advantage. "We want her to feel back-footed," I said. "She might be more likely to talk."

Juniper blinked slowly into the bracing breeze. Now that we were out of town, the sleigh could clip along smartly. The wind was blowing her long hair wild. It looked almost as if her elf cap would fly off. "How would it look, though?" she asked. "I worry Smudge would hear about it and assume I'm jealous of Ivy."

Smudge, Ivy's current love interest.

"He wouldn't think that."

"It just wouldn't feel right," she insisted.

I cut a glance at her and felt bad when I saw her strained expression. This past twenty-four hours had been an emotional snow squall for her.

"Of course, I'll drop you by your place," I said.

"Someone should double-check the locks on your windows and doors," Jake said. "Better stop by Sparkletoe's Mercantile on the way over, April. I can pick up some hardware and meet Juniper at her apartment."

"Locks on my *windows*?" It sounded as if this were a concept Juniper had never considered. Maybe she hadn't. She lived in Christmastown, not Gotham City.

I could understand Jake's thinking. If someone were after Juniper, it would be good to make sure that her apartment was secure. Would locks be enough, though? The sociopath who killed Sterling had done so right before the eyes of several witnesses.

"Maybe you should come stay at the castle until we find who-ever did this," I told Juniper.

She arched a brow at me. "With all the prep for Claire's wedding going on?"

"You're welcome any time. One more guest at Castle Kringle is nothing. That place can absorb fifty guests, no problem."

"I would still feel weird."

"Then maybe you could stay at your parents' for a while."

Juniper liked that idea even less. "My mother's allergic to Dave." Dave was her pet rabbit. She folded her arms. "I'm not going to be run out of my home."

The sun had completely disappeared from the sky, and snow clouds obscured the stars, making it necessary to turn on the sleigh's headlamps. Christmastown had so many lights that they almost mimicked daylight in the afternoons, but here on the path through the Christmas Tree Forest, the darkness was notable. By the time we got to town, shops would be closing, including the florist. I pressed down the accelerator.

"I want to talk to Ivy today." I hadn't foreseen talking to her alone, though. After yesterday she wasn't going to be happy to see me again. I doubted she was going to open up to me.

Jake could have been reading my mind. "It would be a good idea to get the constabulary involved," he said. "Constable Crinkles should be informed that there's a suspect in the murder that hap-pened in his town today."

Having the law in the room while I was talking to Ivy was a good idea. I might think Constable Crinkles was a joke, but most of the elves in Santaland took his authority seriously.

Once we arrived in town, Jake stepped down at Sparkletoe's Mercantile, and then I dropped off Juniper at her apartment build-ing. Mindful of the time, I pressed on to the constabulary.

Crinkles's eyes bugged in alarm when he saw me standing on his doorstep. "You can't come in here. Ollie's finishing his entry for the Nougats and Creams contest tonight. We don't want you to be disqualified again like you have been for Fudge Night." He drew up proudly. "See? I remembered all the ethics stuff."

"I wasn't disqualified. I recused myself."

I hold a Frequent Fudger card at Dash's Candy and Nut Shoppe, so I had to find a substitute judge for the fudge portion of the tournament, which would take place on the third night. On Fudge Night, Mrs. Firlog, the mayor's wife, would be judging.

I was cold and would have appreciated a moment by the fire inside the cozy constabulary, but I understood the constable's hesitation. "I'm not trying to cause problems for Ollie's entry. I just wanted to let you know that there's been a development in the case."

"Which case?"

As if there had been multiple suspicious deaths in Christmastown that day.

"Jake and I think we've found a suspect in the murder of Sterling Redwinkle."

"Murder!" His jowls trembled in shock.

"Haven't you talked to Doc?" I asked. "Or Algid?"

The constable's brow knit. "Is *that* what he was calling about? We've been all atwitter ahead of the contest tonight, we haven't had time to take calls."

I had to fill him in on the poison findings.

Crinkles looked aghast. "Who do you think did it?"

"Right now, all roads lead to Ivy." I told him everything I'd learned that afternoon. This was taking longer than I wanted. My feet were going numb.

The constable listened attentively. Or at least I thought he did. When he spoke, it was clear his mind was gliding along a different track from mine.

"What about Nougats and Creams?"

I tilted my head. "What about them?"

"We don't have time to talk to Ivy now. Nougats and Creams starts in an hour."

"An hour should be plenty of time," I said. "Besides, *you're* not making chocolate."

"I know, but Ollie's entry will be in the name of the Christmastown Constabulary, and so any prize money will benefit Santaland law enforcement. Not that I'm trying to exert any influence on your judging."

Heaven forbid.

"We could just pop over to Ivy's," I said. "It would be good to talk to her before the news that Sterling's death wasn't from natural causes spreads." When he hesitated, I added, "I'm the judge, Constable. They can't start the contest without me."

Grudgingly, he relented and followed me to the florist in the constabulary's snowmobile.

Outside Flock and Ivy's, Bumble the snowman was still standing next to his placard offering hugs for donations. I nodded at him and hurried past.

"Wait!" Crinkles said. He dug into the pocket of his tight tunic. "Darn—I don't have any change."

"That's okay—I'll give." I dug through my purse for change, put a few coins in the jar, and then turned back toward the florist's door.

"What about the hug?" Bumble called after me.

"I'll take a rain check." We were in a hurry, and a snowman hug wasn't overly appealing to me at that moment. I was already chilled through from driving around in the cold all day and then being doorstepped by the constable.

From the incredulous look on Crinkles's face, though, I'd just committed a Santaland faux pas of the highest order.

"What's wrong?" Bumble sounded wounded. "You think I have snow cooties?"

"No, of course not," I assured him.

"Then what's the matter with me?" he asked, practically wailing in that sad, Eeyore voice.

I felt so terrible, I rushed forward and gave him a big bear hug. If you think that's a simple thing to do, try wrapping your arms around a giant blob of packed snow sometime. I attempted to embrace the snowman without either crushing him or inadvertently dislodging one of his body segments. Bumble was a three-blob snowman, and middle sections were notoriously prone to dislocation.

Too late, I felt a tug, like the strap of my shoulder bag catching on something.

"AAAHHHHH!" Bumble cried. "My arm!"

I hopped back, then heard a loud crack.

At the sound, I looked down. So did Crinkles. He gasped. "Look what you did!"

The broken stick on the snowy ground looked almost gruesome under the heel of my snow boot.

"You broke my arm!" Bumble shouted.

My face flushed with heat. "I'm so sorry!" I picked up the two pieces of wood. My heel had snapped the stick arm cleanly in half.

Crinkles tutted. "Won't be able to tape *that* back together."

"What am I going to do?" Bumble moaned. Snowmen might not feel pain quite the way we did, but he was clearly distressed.

Guilt suffused me. "Don't worry—I'll fix this." As the impulsive promise left my lips, I looked over at Flock and Ivy's. A florist had branches, didn't it? I rushed to the door as Ivy was pulling some potted evergreens inside for the night.

"Just a moment," I called out to her.

Her gaze narrowed on me. "We're closed."

"Please, I need to buy an arm." I shook my head. "I mean, a stick." To demonstrate why, I shifted so that she could see what had transpired on her sidewalk.

A little of the stiffness seeped out of her. "We don't have a lot of branches at the moment—except for some dried eucalyptus branches. Would that work?"

It didn't sound like a solid substitute, but maybe a eucalyptus branch would satisfy Bumble until I could find something better. "I guess so."

The florist hurried inside and retrieved the eucalyptus branch.

It was full of fragrant leaves that had dried to a brownish purple. It didn't match his other stick arm at all, but Bumble didn't raise any objection when I poked it into his snowy torso. I had to pack some extra snow into the hole where the old stick had been.

"Pretty exotic, Bumble," Crinkles said when I was done. "I bet you're the only snowman in Christmastown with a eucalyptus arm."

The snowman considered for a moment. "Does it seem odd that my sticks don't match?"

"Makes you look distinctive," I said.

Ivy nodded. "I'll set aside an extra branch for you in case you decide you want to have a match."

Bumble considered. "Thank you. I certainly smell better, even if I look peculiar."

I guiltily dropped another handful of coins into his jar—but by silent mutual agreement I forewent a second hug. Then Crinkles and I followed Ivy inside, where the dulcet tones of Michael Bublé singing "Bewitched, Bothered and Bewildered" combined with the perfumes of hothouse flowers and evergreen. The shop was one Godiva chocolate short of a Valentine sensory explosion.

Ivy was clearly not pleased to see us right on her heels. "Don't worry about the stick. There's no charge."

"Actually, we'd like to speak to you," I told her.

Flock came out of the back room, half hidden by a massive evergreen heart-shaped wreath with the word *LOVE* written across it in roses and sparkly hearts and outlined in red tinsel. Only his elf cap and big eyes poked over the top of the garish, spectacular creation.

"Again?" he asked in exasperation when he saw me. "We answered your questions yesterday." He leaned the wreath on the counter, then flicked his gaze from me to Crinkles. "Has something happened?"

"We need to speak to Ivy," I said.

Still wary but relieved, Flock took this as a dismissal. "I'll go."

"No, stay," Ivy said quickly. "I'd like to have someone on my side during this interrogation."

Crinkles shook his head so vigorously that his chins shook, too. "This isn't an interrogation," he said. "We just need to ask a few questions. Friendly questions."

Ivy's brows arched. "What about? It's been a long, not very good day."

Her ex had died, I reminded myself. If she didn't have anything to do with it, that news must have shaken her.

There was no sense in sugarcoating the news. I wanted to see how she reacted. "Sterling Redwinkle was murdered."

She flinched—maybe from the bluntness of my pronouncement.

Next to her, Flock made a choking sound. "I'll just be in back," he muttered, attempting to retreat to the back room.

Ivy clamped her hand down on his tunic before he could escape. "Stay right here."

Flock did as bid, but his face remained pale and tense. He either hated conflict, or he knew something and he was worried it would spill out.

"That has nothing to do with this shop," Ivy said.

"He was poisoned from the corsage he was giving Juniper."

"Poisoned by a corsage?" Flock asked. "How?"

"The thorny stems were laced in a poison deadly to elves called thallium," I said.

Flock looked horrified, but Ivy blinked at me, unfazed. "So?"

So? That's all she had to say?

"The corsage box, like the box containing the poison-pen poem the day before, had your sticker on it."

Her red lips flattened in an impatient line. "We've been over this. Anyone who ordered something from us in the past two years could have a box with our logo on it." She fixed a questioning stare on her partner. "Flock, did *you* make a corsage for Sterling Redwinkle?"

Eyes wide, he shook his head. "No—no, I didn't."

"People we spoke to in Tinkertown said that Sterling bought arrangements here often," I said.

Flock's head movement pivoted to a vigorous, affirmative bob. "He's been a faithful customer for years."

"That's how I met him," Ivy said.

"There's been a standing order for Mother's Day and Mrs. Redwinkle's birthday for over a decade," Flock added.

He and Ivy exchanged a doleful look.

"That's the end of that," she said.

Cold, I thought. "You don't seem overly upset about his death."

"I'm at work," she said. "Even if I felt like it, I'm not going to break down and start bawling here."

I couldn't help asking, "Do you feel like bawling?"

She lifted her chin. "My feelings are none of your business."

"We know you and Sterling were an item not so long ago," I added.

"I never said we weren't," Ivy said. "In fact, I just told you that Sterling and I met right here."

"That's right, you did." Crinkles took out his pocket watch, checked the time, and then looked at me imploringly. "They said they had nothing to do with the poisoning, so . . ."

None-too-subtly, he jerked his head in the direction of the door.

It wasn't going to be easy to solve this case while Crinkles's mind was on the Tournament of Chocolate. Not that our constable was a crime-fighting dynamo even when his brain was fully engaged.

I gave my own head a shake and turned back to Ivy. Time to change the tone. "I'm sorry, I didn't mean to sound antagonistic. Juniper, who was Sterling's girlfriend, is my friend. I can't help caring about her. She's awfully upset."

"I'll bet," Ivy said, not exactly oozing sympathy.

"She spent the whole afternoon at the Redwinkle house." I didn't mention Juniper's banishment from the Redwinkle sphere.

"Mrs. Redwinkle is probably beside herself with grief," Flock said, hands fluttering. "Poor lady. Maybe we should send her something." He searched Ivy's face for a reaction to the idea. "Sterling was *such* a good customer."

Ivy didn't seem to think much of that idea. "Sterling was, not his mother."

"I take it that Mrs. Redwinkle could be a little tough on elves her son was interested in," I said.

"Let me guess . . ." Ivy crossed her arms. "The old dragon pointed the finger of blame in my direction?"

"No, it was Festa who mentioned that you and Sterling had dated, but only after I asked her."

"Oh, I bet Festa was glad to offer me up as prime suspect." She shook her head. "I swear, the happiest day of my life was when I disentangled myself from that crazy clan."

Odd that she would single out Festa as having been hostile toward her. From my conversation with Festa, I got the sense that she liked Ivy.

"Did you do the disentangling, or did Sterling?" I asked.

"I did—I wised up." Ivy busied herself wiping the already spotless glass counter in anticipation of closing. "Sterling had a lot of good qualities, but he also had one weakness: Mrs. Redwinkle."

This tracked with what Festa had told me, so I knew she was being honest about that.

Ivy continued, "The final straw for me came when Sterling said we couldn't go out on my birthday because it was his mother's Avalanche night."

"Avalanche?" I asked.

"It's a card game," Crinkles explained. "Lots of fun—Ollie and I should teach you how to play." He hitched his throat. "Speaking of Ollie . . . shouldn't we?" He looked longingly toward the door.

I ignored the hint. "So Sterling preferred playing cards to celebrating your birthday?" I asked Ivy.

"Mrs. Redwinkle hosts Avalanche parties every month for all her Tinkertown cronies, and Sterling often sat in if they needed an extra elf to even out the table." Ivy bit her lip. "But I don't think that's the kind of thing that should take precedence over a girlfriend's birthday, do you?"

It sounded like a question that would be in Juniper's *Elf World* quiz. "I can see why you were miffed."

"Actually, playing cards with his mother sounds kind of sweet to me," Crinkles said.

Crinkles, it should be mentioned, is a lifelong bachelor.

"After all," the constable added, "a promise is a promise."

"And a birthday is a birthday," Ivy said. "And a girlfriend isn't a piece of furniture. She can walk right out the door when she feels neglected."

We were getting off track here. "Would you call it an amicable breakup?" I asked.

She shrugged. "As much as a breakup ever can be."

"Sterling never canceled his account or his standing orders here," Flock added.

"And how much later was it that you started seeing Smudge?" I asked Ivy.

"Over six months later. My breakup with Sterling was last Valentine's Day."

I put two and two together. "Valentine's Day is your birthday?"

Crinkles, who was still focused on the door like a Labrador ready for walkies, brightened at the word *birthday*. "Happy Birthday!"

"It's not till Saturday," she said, as if it was somehow bad luck to accept felicitations four days early. "Of course, when my real birthday is, I might never know. Valentine's Day is just what I was told . . . but maybe the folks at the Santaland Home for Orphaned Elves were just making it up to make me feel better. They were very kind to me there."

I'd forgotten that she had no family. Did that account for her impatience with Sterling's overattachment to his mother? Of course, Juniper had been on the verge of backing out of the relationship for the same reason, and she had lots of family of her own.

"Anyway," she continued, "I've been over the whole breakup for months. Why should I want to kill him now when I've moved on? Smudge is great, even if he isn't much to look at." She sighed. "Not like Sterling was."

I felt defensive on Smudge's behalf. He was a friend of mine—we played percussion in the Santaland Concert Band together. Maybe he wasn't the Cary Grant of Santaland. He favored drab clothes and often could use a trip to Tannenbaum's Tonsorial Parlor for a close shave, but I wouldn't have put him in the "not much to look at" category.

Who says something like that about the elf they're dating?

"We're worried that what happened to Sterling was because of Juniper," Crinkles said.

"Then you should be giving *her* the third degree," Ivy said.

She'd misunderstood. "Someone sent that single rose with a threatening poem yesterday, and today Sterling was killed by the corsage," I said. "We suspect that Juniper was the intended victim for both incidents."

"So you're saying that I meant to kill Juniper but poisoned the wrong elf?" Ivy asked.

"I'm not accusing you," I said.

"Right. You're just insinuating that maybe I might have done it." She shook her head. "Believe me, I bear Juniper no ill will. I'm certainly not jealous of her—if she wanted Sterling, that was fine with me. I have Smudge. I think I got the better sweetie bargain."

Except that you just insinuated that he's not as attractive as Sterling.

Then again, Sterling *had* been rather dreamy to look at.

Crinkles cleared his throat. "Speaking of sweeties, Nougats and Creams judging will begin any moment now."

"Not before I'm there," I reminded him.

Ivy looked at the wall clock and sighed. "Oh, snowballs! I'm going to miss Dazzle Winterbright."

Dazzle—I think that was his stage name, but in Santaland it was sometimes hard to tell—was Santaland's dreamiest crooner. Municipal Hall would be packed.

"Dazzle's going to be singing at the Mistletoe Tavern later this week," I said.

I knew this because Juniper and I were planning Claire's bachelorette party for that evening and had arranged with the Tavern to have Dazzle sing that night. He was Claire's favorite Santaland entertainer, too.

"Maybe I'll see him then," Ivy said.

Flock piped up, "Dazzle's a friend of mine."

Ivy rolled her eyes at Crinkles and me. "He acts like he has an inside track with a celebrity because he went to school with him."

"We sat next to each other in third-year Elf History and Lore *and* Candy Chemistry." He lifted his chin. "I helped him study for finals. I even guessed that the essay question would be on syrups and sauces."

I was impressed—it certainly sounded more interesting than my high school's curriculum—but no one else even took note of this. They'd all lived through it.

Crinkles tugged on my sleeve. "We really should get going."

Reluctantly, I nodded. As I turned toward the door, though, my gaze fell on the Valentine spray that Flock had lugged out earlier. It was so preposterously large and showy. "Who's that for?" I asked, adding, "It's beautiful."

Flock puffed up a little. "That's being delivered to Kringle Lodge first thing in the morning."

My jaw dropped. "Amory Claus ordered that?"

He nodded. "It's for his wife. Isn't that sweet?"

Yes it was.

But more significantly, it was hard to believe cranky Amory, Nick's cousin, was giving Midge such a splashy, impractical, romantic gift. "Amazing."

"Mr. Amory Claus is another good customer," Flock added quickly. "Always sending little surprise posies and bouquets to his wife."

I felt strangely deflated . . . and almost jealous. When was the last time Nick had sent me a posy for no reason at all? Splashy, frivolous gestures weren't Nick's strong suit. Last Valentine's, Nick had handed me a card with a message informing me that he'd donated a new set of cymbals to the Santaland Concert Band, which I played in. So thoughtful, but hardly the height of romance.

"Come on," Crinkles said, tugging me by the sleeve toward the door. "We don't want the ravenous crowds to eat all the entries before you can judge them."

Amory's flowers had almost made me forget Nougats and Creams night.

I straightened my shoulders. A meeting hall full of chocolates awaited my taste buds. Tough work, but somebody had to do it.

Chapter 8

"Well! That made me feel better," Crinkles said, hurrying ahead of me. "You?"

The constable and I had decided it would be just as fast to walk to the Christmastown Municipal Hall as to drive there in our separate vehicles and find places to park. Crinkles was cutting down the travel time even more by locomoting as fast as his stubby legs would go. I hadn't seen the elf move this fast since the opening of the buffet line at the last Santaland Infirmary Pancake Supper fundraiser.

"Better about what?" I asked, struggling to keep up with him.

"About Ivy. She told us she didn't do it."

I wasn't certain she'd made an especially strong case for her innocence. "She seems like a very cold person."

"Maybe she was just in a hurry to close up shop and get to the Tournament of Chocolate."

That was some champion-level projecting Crinkles was doing. I had to grab his coat to keep him from running into the street, right into the path of an oncoming sleigh bus.

"The chocolates will still be there whether we arrive in five minutes or seven," I told him.

"I'm just so worried about Ollie. He was fretting over his presentation . . ." He caught my distracted stare and his eyes bugged. "Not that I should be telling you that."

My footsteps slowed. "We should have asked Ivy what her alibi was for yesterday."

"Why?" he asked. "She wasn't there when he was poisoned."

"Somebody had to give Sterling that corsage."

"I'd sure hate for it to have been Ivy, though," he said. "She's not a bad elf. Look how she jumped in to help you with Bumble's arm."

I had to admit, she hadn't hesitated to lend an arm.

"She didn't even charge you," Crinkles reminded me.

All true, yet in the matter of Sterling Redwinkle's death, I didn't quite trust her word. Or maybe it was Flock I was suspicious of. That elf had looked anxious the whole time we were at the florist shop, and he hadn't spoken much. Probably because Ivy was there. She seemed to be the dominant voice in that partnership. Would I ever be able to catch him alone at work and talk to him candidly?

The Tournament of Chocolate was taking place at the reception room of the Christmastown Municipal Hall. Despite how distracted I was by the day's events, I was ready for chocolate. My only fear was that the rumbling of my stomach would echo through the hall. But I needn't have worried. The hall echoed with the sounds of bells and stomping.

Crinkles and I stopped, frowning. "Elf cloggers?" I said. "They weren't scheduled for this week."

Yet we heard more stomping, clapping, and then a high male elf voice raised in song. Not Dazzle Winterbright. This sounded more like a Santaland hootenanny.

Crinkles, who'd been racing like a snowshoe hare to get here, now stood rooted to the spot, his head tilted to listen. "That's old Blizzard Goldstocking."

The name was somewhat familiar to me, although I hadn't yet met this particular elf. "Another singer?"

"His specialty is old-timey elf songs. Good stuff." He frowned. "Only trouble is, once he takes the stage, he never wants to leave."

Inside the hall, the traditional red-and-green decor had been tarted up with a lot more red, white, and pink. Sparkling heart balloons hung from the hall's high ceiling, along with pink and white paper streamers. The tasting tables, covered in pink cloths with tiny red hearts, were arranged around three walls in a giant horseshoe. The crowd, for the most part, stood apart from the candy displays on the tables, gathering instead around the musician and the dancers.

In the center of the crowd, an old, white-bearded elf in faded green was seated on a high stool. He was playing a guitar and singing an old chestnut called "The Apple in Your Stocking." A group of elf cloggers were dancing to the music and teaching a few of the crowd to dance.

Just what Santaland needed. *More* elf cloggers.

As I was scanning the crowd for a friendly face, Dolly found me. And she was accompanied by Jake.

I sent him a questioning look. "I thought you were at Juniper's."

"He was." Dolly gripped his arm. "I tracked him down there. It seemed silly for Jake to waste his whole evening with locks and have both of us miss the Tournament of Chocolate."

"Why would both of you miss it?" I asked.

"I didn't want to come here alone," she said. "Anyway, Juniper finally did the sensible thing and called a locksmith."

Jake looked apologetic. "Better Watch Out Alarms and Locks is over there now. They'll do a more thorough job than I could."

"I doubt that," Dolly said. "But I'm still glad they're tending to it and not you." She looked around, eyes sparkling.

"Claire didn't feel like going out," Jake explained to me.

I could understand that. It had been a long day.

"Isn't this exciting?" Dolly asked in a rush. "Apparently Dazzle Winterbright has a sore throat. Elves were saying that everyone was *really* disappointed, and then that old elf started singing and elves began clogging. I even joined in a dance before we saw you over here."

The news about Dazzle's throat alarmed me. Would he be better two nights from now, for Claire's bachelorette party? We were counting on his performance to make the evening more special than just another night at the Mistletoe Tavern.

"Did you find out anything?" Jake asked, sounding not remotely interested in the evening's entertainment woes.

I shook my head. "Just got denials. As expected."

"Was Crinkles there?" he asked.

"Yes." Where had the constable disappeared to? I looked around the walls of the room, which were lined with long folding tables that had been decorated with pink and red crepe paper. Crinkles was standing next to Ollie, sneaking a chocolate into his mouth from the tidy pyramid Ollie had carefully constructed on a decorative platter.

"Crinkles doesn't seem to agree with my suspicions," I told Jake in a low voice.

"You mean he didn't arrest Ivy for murder?" Dolly asked loudly.

"Shh," I said. The last thing this evening needed was gossip about a murder.

At that moment, Mrs. Firlog was steaming her way over to me. She was head of the organizing committee for the Tournament of Chocolate, and if her laser stare was any indication, my tardiness had earned her official displeasure.

"Thank goodness you're finally here," she said, grabbing my shoulders and spinning me around toward the long tables where the chocolate contestants were set up. "What an evening! First Dazzle Winterbright was a no-show, and then you didn't arrive. I was beginning to worry that I was going to have to step in as judge for tonight, too."

"Would that have been so awful?" I asked.

"I don't like nougats." Mrs. Firlog clamped her hand onto my arm and dragged me toward the tables.

That was the trouble. Nobody liked nougats . . . at least not as much as other chocolate categories. My motto was that any chocolate was better than no chocolate, but mention of nougats didn't set off the Pavlovian response in my taste buds that, say, a chocolate-covered caramel did.

As the crowd parted to let us through, Blizzard took up his guitar again. "Shall I play 'Ballad of the Ice Fisher's Sweetheart'?"

I could tell Mrs. Firlog was about to stop him, but I called out, "Yes, please!"

A little folk song accompaniment was preferable to everyone watching me sampling chocolates in silence.

We arrived at the first table, which had six chocolate entries lined up for me. The first was something called Dark Chocolate Leaves. The glossy, rich chocolate had been molded into perfectly shaped maple leaves. And for good reason. When I bit into one, I discovered they had maple cream inside. Dark chocolate and maple was not my favorite combo, but it was still pretty good. I marked it six out of ten.

Down the long row of tables I went, tasting every entry, tapping my feet to the tunes of Blizzard Goldstocking, and trying not to dwell on the hopeful gazes pinned on me. Elves in Santaland took their chocolate very seriously. I couldn't forget that my decision tonight would make one elf very happy—and disappoint about thirty others.

After a few entries, Mrs. Firlog allowed me a brief coffee break. A hot beverage was essential as a sort of palate cleanser. Much as I loved chocolate, I could only eat a nibble or two of each entry. Even so, I was going to end up consuming the equivalent of an entire Whitman's Sampler this evening.

By the time I was halfway through, I already had that Halloween-night candy bloat feeling. In fact, I worried that I wouldn't have the stamina to make it through all the tables. Then I tasted Happy Greenberry's white chocolate almond nougats.

"Wow!" I couldn't help blurting out.

Heavenly. Forget one bite. I couldn't help gobbling down the whole thing.

Happy, a short elf in a green cap, pinned me with a hopeful stare when he saw my reaction. "It was my grandmother's recipe," he told me. "That's why I call them Granny Greenberry's Nougats—in honor of her."

Full as I was, I would have been happy to grab a second one. But I had a table to sample yet.

Still, this was my first ten out of ten. A perfect ten for a nougat. Who would have predicted that?

At the very end of the last table, Crinkles and Ollie stood on the other side of a slightly depleted pyramid of round milk chocolates. They were both standing at attention in their uniforms as I approached. Ollie looked like the stringbean shadow of his uncle. The sign at the front of their platter read *Constable Creams*.

"Hope you like them," Ollie said breathlessly.

I nodded, ready to give him a polite response after I bit into the candy.

What a shock! I knew Ollie was a good baker, but his chocolates were a revelation. The milk chocolate was rich and smooth as it should have been, and the cream tasted like a pink sugary cloud with little bits of cherries in it.

My face must have been a window into my ecstatic tastebuds.

"They're good, aren't they?" Crinkles asked, beaming.

It was hard not to gush, but I held myself back. The fact that this was Ollie's confection was slightly problematic. Everybody knew I liked Crinkles and Ollie—not enough that I couldn't be objective, but I didn't want to appear to rush to give the Constabulary Creams the blue ribbon.

"Very good," I said noncommittally. It was the same remark I'd made to several other entrants.

Except Ollie's chocolates were *so flippin' good*. Blue-ribbon-worthy. Unfortunately, they would be bumping Happy Greenberry's nougats down a peg in the ranking. I remembered the pride in his eyes as he spoke of Granny Greenberry. This was agonizing.

But what could I do? I was here to give my honest opinion, and to my mind the Constable Creams were the hands-down winner. In fact, if Ollie were ever to tire of being his uncle's deputy constable, I could see him making a go at opening his own chocolate store. I might even be his first investor.

I retreated to the coffee urn to wrestle with my conscience. Mrs. Firlog twitched impatiently as I agonized.

Finally, I asked, "Can there be a tie?"

Her eyes widened in shock. "What?"

"There are two excellent entries," I said. "It's hard to decide what to do."

She leveled an exasperated look at me. "Of course it's hard to decide—that's why you're the judge. You're supposed to make a decision."

"But I hate to disappoint someone."

She planted her fists on her hips. "April, we have a blue ribbon and a red ribbon. We can't split them."

"Why not?" I asked.

Mrs. Firlog lowered her voice and laid down the law. "The blue ribbon from each night goes on to the finals on Saturday morning. If we send two winners from Nougats and Creams night, would that be fair to Caramels and Nuts? Would I need to pick two fudge entries to even out the unbalance you created because you were too wimpy to pick a winner?"

"I see what you're saying, but . . ." Clearly I wasn't cut out for this kind of pressure.

In disgust, she snatched my judging sheet from me and looked it over, clucking as she read my scrawled notes. "You have an obvious preference. Go with that."

It was probably silly to agonize over chocolate judging. The big blue ribbon was produced, as well as a red one. With ceremony, Mrs. Firlog and I gave the red ribbon to Happy Greenberry, who bravely wore the frozen, devastated smile of all first runners-up. Then I walked down the length of the tables again and presented the blue ribbon to Ollie.

Ecstatic didn't begin to describe the constables' reaction. You'd think they'd just won the Powerball jackpot. Ollie grabbed the ribbon, while Crinkles hopped up and down with joy. Then the two of them jigged around in joy as Blizzard launched into an old chestnut, "The Reindeer Reel."

Soon, half the hall was dancing.

"You did it!" Crinkles whooped to Ollie. "Now it's on to the finals!"

Seeing them so happy made me feel better. My work done, I looked forward to going home and crawling into bed before the chocolate high I was zooming on turned into a sugar crash. I was just putting my coat on when Happy Greenberry stomped over to Mrs. Firlog. "This is an outrage!" he bellowed. "I'm going to lodge a complaint."

The music stopped, and the elves stopped jigging.

Mrs. Firlog eyed the little elf as if he were mad. "A complaint about what?"

"The contest! It was rigged." He planted his hands on his hips. "Nougats were at a distinct disadvantage in this contest. It wasn't fair to make us go up against creams. Everybody likes creams—it's like children's candy. Nougats require a discerning palate."

"Your nougat was fantastic," I assured him. "That's why you won the red ribbon."

I wanted to tell him that I'd really wanted it to be a tie, but that confession would have thrown the whole event into turmoil.

"Behind a cream," he said, as if there were something shameful about that. "I'm telling you, it's not fair. This so-called contest is a disgrace!"

The mayor's wife, the tournament's organizer, puffed up in offense. "Don't be ridiculous."

"The judge came into the hall with the elf who won the contest." He pointed at me and Crinkles, who was now by my side. "And then surprise, surprise! That elf wins."

I blinked. "What did you say?"

"I'm saying that this whole setup is hinky!"

"No, you said 'Surprise, surprise.'"

He rolled his eyes. "That was sarcasm."

Surprise, surprise. Someone wants you dead.

A shiver went through me.

It was probably just a coincidence, though. Right?

Crinkles shook his head, bug-eyed with worry that his nephew's victory could be overturned. "Ollie was the confectioner, not me. And Mrs. Claus and I only entered the hall together because we were working on an unrelated matter. There's been a murder in town!"

I groaned inwardly. *Here we go.*

"Murder?" Mrs. Firlog repeated, horrified.

Unhelpfully, Crinkles blurted out, "Sterling Redwinkle was poisoned by a deadly corsage delivered from Flock and Ivy's!"

At that, the whole hall was abuzz.

"Flowers were poisoned?" Mrs. Firlog asked, aghast. "From Flock and Ivy's?"

I struggled to find some words to calm the situation. "Artificial ones. The stems had thorns, and that was the way the poison was transmitted."

"So *crafty* things are all we have to worry about," one elf said. "Suffering snowballs!"

Flowers in Santaland in February were luxury items, but crafts went on all year round. Every elf in the hall gawped in horror.

"If we can't trust Valentine gifts, what *can* we trust?" someone asked.

"Chocolates," Crinkles said.

Mrs. Firlog scowled at him. "You think *candy* can't be poisoned?"

"But whoever killed Sterling seemed intent on killing someone in particular, not causing chaos," I explained over the hubbub.

"Weren't Sterling and Ivy the florist an item once upon a time?" someone asked.

"And then he's killed by a flower!"

While the hall buzzed with speculation, I hurried for the exit. It's not easy to slip out of a room when you're at least half a foot taller than everyone in it, but I grabbed my overcoat, hunched into it, and made a dive for the side door.

Maybe we *should* have separated out the nougats into their own category, I thought as I wound my muffler around my neck several times. But there had only been so much time for the tournament. And how many elves wanted to make nougats? They'd been out-numbered five-to-one in the contest this evening.

Happy's sarcastic "surprise, surprise" kept rattling through my mind. Could there be some connection between the chocolatier elf and Sterling Redwinkle's death?

The night was blustery cold and snowy, and I had to walk all the way back to the florist shop where my sleigh was parked. Even double-gloved, hatted, wearing snow boots and my puffiest coat, I shivered. Elves gamboled about in these conditions as if it was just slightly chilly, but I felt the cold down in the marrow of my bones. After four years at the North Pole, my chattering teeth and perpetual whining about the weather still marked me as an outsider.

"Good evening, Mrs. Claus!" Bumble called out to me as I passed him. The light from a pink-beribboned streetlamp puddled around him, but the windows of the florist behind him were dark.

I paused. His new stick was still firmly in place. The eucalyptus branch had several offshoots to it, I couldn't help noticing now, so that it looked like a piece of shrubbery growing improbably out of his side. The leaves had a dusting of snow.

"How are you feeling?" I asked him.

"Never better!" He paused, and for a moment I wasn't certain what was going on. Then he blurted out, "I can breathe!"

The pause had evidently been him taking a deep breath.

"I feel like a newly rolled snowman!"

"You were congested?" I'd never heard of snowmen suffering from bad sinuses. I hadn't even known that they *had* sinuses. But now that he mentioned it, his voice did sound clearer, less stuffy and lugubrious.

"It was bad," he said. "I thought I was going to have to get a new carrot. But come to find out, all I really needed was a new arm." As he spoke, a eucalyptus leaf dropped to the snow. Maybe Flock and Ivy would get some more eucalyptus in someday soon and we could get him a fresher branch.

"I have you to thank for this," he said.

"Me?"

"Of course. If you hadn't been so clumsy, I never would have gotten my new stick. Thank you!"

It was the first time my klutziness had drawn a rave.

I bid the snowman good night and found my sleigh at the end of the block, where I'd left it. When I hopped on and tried to turn on the ignition, all I got were a few clicks from inside the dashboard. I looked down at the power gauge. The battery was drained to zip.

Luckily, at that moment I heard the jangling harness bells of the sleigh bus coming up Celebration Boulevard. Pulled by a team of six sturdy reindeer in full winter coats, the sleigh bus went all the way up Sugarplum Mountain, and made a stop by Castle Kringle. I hurried to the corner and the driver stopped to let me on. The bus was full of elves going home from the Tournament of Chocolate, and there was a chorus of "A Marshmallow World" as I climbed onto the back bench. It might be the season for love songs, but elves loved to sing Christmas music all year long.

All the elves around me seemed paired off. They sat snugly shoulder-to-shoulder, holding hands. Some held heart-shaped Mylar balloons I'd seen street vendors selling in Christmastown. The one in front of me was white and had *ME + YOU* written in big red letters.

I joined my fellow passengers for a chorus until I noticed a copy of *Elf World* that a rider had left behind.

I picked up the magazine and flipped through it. Sure enough, the issue contained the "What's Your Sweetie Level?" quiz. My gaze landed on a random question.

How long can you stay angry with your sweetie?
a) Longer than the shelf life of a candy cane.
b) A cup of hot cocoa and a good night's sleep and I'm over it.
c) Angry? Who gets angry?

Humph. I couldn't see what Juniper saw in this nonsense. Not a lot of subtlety here. I read on.

How close should a couple be?
a) Totally independent but complementary, like pieces in a bridge mix.
b) Chocolate-covered caramel—distinct flavors, together forever!
c) Completely blended, like chocolate-hazelnut spread.

I shook my head. Juniper had been ready to reject Sterling because she didn't want to be a chocolate-covered caramel with him?

Or maybe she thought he was the Nutella type . . .

Which best described Nick and me?

I was so lost in thought that I almost missed the sleigh bus pulling up to my home. *Hard to miss a castle, April.* Luckily, the driver knew me.

"Castle Kringle!" he called out, as if anyone else would be hopping off there. When I snapped to, I was shocked by how much the sleigh bus had emptied out. Most all the other elves had already gotten off, and now it was just me and a few lodge elves who worked for Amory and Midge at Kringle Lodge, at the timberline of Sugarplum Mountain. I bade them and the driver a good night and hopped off the bus.

The driver had been kind enough to drive up to the castle so that I didn't have to trudge up the long driveway. Salty came around from the side building, shocked to see me disembarking from the bus.

"What happened to your sleigh?" he asked.

"I ran out of juice. I had to leave it in Christmastown."

He shook his head. "Wobbler shouldn't have abandoned you. I knew something was off when he came back on his own."

"Don't blame him—I told him he could have some time off to make up for the free time I gave Cannonball."

My assurances didn't ease the worry in his eyes. "Those two are losing their heads over that doe. Now they're refusing to sleep in the same reindeer barn. Wobbler said he'd rather stay in the sleigh shed."

"Do you have any sense of which one Flouncy prefers?"

He crossed his arms. "Wobbler definitely thinks he has the inside track. But then Cannonball is also convinced that he'll be escorting Flouncy to the Muzzle Nuzzle."

Oh dear. "May the best reindeer win, I guess."

Salty sighed. "What if they're two equally good reindeer vying for a heap of trouble?"

On that note, he left me standing under the light of the portico. I couldn't help noticing that someone—probably Salty himself—had put a pink lightbulb in the fixture. Pink and white tinsel wound around the columns. I was surprised Pamela hadn't ordered it to be replaced by the ribbon she'd picked out for Claire's wedding.

Jingles greeted me at the door holding a tray of hot cocoa aloft. Liquid chocolate was the last thing I needed, but I was still touched. "How nice," I said.

His lips turned down. "The cocoa's for Santa."

"Oh." Actually, that gave me an idea. I unwrapped myself from my outer layers and traded Jingles my muffler, coat, and hat for the cocoa tray. "I'll take this to Nick."

I found him behind his desk in the long office that was Command Central for all official Santa work. Behind him was the all-year Christmas tree, although at the moment it was decorated in pink and white lights, with red tinsel and sparkly ornaments shaped like hearts and cupids. A few looked as if they were aiming their arrows directly at Nick.

I set the tray down on his desk and jealously eyed the page spread out before him. Nick loved going over Santaland's account books, inventories, and other financial minutiae. It was the job he'd trained for before his older brother, Chris, had died and left him to fulfill the official Santa duties until Nick's nephew, Christopher, reached his majority.

Tonight, though, he had a world map spread open before him and was studying it with intense scrutiny.

"Isn't it a little early in the year for obsessing over the route for your big night?" I asked.

I mean, honestly. I knew delivering toys around the globe was a big job and a planning nightmare, but Christmas was ten months away.

He slapped the atlas closed and smiled up at me. "Sorry, darling. I was expecting Jingles." He gave me a kiss. "You're a definite upgrade."

"Don't let Jingles hear you say that." I frowned at the atlas. Why *was* he looking at maps now? "Are you worried that your usual route needs to change for some reason?" I asked. "Is it a safety worry?"

He shrugged. "You know me—I just like to nail down details early. How was your day?" Just after the question left his lips, his smile faded. "Doc Honeytree called to let me know that Sterling was poisoned. It's very disturbing."

"Claire's freaked out," I said. "She believes her wedding is cursed. She's even rumbling about calling it off."

"She shouldn't do that."

"Jake doesn't want to cancel, especially since we think the victim was actually intended to be Juniper." I frowned. "Of course, that's not great for the wedding, either, since Juniper's a bridesmaid."

Nick frowned. "Who would want to kill Juniper?"

"That's what we're trying to figure out."

"We?"

"Jake and I." Catching Nick's arched-brow expression, I explained, "I can't just stand aside as one friend's wedding hangs in the balance and another friend is the target of a Valentine's Day maniac."

Nick looked thoughtful as he poured out a mug of cocoa. "You'd better take this," he said, trying to hand the hot steaming cup to me. "I think you need a soothing beverage more than I do."

I hesitated, then shook my head in a rare show of willpower. "I'm full of chocolate already from the tournament." The memory of that event made me flop into the nearest chair in exhaustion. "You won't believe what happened with Happy Greenberry's nougats."

"Did he win?" Nick asked.

"No—Ollie did. You can't imagine how good—"

Nick held up a hand. "Don't say any more."

"Why? What's the matter?"

"I'm judging the grand finale on Valentine's Day," he reminded me. "I don't want there to be any appearance of bias against any of the contest entrants."

"Seriously?" I asked. "Two married people can't talk about it? It's a chocolate tournament, not a Supreme Court decision."

His face morphed into that judgy Santa expression—as if I were at risk of being on the naughty list. "These contests mean a lot to the elves. I don't want to behave in a way that could taint the result."

"Even if it's just a little harmless gossip?" I asked.

"Gossip usually isn't worth the breath it takes to spread it."

I frowned, feeling disgruntled. I didn't consider myself a blabbermouth. Could telling your husband something even be considered gossip? Wasn't that just talking, or sharing?

Maybe I *was* a blabbermouth . . .

And maybe my irritation over Nick's insinuation that I was a gossip was the sugar crash hitting me. I forced myself to change the subject. "You should have seen the flower arrangement Amory bought for Midge for Valentine's. It was huge."

"Amory never can curb his liking for frivolous, impractical things." Nick looked down at his ledger pad again. Back to accounts.

"Frivolous and impractical is sort of what Valentine's is," I said.

"You can say that again." He was already lost in his tangles of scribbles.

"It really was a beautiful spray."

"Mm."

I tilted my head. "Has it ever occurred to you that we're becoming bridge mix?"

He dropped his pen on his desk blotter and fixed me with a puzzled stare. "What are you talking about?"

"Bridge mix," I repeated. "Independent, but tossed together."

His lips screwed up. "That sounds . . . ridiculous."

"Yes, it is."

But couldn't something be both ridiculous and true?

His gaze narrowed on me. "Is this some kind of hint for something you'd want for Valentine's. Bridge mix?"

I laughed. "No."

"I was going to renew your Frequent Fudger card for you, but you'd already done that."

"Some things are too important to let lapse," I joked. "Don't worry about Valentine's."

He nodded. "Okay. Sounds good."

I hadn't expected him to agree so quickly. "I mean, of course little silly romantic gestures are nice . . ."

He smiled and finished, "But once you've been married four whole years, they don't seem sensible."

Sensible. I needed to shut up or I'd end up as one of those women whose husbands gave them appliances and vacuum cleaners.

Or concert band cymbal donations . . .

I was a sensible person, but there were times when sensible didn't seem as good as ridiculous.

Chapter 9

Usually Jingles would bring me my morning coffee and deliver whatever tidbits of gossip were floating around Christmastown or the castle. But this morning I managed to sleep until hammering echoing through the halls from a distant part of the castle woke me. The elves were still fixing up the Old Keep for Claire's wedding on Saturday afternoon. We didn't want another ceiling collapse on the overflow wedding guests.

The thought of the wedding made me bolt out of bed. I had a lot to do—including once again traipsing over to the Order of Elven Seamstresses to see how my dress would fit today. I felt like I was one nougat away from needing the seams let out again. And that reminded me: tonight was Caramels and Nuts, which was bound to be competitive. My taste buds needed to be in tiptop condition.

At the thought of the Tournament of Chocolate, I couldn't help thinking about the scene that had occurred last night with Happy Greenberry. *Surprise, surprise . . .*

But it was just a phrase. It didn't mean that he was the one who'd written that poem.

I reached for the phone on my bedside table and texted Juniper. She would be at the library already.

Time for a coffee break later this morning?

Tiny pulsing snowflakes appeared within seconds, indicating that Juniper was typing.

Merry Muffins @ 11?

I gave that suggestion an enthusiastic mittened thumbs-up.

I thought about asking her to come up with a list of anyone who might want to kill her, but decided that might be something that could be handled better in person, over a warm muffin.

What *didn't* go over better with a warm, buttered muffin?

My stomach rumbled at the thought. Jingles was AWOL with my usual morning tray, so I headed downstairs to see if I could scare up a cup of coffee. On the way to the breakfast room, I was nearly mowed down by a battalion of elves transporting a piece of the heaviest, gaudiest furniture I'd ever seen. It appeared to be something between a sideboard table and a breakfront cabinet. The wood was heavily carved with swirling leaves, blossoms, and cupids, all covered in gilt. The gold was eye-strainingly shiny. Castle Kringle had some magnificent old furniture, but this looked like something straight from Versailles—the Vegas version.

Jingles appeared just in time to steer me against the wall, out of harm's way.

"What is that?" I asked him.

"The display table Mrs. Claus—the Dowager Mrs. Claus—ordered."

I knew Pamela and I had different decorative taste, but when had she decided to go full-bore Liberace?

With big arm gestures, Jingles gestured to the elves to stop and then maneuver the piece toward the wall. Like he was docking the *Queen Mary*.

"What is Pamela going to display?" I asked.

Jingles looked at me as if I were thick. "The wedding gifts." He frowned. "Some of them. Obviously, we're not going to display every set of toasting tongs that comes in."

I shook my head. "Toasting tongs?"

"Have you never been to a wedding? Brides always get too many toasting tongs—although some are purely ornamental. Almost all of them, actually. Most elves use toasters now."

I had a vague recollection of seeing odd objects hanging near hearths in some of the elf cottages I'd visited. I'd just assumed they were fireplace utensils, which I suppose they were. Fireplace utensils that were vestiges of a time when elves used to toast their bread over open flames in the family hearth.

"Amazing," I said. "I'm still bumbling into little bits of elf culture I didn't know about."

"It's not just elf culture." My sister-in-law, Lucia, swooped in out of nowhere. "It's Claus culture, too. Who doesn't like toast?"

I smiled. "Let me guess—*you're* giving Claire toasting tongs."

"Not just any kind of tongs. Mine are carved from reindeer antlers."

I drew back. "Is that sanitary? Or even legal?"

Reindeer were protected citizens in Santaland. I couldn't imagine that the reindeer herds looked favorably on having their antlers harvested to make outmoded cooking utensils.

She rolled her eyes. "They're from naturally shed antlers. Quasar's, in fact."

Next to her, Quasar dropped his head modestly, his red nose fizzling like a wonky light bulb. He wasn't comfortable being the center of a conversation. "Not that anyone will recognize the antlers as mine. It's a w-work of art."

"The antlers are twisted to look like a heart when the tongs clasp together. It was done by Emerald Goldpuff, the premier antlerist in the North Pole. Do you want to see them? They haven't been wrapped yet."

"That's okay—I'm sure Claire will love them." I did want to ask Quasar a few questions, though. "Do you know a reindeer named Flouncy?" When he didn't respond immediately, I prompted, "Vixen herd?"

"I–I've *seen* her," Quasar said carefully. "But we've never spoken."

"I think she's caught the interest of my reindeer," I said.

"*Both* of them?" Lucia asked.

I nodded.

"That can get ugly," Lucia said.

"Cannonball and Wobbler have always been such friends."

"Y-you know what the elves say," Quasar said. "'Y-you can't split a snowball in two.'"

I hadn't heard that. Like a lot of elf sayings, I had to puzzle over it for a moment.

Lucia gave me a firm pat on the shoulder. "Maybe it's not as serious as you think," she said. "A Valentine crush that'll be over in a week."

Somehow, having Lucia trying to reassure me only made me worry that the situation was more fraught than I assumed. Lucia was not a reassuring kind of person. A situation had to be dire to impel her to express sympathy.

I had a hard time imagining Wobbler and Cannonball crossing antlers. On the other hand, I wouldn't have thought they were the types to snipe at each other, either. But they'd both been doing that for the past couple of days.

A delighted clap of hands interrupted my thoughts.

"Isn't this wonderful?" Pamela still held her hands together, her face lit up like a delighted child's on Christmas morning. More than her enthusiasm for the display, however, I was more struck by what she was wearing. Her formal dress, which was vaguely familiar to me, was fashioned from creamy beige taffeta, gathered at the waist, with puffy sleeves and a full skirt. It even had a modest train, like something out of a fairy tale.

Where had I seen that dress before?

"Are you going somewhere?" Lucia asked, bemused. "It seems kind of early in the day for ball gowns."

Pamela's eyes sparkled. "Isn't it a dream? Madame Neige sent it over this morning and I just had to try it on." She performed an elegant twirl. "It's an old dress that I had altered to wear at Claire's wedding. Do you like it?"

Wedding. Suddenly, the answer hit me. "That looks like Princess Di's wedding dress."

"That's exactly what I wanted when I got married," she said. "I always loved Princess Di. What a lady."

"You mean that's *your* wedding dress?" I asked.

Lucia and I exchanged bemused glances.

She plucked at the skirt's fabric in satisfaction. "It certainly is—and it still fits."

"It's r-r-ravishing," Quasar said.

Pamela didn't usually relish having a reindeer wandering around the castle—especially one with a tendency to munch on floral decorations—but now she bestowed her most brightest on him. "How sweet of you to say that!" Leaning in to him, she confessed, "Madame Neige had to let out a few seams, of course."

Madame Neige really was a miracle worker. But what could I say about that dress? It screamed wedding gown. How would Claire feel about being out-brided by Pamela?

"Are you going to have it dyed?" I asked.

Pamela goggled at me in shock. "Dye it! Why?"

How could I put this diplomatically? "Isn't it sort of not the thing to dress in bridal white when you're not the bride?"

You would have thought I'd just tossed a can of black paint over her. "This dress is *not* bridal white. It's cream. Is there a law against wearing cream?"

"It's not a matter of laws—it's just that the bride usually gets dibs on white," I said.

"Don't be ridiculous. It's not as if anyone would mistake me for Claire." She twitched her train and sighed. "*My* wedding was so wonderful. I do wish you all could have seen it."

"That would have involved time travel, Mother," Lucia reminded her.

Pamela was so absorbed in her own memories, I'm not sure she heard her. "The castle looked so beautiful that day—it was truly magical. You wouldn't believe the number of guests who showed up."

I had a hunch that it was around 543. And that the day involved a whole bunch of harps. Pamela's fixation on Claire's wedding made a little more sense to me now. It was she herself who wanted to step into a time machine and relive the past—back to when she was young and the love of her life was still with her.

I held my tongue.

Maybe normal Claire might get a little spicy about too many bridal gowns showing up at the wedding, but the distracted Claire of this week might not even notice.

On the way into town, I had to stop by the Order of Elven Seamstresses to see if they wanted me to try on the dress again after their alterations. That was my pretext, at least. I was also curious to see if anyone had seen Sterling enter the building yesterday.

Button greeted me at the door dressed in a thick, red, boiled wool tunic with the Order's red cloak draped over her shoulders. She glanced at my sleigh. "What's the matter with your reindeer?"

Cannonball had a bandage on the side of his snout. According to Salty, Wobbler and Cannonball had been in a shoving match this morning before he broke it up.

Noticing our stares, Cannonball looked sheepish. "I'm fine," he called out. "It's just a scratch. He barely touched me."

It was lucky that the male reindeer had shed their antlers for the winter. Otherwise it could have been much worse.

"You were here at the door yesterday when Sterling Redwinkle arrived, weren't you?" I asked Button.

She paled at the mention of yesterday's tragedy. "Oh, yes. I let him in. I was so sorry to hear what happened to him."

"You've probably been asked all this by the constable, but did you notice anything about his appearance?"

Her forehead cracked into puzzled lines. "Constable Crinkles never spoke to me."

That figured.

"He probably has a lot on his mind," she said, "what with the Tournament of Chocolate going on. I heard the constabulary won Nougats and Creams."

I was determined not to get sidetracked by nougats and creams again. "I was just curious about how Sterling seemed when you saw him. To us, his collapse seemed to come out of the blue."

She nodded. "Yes—that's how it seemed to me, too. When he came in, he was just his usual friendly self. If you want to know the truth, his greeting put me a little aflutter. He was so handsome." Tears stood in her eyes. "And then the next thing I heard, he was gone." She snapped her gloved fingers. "Just like that."

"So all you did was open the door for him? He must have run into Blanchette in the main corridor." She was the one who'd escorted him into the viewing room.

"Maybe so . . . although *I* only saw him briefly greeting that other bridesmaid."

"Dolly Frost?"

"I guess that's her name," Button said, her barely disguised distaste revealing a prejudice many elves here had against the denizens of the Farthest Frozen Reaches.

Dolly had misplaced her bag, I remembered. "What did they say?"

"I didn't *listen*, ma'am. I'm just the door elf. I did notice that she seemed to be looking for something, and he set down his box to help her search."

"So he had the florist box when he came in."

She frowned. "I don't recall. But he must have—it was on the table over there. I remember that."

"The florists deny that the corsage came from there."

"The box had their sticker." She glanced furtively around the foyer and into the main corridor, then lowered her voice. "The rumor is that the Order is going to stop sending our roses to the florist's now. Madame Neige is worried that this incident is going to blacken our name."

Incident? This was *murder*. And Madame Neige seemed to be ready to assign guilt quickly. I wondered if she would talk to me— she was usually so tight-lipped. I could probably coax more information out of Blanchette.

"I need to speak to Blanchette."

The elf shifted. "Is Mrs. Claus expected?"

"I have a dress here being altered."

As if she didn't know. I'd been here every day this week.

"Things have been thrown into a bit of confusion here today, Mrs. Claus. Madame had to leave unexpectedly, and Miss Blanchette has had to meet with the chief of the Santaland Fire Brigade."

"About Sterling's death?"

She blinked. "Oh, no. The Order does their uniforms, so they're probably discussing that. But he's also going to take Sterling's snowmobile back to Tinkertown. You probably saw it outside."

"I did." The snowmobile was where Sterling had left it, but the workers at the Order had draped it in black crepe overnight.

Button dashed a tear from her eye. "So sad."

"Maybe I can speak to Snowbell," I suggested. "She knows my dress."

Hopefully by the time I was finished asking Snowbell for her memories of yesterday, Blanchette would be free.

Button shifted. "Snowbell's belowstairs today, in Hades"—she flushed—"I mean, in the ironing room."

My eyes were drawn to the narrow arched door in the corner of the foyer that Button had instinctively looked at when she was talking about belowstairs. "Does that lead to the staircase?"

Panic overcame her. "You can't go down there, ma'am. If you'll just wait—"

"That's all right. I'll find the way."

If I waited, I worried I'd be stonewalled all day. Much as I wanted to ask questions here, I also didn't want to be late for my appointment with Juniper at Merry Muffins. I darted for the arched door and found myself descending steep stone steps lighted only by a few dim candles in wall sconces. It reminded me of the Old Keep at Castle Kringle . . . the wing where the roof had caved in.

At that unpleasant thought, my feet tapped more quickly down the steps.

Unlike Algid Honeytree's basement, the farther down I went

here, the higher the temperature rose. By the time I reached the bottom of the stairs and stepped on level ground—semi-level, since the stone beneath my feet was uneven—sweat was pouring off me. I dug into my purse for a handkerchief and mopped my face.

I'd say that it was like a sauna, but saunas usually have at least a pretense of relaxation. A few steps down a long, coved-ceilinged corridor, and arched doorway opened onto a large workroom, I could see that this was a place of work. Steam emanated from a massive industrial flatwork press. It was fashioned from metal—as ornate in its way as a Beaux Arts sculpture. A large handle crank-turned a wheel that controlled the motion of the top of the press.

Through the steam I could make out Snowbell at the crank, which lifted her little feet off the floor as she turned it and the crank reached its zenith. The press rose off a wrinkle-free length of plain cloth bleached to a snowy white. The poor elf looked half wilted. No mystery why this place was called Hades.

Her eyes went wide as a snowy owl's when she caught sight of me. "Mrs. Claus—you shouldn't be down here. Are you lost?"

Unwinding my muffler, I crossed to her. "I came down to talk to you."

She appeared to gulp, but that might have just been because she was dehydrated from working in this sweat box. I ripped off my hat and gloves. I was ready to do an entire striptease. I didn't know how Snowbell could stand to work down here in the standard cap, tunic, tights, and booties of the Order of Elven Seamstresses.

"Madame will be very unhappy to learn that you've been here. This isn't a place for people from Castle Kringle—especially not Mrs. Claus."

"I wouldn't think it's a great place for elves, either," I said, fanning myself with my wool cap. "What are you doing down here? I thought you worked in the fitting and viewing room."

She ducked her head. "I usually do, but Blanchette sent me down here today."

"What did you do, murder someone?"

I was joking, but the moment the words slipped out, their inappropriateness made me want to kick myself. My thoughtless flippancy struck poor Snowbell like a slap. She reacted as if I'd accused her of actual murder.

"Of course not," she said. "I had nothing to do with Mr. Redwinkle's murder."

"So you know foul play was involved."

"Oh, everyone knows! Several of our Order came back from the Tournament of Chocolate and said it was all anyone talked about afterward. I still can't believe it—it's too terrible."

She visibly shook at the memory.

"Did you see anything yesterday?"

Her face looked as white as the sheet that she pulled off the iron press and began to fold with crisp, precise movements. In no time, she had that bedsheet chunked down to the size of a hardcover book. She tossed it on a pile of identical rectangles, then took another sheet from the rolling bin behind her and flapped it over the press.

"Better stand back," she warned as she took hold of the crank.

I was too mesmerized by the large piece of hot, flat metal coming down to heed her advice. It landed on the white cloth in an explosion of steam and all at once I felt as if I were standing next to a fire-breathing dragon. I flapped my hands in front of me, but it was like trying to bat away a Santa Ana wind.

"There are a lot of these for me to do today," she said.

"Don't you mind being down here?" I said. "It's like a furnace."

"I go where I'm told."

Why would they send an accomplished seamstress apprentice down here to iron sheets, though? To say that this was drudge work was an understatement.

"I was wondering what you saw yesterday."

Snowbell turned away from me and went back to the crank. "I didn't see anything." Her face was flushed—from exertion, I supposed. But the ways of this place were weird even by Santaland standards.

"Is it typical for an elf of your skill to do this?" I asked.

"Madame Neige says that there's no such thing as an unimportant job."

Those were words I agreed with. Still, I wondered how often Madame Neige ironed sheets.

I realized I was letting myself be distracted. *Focus, April.*

"I'm curious if you noticed anything out of the ordinary yesterday."

Snowbell turned away from me and went back to the crank. "I didn't see anything," she repeated. Her face was almost beet red.

Mine probably was, too. "Were you in the corridor when Blanchette escorted Sterling in, or were you already in the viewing room?"

"Neither. I was tidying a changing room. I couldn't have seen anything. If you're trying to gather information about what happened to Mr. Redwinkle, I can't be of any help to you."

She was adamant about that last statement—and yet I sensed anxiety in her gaze. She, like Button, didn't like my being here.

The corner of my mouth twisted in disappointment. "Maybe Blanchette remembers something."

"Ouch!"

Snowbell hopped back from the press, flapping her hand and then lifting it to her mouth.

I hurried to her. "Are you all right?"

"I just brushed my hand against the hot metal. So careless—but it happens all the time down here."

"That machine's a hazard," I said, glancing back at the press. It was a beast. And it seemed like extremely hard, hazardous labor just to have wrinkle-free bedding. "Why are you ironing sheets?"

"Madame insists we all sleep on starched and pressed bed linens," Snowbell explained. "She wants us to feel refined. We come from all walks of life here, you know. Some are from the premier elf families of Santaland—but some of us had more humble backgrounds. My parents both worked at the Tinkertown Gumdrop Factory. They wanted me to do better."

"Nothing wrong with making gumdrops." I was rather fond of them.

"I agree—but they thought I would be able to learn skills here that might allow me to open my own shop someday. That was their dream, at least." She lowered her head. "They're gone now."

And now she was ironing sheets in Hades.

"You aren't down here permanently," I said, hoping. This seemed like punishment.

"Oh no. I'm sure I'll be assigned upstairs again. Or maybe to the sewing room—or crafts and millinery."

"Crafts and millinery would be where they make the roses?" I asked. "The ones that got sold to Flock and Ivy's?"

She nodded. "That department is on the third floor, just below the dormitories."

"I'd like to see it."

Her eyes widened. "Madame doesn't allow visitors."

"No one?"

She shook her head, but the gesture was belied by a voice behind us. "We'll surely make an exception for Mrs. Claus," Blanchette said.

I turned. Even though her face seemed a little red and glistened in the steamy heat, her fitted tunic was starched and neat. "I will take you on a tour, Mrs. Claus. I had no idea that you were so curious about our Order."

"I'd love to see where all the work gets done." And maybe I could also see if any elves had a guilty look.

As the press hissed and billowed steam behind us, Blanchette escorted me back up the staircase. "Your dress is done. You can take it with you if you like. I will be at the castle on Valentine's morning to see if there are any last-minute alterations to be made."

"That's very kind of you."

"It's part of our service."

I had a feeling it was part of their service only for Castle Kringle. I can't imagine that the average elf received blue-ribbon treatment.

Instead of going into the viewing room, I followed Blanchette up another staircase—wider and grander, with walls crammed with framed artist sketches of fashions during Madame Neige's career here. The bright colors perked up the dark stone walls.

Walking slightly ahead of me, Blanchette turned her head to speak. "I hope the elves haven't been spreading gossip to you here. What happened yesterday has upset us all, to be sure, but Madame gave us strict instructions not to rush to judgment and to keep our own counsel as the matter was being investigated."

That was interesting. "I heard that Madame Neige was away on business."

"Yes, ma'am. But last night at dinner she spoke to the entire Order. It was quite moving—all about the profound mark death leaves on a place where it occurs so tragically, so unexpectedly." As she waited at the second landing for me to catch up with her, she added, "Madame is a sensitive soul."

I attempted to keep my expression neutral. Madame Neige always struck me as hard as nails, and not especially empathetic. But maybe having an unnatural death occur here had spurred her to rise the occasion and comfort the elves beneath her roof, who were all devoted to her.

Blanchette led me down a stark hallway with whitewashed walls. No decorations up here. A whirring sound that grew louder the farther down the hallway we went. She pushed open a door to a long room with three rows of individual tables, each with a sewing machine atop it. This is where the noise I'd heard in the corridor had come from. It was loud enough to drive one to distraction, and was certainly too loud to talk over comfortably. Noting that I'd gotten a good look, Blanchette shut the door again.

The next door opened up on a room of equal size, but this one had three rows of long, connected tables. Every few feet an elf sat bent over a project in painstaking concentration. Some were making flowers, some hats, some embroidering fabric. Blanchette led me to where one elf was busy tying perfect bows in the creamy pink fabric I was now quite familiar with. Each bow was finished off with sparkly tinsel.

"For the wedding," Blanchette explained to me. "We are working very hard to make sure all is ready in time for Valentine's Day."

I smiled at an elf sitting at the table, and she blushed the same pink as the ribbon in her hands.

"This is Hope," Blanchette said, making the introduction. "She will be assisting me at the castle on Saturday."

"Wonderful." I turned to Blanchette. "You should definitely ask Snowbell to be there, too."

Blanchette's brow furrowed. "Why?"

"She's always been a calm presence in the fitting room. She will probably know exactly how to soothe ruffled feathers and jittery nerves."

"That's a very nice compliment you pay her, Mrs. Claus," Blanchette said. "I've heard that you are very kind. I'll make sure Snowbell is with me the morning of the wedding."

"Thank you." As she escorted me out of the craft room, I asked, "I suppose there's no sense in waiting to speak to Madame Neige. I'm curious about what she thinks about what happened here yesterday."

Blanchette's face pinched slightly into a frown. "Madame is in town. I believe she is cutting off our association with Flock and Ivy's."

"Cutting off the Order's association because she believes Ivy poisoned Sterling Redwinkle?"

"I've probably said too much."

But not enough for my liking. "For someone who was counseling the elves working for her not to rush to judgment, it sounds as if Madame Neige has already made up her mind about who the culprit was."

Blanchette's face became a blank mask. "Madame doesn't share all her thoughts with me."

"Not even about the business? Aren't you second-in-command here?"

She squared her shoulders. "This is Madame's empire. Second-in-command is still only a slight step above the lowliest seamstress."

I could see that. Madame Neige might be a small woman, but she cast a long shadow.

"Did you see anything unusual yesterday?" I asked.

Her brow furrowed. "I saw an elf dying. That was unusual—and terrible."

"You led Sterling into the view room, didn't you?"

"Yes—he was in the corridor. I knew the bridesmaids were all in a present state of dress, so I escorted him in as he asked me to. Was I wrong to do so?"

"I don't think so."

She looked doubtful. "In retrospect, knowing what happened, I wish I would have turned him away."

"That corsage would have ended up in *someone's* hands."

"True. Still, one can't help engaging in what-ifs."

I could see that. "So I guess Sterling had a box when he came in."

She cocked her head, thinking back. "I just assumed so—but I didn't actually see him walk through the door. You'd have to ask Button."

"Button doesn't remember."

Blanchette lifted her hands. "Well, there you are. No one expects bad things to happen. We don't live life as if we're going to be called to testify as witnesses."

Blanchette started to lead me back down the staircase, but a light from above made me twist around. Overhead, high about the landing on the fourth floor, cherished daylight shone through the windowed turret above. "Is that where the cupola is?"

The cupola was the one rather fanciful architectural feature on the rather austere gray stone building.

"Yes. There's a wonderful view from there, but probably nothing as spectacular as what you see looking out from the castle."

There were vantages from Castle Kringle where it was possible to view Christmastown and the entire valley around it. And, in the distance, we could see the formidable peaks of Mount Myrrh in the distant Farthest Frozen Reaches.

"I've always liked that cupola."

Blanchette's lips turned up in a genuine smile. "And the light coming in is so welcome—even what little light we get in winter."

Daylight still didn't last long these days. Which reminded me, I needed to get to Merry Muffins to meet Juniper.

Chapter 10

I was running late getting down the mountain, but once we were in town, I noticed something odd and asked Cannonball to stop. The reindeer pulled up to the curb and I hopped out. Bumble the snowman was heading in my direction—at a glacial pace. He'd moved perhaps half a block from where I'd seen him last.

He also now had matching eucalyptus branch arms. Ivy must have found another branch to match his replacement limb. He looked oddly bushy-armed, but symmetrical.

"Hi, Bumble," I said. "I thought you liked your spot in front of the florist. Where are you going?"

"It's a secret. I'm headed to the constabulary."

Apparently he wasn't quite clear on the definition of *secret*. Then again, at the rate he was moving, it would take him a week or so to reach the constabulary, which was a long time for a snowman to keep something under his hat.

"You want to talk to Crinkles about something?" I asked.

"That's the idea."

"Is it an emergency? It might take you a while to get there." *Might* made that a laughable understatement, but I didn't want to insult him. "Perhaps I could get him for you."

He chewed over my offer. "I don't want to inconvenience the

constable, but you're right. In matters of life and death, there's no time to lose."

Life and death? I was already pulling out my phone. "I'll call him. How about that?"

"Yes, thank you. That will save me quite a bit of effort."

I waited through a few rings. "Christmastown Constabulary, home of award-winning confections," Crinkles answered in a chirpy voice. "How may we be of help to you today?"

That blue ribbon might be going to the constables' heads.

"Hello, Constable, this is Mrs. Claus."

"Oh—hello!" He chuckled. "Ollie's busy making caramels for tonight."

Last night I'd been so full of chocolate that the idea of another night of tournament judging had made me nauseous. Twelve hours later, the mere mention of caramels perked me up. Ah, the cycle of carbohydrate consumption.

"I realize that we'll be handicapped after winning the round last night," he said.

"Every night of the contest is a blank slate," I assured him.

Next to me, the snowman cleared his throat. I'd gotten side-tracked by sweets.

"I have Bumble here," I told Crinkles. "He wants to speak to you."

"About a very important matter." Bumble enunciated loudly toward the phone.

As if Crinkles wouldn't guess a matter was important if a snowman was calling him.

I nearly handed the phone over to the eucalyptus limb before I remembered that Bumble wouldn't be able to hold it. I thrust it out at arm's length at the side of the snowman's head and turned slightly to give him privacy.

"Hello?" Bumble's voice was still loud and stiff. I guess he wasn't used to talking on the phone. "Am I speaking to Constable Crinkles of the Christmastown Constabulary?"

A tinny reply bleated out of the phone.

"Could you speak a little louder, Constable?" Bumble asked. "I'm having trouble hearing you."

I looked around, noting that we were alone on this stretch of sidewalk, and then volunteered, "Let me put you on speakerphone."

Now the constable's voice came through loud and clear. "What's happening?"

"I heard about the murder of Sterling Redwinkle this morning," Bumble said. "I would like to report that I saw him talking to his probable killer."

"When?" I asked, before Crinkles had a chance to.

So much for giving them privacy. I was just too nosey to stand by silently.

"The night before last. Sterling came to the florist shop just before closing time."

I cast my mind back. That would have been the night of Juniper's dinner with the Redwinkles. Had Sterling come by the florist before picking her up?

"When he left, he crossed the street," Bumble continued. "Jaywalked, I'm sorry to tell you, Constable."

Crinkles harrumphed over the phone. "That's not good to hear."

I took a breath for patience. I was still focused on the fact that Sterling had gone into the florist's. Ivy and Flock had sworn that the corsage hadn't come from their shop. But why else would Sterling have been there the night before his death? To *not* order a corsage?

"What happened when he crossed the street?" I asked.

"That's when he stopped to speak to a female elf in a red coat, right over there in front of the podiatrist's office. Dr. Winkle was already closed by then, though."

That was too bad. Otherwise someone at Dr. Winkle's might have witnessed the encounter, too.

"Was Sterling carrying anything when he left the florist?" I asked.

Bumble thought about this. "I don't think so, but I was turned at a bad angle. I'm not as agile as I used to be."

I was hoping he would have noticed a corsage box.

"Did you recognize the elf?" Crinkles asked through the phone.

"No, sir." He let out a regretful sigh. "I could have told you all this yesterday, but I didn't know there had been a murder."

My arm began to protest holding the phone out rigidly. I needed to do some muscle conditioning. "You must have received some impression of her," I said. "Enough to make you suspicious later when you did hear about the murder."

Enough to make him decide to expend a lot of snowman energy to go to the constabulary.

"I could only see them through my peripheral vision, but they were talking like they were in a huddle. I couldn't hear words, but they were being very furtive."

I usually set store by snowmen as crime witnesses. They spend all their time out in the open, on the street, not moving, and not sleeping much, either. They were like sentries stationed all over Santaland.

But all Bumble was giving us was a vague description of the elf Sterling had exchanged a word with on the sidewalk one evening. It could have been a conversation with his killer, or it could have been a random encounter. Or an assignation . . .

That last thought popped into my head out of the blue, and I batted it around uncomfortably before dismissing it. Would Sterling have come to the Order of Elven Seamstresses the next morning to drop to one knee, presumably intending to ask Juniper to marry him, if he'd been seeing another elf on the sly? What would be the point of that?

Unless there was more love left over than both Sterling and Ivy had wanted to admit.

"The elf couldn't have been Ivy, could it?" I asked Bumble.

"Oh no!" he said, sounding shocked. "I'd know Ivy. She's my friend. She gave me my new arms."

"We're very grateful to you for coming forward," Crinkles said.

I could have sworn the snowman swelled with pride. "Only doing my duty, sir."

I took the phone off speaker and said to Crinkles, "This tells me that the corsage did come from here."

"Bumble didn't see a box, though."

"He might have ordered it and had it delivered later," I said.

"Ivy denies it. Flock does, too. I've never known Flock to lie."

My impression had been that he was nervous about something. "What about this elf in the red coat?"

Crinkles chuckled. "Weeping Walruses! Every elf I know has a red coat."

He wasn't wrong. In Santaland, it was the favorite color in winter wear.

Also, I didn't want to say anything in front of Bumble, but I was beginning to worry that he wasn't a reliable witness. He admitted he'd only been able to see out of the corner of his eye. Maybe hearing talk of murder had made him imagine more drama in the simple encounter between Sterling and the elf across the street.

"If you have any ideas, let me know," Crinkles said. "I'll see you tonight at the tournament, I guess."

"I'll put my thinking cap on," I said, trying not to betray Crinkles's skepticism in my tone of voice. Bumbles was eyeing me curiously.

When I ended the call with the constable, he asked, "Do you really have one of those?"

"One of those what?"

"A thinking cap," he said. "I could sure use one."

"It's just a figure of speech," I told him. "Like the elf saying about not being able to cut a snowball in half."

"But you *can't* cut a snowball in half," he said. "I should know—I'm made of them. But if there's a real thinking cap, I'd sure like to have one."

I think I'd just managed to confuse him more.

"Your hat suits you well," I said, straightening his old bowler. "You don't need a thinking cap. You've been very helpful to the constable."

"I'll keep my eyes open," he promised. "Maybe I'll see that elf again."

"You've done all you can," I told Bumble. "Don't go looking for trouble."

"You don't have to worry about that. I've already had more excitement in a week than I usually have in a year."

I thanked him again and hurried on to Merry Muffins.

Because I'd been waylaid, Juniper was already installed at our usual window table, and like the stellar friend she was, she'd ordered me a coffee and my favorite apple-ginger muffin.

"Oh good—you're here," she said, swallowing a bite of the eggnog-spice muffin she preferred. "I was just finishing up drawing up my list."

I was busy getting out of my coat and unwinding my scarf, but I couldn't hide my surprise. "How did you know we needed to draw up a list?" I'd intended to broach the idea of making a possible enemies list once we'd eaten a muffin or two.

"Because there's so much we need to do." She nibbled at the muffin as she looked over a page full of her tidy writing. "I've got Trumpet at the top."

"Trumpet?" That shocked me. Trumpet was the proprietor of We Three Beans coffeehouse, our favorite hangout. He was a prince among elves . . . and made the best latte in the North Pole. "Surely not."

She tilted her head. "Surely not what?"

"Surely you don't think Trumpet would want to kill you."

She drew back in confusion. "*Kill* me? What are you talking about?"

After draping my coat over the seatback, I sank into my chair. "Sterling's murder. What are *you* talking about?"

"Claire's wedding shower. We need to talk to Trumpet to see when we can get into the coffeehouse and decorate."

I breathed a sigh of relief. "Oh—yes." My thoughts had been so consumed by the murder and what had happened to Sterling, the plans for Claire's hen party had completely escaped me. The timing worked out particularly well, since I didn't have to be a judge at the Tournament of Chocolate tomorrow evening. We were going to start with a surprise shower at We Three Beans and then move on to the Mistletoe Tavern for some more raucous celebrating.

At least, as raucous as Christmastown could offer. Grog, darts, and some frenzied elf polkas, maybe. Although Dazzle Winterbright's set list leaned heavily on love songs and ballads, he could also let his hair down and lead his combo in more upbeat numbers.

I hoped Dazzle's throat was okay. I should probably check up on that, too. Otherwise we would end up having to get a last-minute replacement. Blizzard Goldstocking, maybe.

"I'll call on Trumpet," Juniper said, marking a star by his name. "You obviously have other things on your mind." She aimed a wry smile at me. "Like people trying to kill me . . ."

I took a sip of coffee. "I would think you'd have that on your mind, too."

She blurted out a laugh. "What do you think I did last night while You Better Watch Out installed locks all over my apartment? I've got more security now than the Strategic Candy Cane Reserves, by the way."

"I'm sorry if you were freaked out. I should have called you."

"No, it was good. I got a lot done while I was freaking out." She flipped back a few pages. "I drew up a list of names."

When she pushed it across the table at me, I was shocked at how long it was. "A whole page of names of elves who want to kill you?"

"Who *might* have motive to," she said. "The bottom half are mostly library patrons."

I gave those a quick scan until one name jumped out at me. "Happy Greenberry?" I said. "He was the runner-up at Nougats and Creams."

She bit her lip. "I hesitated to put him on there, actually. That was just a library fine thing, although he did pitch a fit after we revoked his card."

"He must have had a lot of fines."

"Actually, he was the one whose complaints to the municipal council caused us to do away with late fees. But I was all for that. By the time the policy went through, I think he knew I was on his side."

The decision to do away with late return fees at the library had created a firestorm of controversy last year. Many Santalanders thought allowing patrons to hang onto books past their return date was the beginning of the end of civilization. Without deterrents, who would follow any rules?

But Juniper, who trusted in the innate goodness of all living creatures, was certain Santaland library users would not take advantage of the new honor system. So far, she'd been proven right. Books were still being returned at about the same on-time rate as before.

"If he's had his slate wiped clean, I don't understand why Happy would be on your list."

She shrugged. "I just remembered that he seemed very temperamental. A lot of pent-up frustration in that elf."

No kidding. On the other hand, I still felt guilty and torn over giving him the red ribbon.

I continued to scan down the list. "Otto Henberry? Your *landlord*?" I asked incredulously.

"Dave got out one day and ate his peppermint plant."

Dave was her pet rabbit. "I would worry about him poisoning the rabbit, not his paying tenant."

"Maybe you're right," Juniper said.

I crossed out the landlord's name and went on to the next one. "Ginger Whitesong?"

"We were friends in school. When I told her I couldn't go to her skating party because it was my volunteer day at the library, she followed me down Celebration Boulevard one day after school and threw a snowball at me. Constable Crinkles, who was just a young constable at the time, saw the whole thing and gave her a stern talking to."

"I bet that terrified her."

"Well, she never bothered me again after being called out for that bit of naughtiness." She sighed. "She never invited me to any more parties, either."

We went through the rest of her list of acquaintances, ex-boyfriends, and various elves around town who might harbor some kind of resentment against her. But just from her descriptions of the quarrels they might have with her, I couldn't see that any of the situations rose to the level of murder.

"One name you *don't* have here is Ivy," I noted.

"Why would I? I don't think Ivy has a grudge against me. Ivy said she and Sterling parted ways amicably."

"Yet there's something fishy about her, isn't it? I keep thinking that she wouldn't be involved because what few clues there are to Sterling's death link the murder so clearly to Flock and Ivy's. She'd have to have been crazy to kill Sterling—or try to kill you—using flowers that came from her own store."

"And she said they *didn't* come from her store," Juniper said.

"I think she might be lying about that. On the way over here, Bumble the snowman said he saw Sterling talking to a female elf in a red coat near the florist's the night before he was killed. He said Sterling had just left the florist's."

Her mouth dropped open. "When was this?"

"Late evening, right before the shop closed."

"Sterling picked me up to take me to dinner around then, I'll bet." Her brows knit. "Who could he have been talking to? A red coat isn't much to go on. Everybody has a red coat." Juniper nibbled a little more of her muffin and thought about it. "*I* have a red coat—but it's a puffy coat and I don't like it. It makes me look like a cranberry."

I frowned. "Someone else we know has a red coat."

"Who?"

"Dolly," I said. "It's bright red, and brand new."

She let out another little laugh. "I could imagine Dolly as a poisoner if Claire had been the victim."

That was the truth. "Well, if we think Sterling wasn't the intended victim . . . maybe you weren't, either."

"That would be nice for me, but I don't wish anyone else to have a target on their back," Juniper said. "Especially not Claire. That would be horrible! This should be the best week of her life."

"Looking at her recently, that doesn't seem to be panning out."

She shook her head. "I don't think it's just the murder that's bugging her, do you?"

"No. It seemed to start before this week. In the beginning, I thought she was coming down with something."

"Maybe she's coming down with cold feet."

"But why?" I asked. "She and Jake were deliriously, disgustingly happy. Now my mother-in-law's planning a ginormous bash for a wedding that at this point only seems to have about a fifty-fifty chance of coming off."

"Surely things aren't that bad," Juniper said. "Why would Claire suddenly look at this guy she's been head over heels for—that she uprooted her entire life for—and think that she might be making a mistake?" She drummed her fingers, then gasped. "Do you think it's some kind of hex?"

We knew a snow witch named Imelda who was no stranger to hexing people. Imelda also had a thing for Jake. Then again, the witch had an even bigger passion for donuts.

"If Imelda had hexed Claire, she would've done something more dramatic, like turn her into a newt," I said.

Juniper allowed that this was true. "Do you think it's possible that Claire's fallen out of love with Jake? I don't."

"Me neither." I ate the last of my muffin and thought this over. "It's more likely that she worries that they'll be Bridge Mix."

Juniper gasped. "You read the quiz."

I nodded glumly. "I don't think Nick and I are the Full Heart-Shaped Chocolate Box, either."

"How can you say that? You two are perfect together."

"The romancy part is dimming, though. A few weeks ago I went into the Naughty or Nice lingerie store and bought a sexy negligee."

She smiled. "That sounds spicy and romancy."

"I thought so. But Nick took one look and retrieved my wool robe for me because he said he was afraid I was cold."

Juniper released a sympathetic laugh. "That's so like Nick! He loves you—and you always *are* cold."

I nodded. "I know, I shouldn't complain. I guess with seeing all the Valentine fun and happy couples this week, I feel a little conflicted."

"Not to sound like Dolly," Juniper said more carefully, "but I bet that's normal with married couples, right?"

"It's only been four years," I lamented, probably louder than I should have. I lowered my voice. "I don't mean to complain, but Pamela's going so over-the-top for Claire's wedding is reminding me of what a low-key event our wedding was. I didn't even know about toasting tongs."

She looked shocked. "You didn't receive *any*?"

"Nick thought it wouldn't be right to have a big wedding or ask for gifts when everyone was in mourning for his brother."

She nodded. "And you didn't have a honeymoon, either."

"We met while Nick was on vacation, and we were always traveling to see each other. At the time, it seemed like more of a novelty to be together at home than to travel somewhere."

"All relationships are different, I guess," Juniper said. "But I can tell how much he loves you when he looks at you. That's the important thing, isn't it? And you two just gravitate toward each other."

I felt that too, most of the time. Only it seemed like our private moments were fewer and farther between these days. We were so quick to settle into old married coupledom. Maybe we should have spent longer in the awkward newlywed phase.

"Sometimes I feel like he's not noticing me anymore. Then again, I haven't been trying very hard to attract his attention." I looked down at myself. I was wearing practical wool slacks and two layers of sweaters. "I'm not quite Lucia yet, but I'm getting there."

"I know what you need," Juniper said, getting out her phone and tapping on her keyboard.

"What are you doing?"

"I'm emailing Sparkle at Three French Hens to see if she can fit you in today."

"Oh no," I said quickly. "There's so much to do." Suspects to track down, hen-night plans to finalize.

Juniper waved away my concerns. "It's just be an hour of your time. Sparkle will have you feeling like a new woman."

"It's very nice of you . . ." I said.

She watched her screen for a moment and then let out a sound of satisfaction when an answer bubble popped up on her text screen. "Sparkle says to send you over right away and she'll fix you up."

"I don't know . . . I was going to call Dazzle Winterbright to make sure he'll be well for Claire's bachelorette party."

"I'll do that," Juniper said. "You just go enjoy your time at Three French Hens. Sparkle can make a shampoo feel like the most luxurious scalp massage ever."

That decided it. Between my worries about the murder, and Claire, and my own marriage, my head could definitely use a little TLC.

Chapter 11

Instead of finding myself a reindeer short, when I left Merry Muffins, a spare reindeer had appeared at my sleigh. Wobbler had joined Cannonball. The former wasn't in harness, but he stood stiffly next to his comrade as if he were. He also had a bandage—his was on his ear. The two of them looked like veterans of a reindeer skirmish, but the skirmish had been with each other.

I'd barreled out of the bakery full of purpose—I needed to hurry to Three French Hens so Sparkle Greenleaf could squeeze me in. Seeing the two reindeer side by side, standing with so much tension, I faltered midstep.

Had Wobbler been sent from the castle with a message? Wouldn't Jingles or Nick have called me or come in person in the event of an emergency?

"What's going on?" I asked. "Is something wrong?"

"I'll say there is." Cannonball shook his head in disgust. "Wobbler here doesn't seem to trust me to do my job."

"Why should I?" Wobbler shot back. "Why should anyone? Everyone heard about how you shamefully went running off to visit Flouncy the other day, leaving Mrs. Claus high and dry."

I sank into my heels, relieved. Also a bit annoyed. At least there wasn't an emergency. I just had two squabbling reindeer on my hands.

"You're just jealous because I was there and you weren't. You only hang around mooning after her when you're not needed at all . . ."

"As if she would ever need a chunker like you around her."

"Hey!" I said, trying to break it up.

Steam blew out of Cannonball's snout. "Better a buck on the burly side than a knobby-kneed weakling."

"Weakling! Who's the reindeer Santa's called on to help in an emergency?" He hoofed the snowy ground adamantly. "*This* reindeer, that's who."

I held up my hands. "Would you both stop? This is nonsense."

"He started it," Cannonball muttered. "He shouldn't even be here. I was just minding my own business."

"Probably dreaming of slipping your harness again," Wobbler muttered. "Ready to run off to make a nuisance of yourself with Flouncy at the first opportunity."

"I don't have time to referee this argument," I said. "I have to get to Three French Hens salon."

Both of them stood at attention. "We're ready," they said in unison.

Which was weird, since Wobbler wasn't even harnessed to the sleigh.

Cannonball shot him a look. "Do you really think you're needed here?"

I jumped on the sleigh. "It's fine. Wobbler, you can trot alongside us."

And that's what he did. The two of them, each unable to trust the other, trotted through the streets of Christmastown in stiff silence. This uneasy truce didn't fool me. The moment I was out of ear range, their sniping would probably begin all over again.

Part of me just wished Flouncy would make up her mind. Hopefully things would return to normal after the Muzzle Nuzzle.

"You shouldn't argue in public," I told them when we'd arrived in front of the salon. "Remember, you represent the castle. Bickering is unseemly." I hated to lecture, but it was time for some tough love. I channeled my inner Pamela. "If this kind of behavior goes on, I'll have to find two other reindeer to pull my sleigh."

Cannonball's big round eyes widened in shock. "You would replace *us*?"

"I wouldn't want to," I confessed. "I know the Muzzle Nuzzle has you out of sorts, but if this behavior continues . . ."

The two exchanged startled expressions.

Wobbler dipped his long neck. "I'm sorry."

"Me too," Cannonball echoed grudgingly. "I *might* have started it."

"No, I did," Wobbler said.

Cannonball eyed him impatiently. "You just can't let me have the last word, can you?"

So much for my getting reindeer in touch with the better angels of their natures. Although at least they seemed to be trying. "I'll probably be a while, but hopefully no more than two hours."

I hurried inside the Three French Hens Beauty Salon.

Sparkle, waiting in her pink smock, pounced on me as I came in the door.

"Thank you for squeezing me in," I said.

"Of course," she said, wasting no time steering me toward the sinks in the back of the salon.

I'd always found salon sinks so uncomfortable—the porcelain neck holder always seemed to hit the base of my skull in the most torturous spot. But elf sinks were built on a smaller scale, and even though my head hung over the sink more, it was more like a good stretch than a porcelain vise gripping my head. And Juniper hadn't been wrong about her cousin's shampooing technique. Her magic fingers on my scalp lulled me into a state of bliss.

And then I opened my eyes. Just behind Sparkle stood Ivy.

Ivy in a blazing red coat. Her eyes were blazing, too. At me.

I let out a sound of distress, probably like a seal on an ice floe who doesn't spot the polar bear till it's dangerously close. Sparkle frowned at my grunts and flailing limbs for a moment before turning.

"I had an appointment at twelve thirty," Ivy reminded her. "Cut and highlights."

"You do. If you'll just take a seat, I'll get right to you," she assured Ivy.

Ivy wasn't convinced. "You can hardly get right to me when you've just started shampooing Mrs. Claus."

"You're early."

"Five minutes," Ivy said. "You can't cut her hair in five minutes."

I hadn't meant to create a situation. I often forgot that being Mrs. Claus carried privilege that sometimes inconvenienced others. People didn't like to say no to Santa's wife—and Sparkle had probably wanted to accommodate me *and* do a favor for Juniper, her cousin.

"Yes, she can," I piped up. "I just came in for a shampoo and a quick"—my mind frantically searched for something that wouldn't take long—"bang trim."

They both frowned at me.

"You don't have bangs," Ivy pointed out.

Right. "But I've been thinking about getting them."

And now I was just thinking about getting out of here as soon as possible. It was hard to keep my eyes off that coat. My brain whirred with unpleasant thoughts. What if Sterling had gone into the florist, spoke to Flock, and then run into Ivy outside the podiatrist's office? What would they have been talking about? Sterling's upcoming proposal to Juniper?

She'd lied about the corsage . . .

Was Ivy Sterling's killer?

She certainly looked as if she wanted to kill someone now. Namely, me.

"Just have a seat," Sparkle repeated to her.

Reluctantly, Ivy retreated. As she sat down, two other elves waiting for other stylists got up and moved to seats farther from her.

Ivy clucked her tongue at them. "Really? You think I'm going to poison you here at the hairdressers?"

The other elves shifted uncomfortably and looked intently at their magazines.

Sparkle turbaned a towel around my head and guided me toward her station. I sank into the offered chair and looked into the mirror, saying a silent goodbye to my forehead. It didn't take long for it to be obscured. Under the impatient eye of her next customer, Sparkle worked her scissors like a samurai, cutting and trimming with astonishing speed. I held my breath, watching the stainless steel blades glinting and the hair falling in hanks to the ground.

All the while, Ivy kept glaring at me. So much for trying to appease her with a quick trim.

Yesterday I'd been skeptical that she would have killed Sterling. Now I was leaning the other way. Fatally poisoning someone using a box bearing your business's label still seemed like a crackbrained murder method. But maybe Dolly was right and this was one of those double-bluff situations: Ivy thought she would be able to get away with it because no one would believe that a killer would practically affix their label to the murder weapon.

Though, judging from the reaction to her by the other customers in the waiting area, plenty of elves were entertaining suspicions against her.

An idea struck me. If Ivy was getting her hair done, this would be a perfect time to catch Flock at the florist's shop by himself. A cut and highlights could take a while.

Suddenly, I felt as impatient as Ivy. "You know what?" I told Sparkle, who was finishing up with a few tiny snips. "I just remembered an appointment I have. I'll need to go."

"But you can't leave like this," she insisted. "Your hair's wet."

"It'll dry," I said, ready to bolt for the door.

She put a hand on my shoulder. "Ten minutes under the dryer, at least," she said. "I won't be responsible for Mrs. Claus ending up in the infirmary with pneumonia."

She was right. If I left like this, my head would be a block of ice before I made it the few blocks over to Flock and Ivy's.

Sparkle snapped her fingers and an assistant hurried over to take me in hand.

"Put Mrs. Claus under dryer number two."

Elves in Santaland still favored chair dryers with the space-age-looking helmet that blew hot air all over your head. There was usually something lulling about sitting under the dryer and thumbing through the latest *Elf World* magazine. Today, however, I wasn't in a leisurely mood.

It didn't help that the dryer faced the salon's plate glass front window, giving me a perfect vantage of the street. I was seated just in time to see a reindeer with a fluffy winter hide the color of vicuña chatting with Wobbler and Cannonball. The two males were both at sharp attention; neither could take their eyes off the fetching doe who had deep brown eyes that looked more dramatic because of the long black lashes and dark markings around the eye. It almost looked as if she'd dolled herself up with eye pencil.

Flouncy, I presumed. No wonder they were crazy about her. I wasn't exactly a connoisseur of ruminant beauty, but even I could tell that this was one good-looking reindeer.

Flouncy dipped her head to say goodbye to them and sashayed elegantly away from them.

Cannonball and Wobbler were practically salivating after her, and sure enough, Wobbler followed her.

Within seconds, Cannonball was struggling to shed the harness and trotting after them both. Unfortunately, he wasn't able to pull off his Houdini act today—Salty must have secured the buckles to make his escaping more difficult. After a moment of indecision, Cannonball took off, sleigh and all, reins flapping.

Seeing my sleigh disappear down the street, I instinctively jumped up. My head whacked against the hard plastic of the dryer helmet and I sank back down.

I definitely had a reindeer staffing problem on my hands.

My movements caught Sparkle's attention. She apparently thought I was trying to leave before my drying time was up.

"Five more minutes, Mrs. Claus!" she called out to me, over-enunciating in case I couldn't hear her.

No telling where my reindeer would be in five minutes. What's more, I didn't have time to go looking for them, or to wait for one or both of them to return. I needed to get to Flock and Ivy's. As soon as the bell dinged on my dryer, I was up and out the door. My hair still felt damp—and of course my sleigh was nowhere in sight.

So much for tough love. During Valentine's Week, nothing could compete with good old-fashioned romantic love.

Chapter 12

Even on foot, it didn't take me long to get to the florist shop. Christmastown might be a metropolis by Santaland standards, but it's still a small town. The only traffic jams occur when there's a big reindeer race through town or during one of our many parades. Otherwise, the well-tended sidewalks never get too busy.

The only thing that slowed me down was coming across a chorus of elves singing "Mr. Sandman"—except to add a little local flavor, they'd changed the words to "Mr. Snowman." Sand wasn't a big thing here at the North Pole, so it was natural that the elves might want to substitute snow. I tossed several coins into the cap on the ground at the chorus's feet.

I breezed past Bumble, who was back next to his sandwich board and had someone offering him money for a snowman hug. I didn't want to interrupt that.

As I was about to push open the door to Flock and Ivy's, Smudge was just leaving. From afar, I wouldn't have known him. He was wearing a purple-and-yellow cap and matching tunic. His booties were shiny leather with a fashionable extra swirl at the toe. It was a big switch from his usual dark colors.

He was as surprised to see me as I was to nearly run into him. "April!"

Smudge and I both played percussion in the Santaland Concert

Band. He was on drum kit, I was on triangle. Occasionally he and Luther Partridge, the conductor, trusted me enough to let me do a cymbal crash. I hadn't seen him in a while, though, because the band was on hiatus in January and February.

"I almost didn't recognize you," I said. Ivy's influence had clearly brought about the wardrobe brightening. She had striking natural style. It didn't look quite so natural on Smudge, though.

He shrugged and said, "Seemed time for a change." Then he peered at me more closely. "You look different, too."

My damp bangs. I'd almost forgotten them.

"Were you here looking for Ivy?" I asked him. "I just saw her at the Three French Hens salon."

"That's what Flock just told me. Bad timing." He tilted a glance up at me. "Except that it's not, because I'm glad for a chance to talk to you."

"I'm worried about Juniper," he said. "Is she okay?"

"Why don't you ask her yourself? You know where to find her."

He ground the toe of one of his new booties into the snow-covered sidewalk. The walk had probably been shoveled not long ago, but it had been snowing on and off since morning. "I don't like to bother her."

"How could you? You two are still friends."

"Right." He looked off into the distance, as if his vision could laser right through all the buildings standing between us and the Christmastown Public Library several blocks away. "But given all that's happened this week, I don't want it to look like . . . you know."

"Like you care?"

He cleared his throat. "That I'm rushing over first thing now that Sterling's out of the picture."

"I doubt she'd take it that way. She knows that you're involved with Ivy."

"Yes, but that's the thing."

Suddenly, the penny dropped. He was worried that Ivy might

take it the wrong way if he expressed his condolences to Juniper. And he was clearly not happy about that.

I hesitated to involve myself in his relationships, but I had a hunch that he was missing an important detail from the past two days. "Crinkles, Jake, and I suspect that whoever killed Sterling actually meant to kill Juniper."

It wasn't often that Smudge lost his cool, but now his eyes widened and he bobbed in agitation.

"You wouldn't know of anyone who has strong ill feelings toward Juniper, do you?"

"No! This is terrible. How could anyone . . ."

He didn't finish the sentence, either because it was so obvious what he was trying to say—or because he suddenly thought of someone. I wasn't sure which.

"Is Juniper okay?" he continued in a rush. "I should have called her, or gone to her apartment last night after I heard the news about Sterling."

"You know Juniper," I said. "She's strong."

"I'll bet she's at the library today, same as usual," he said.

"Yes."

"Excuse me, April," he said, edging past me on the stoop. "I need to get going."

But for a moment, he looked off-balance, as if he didn't know where to go next, the salon or the library. Which was stronger—the urge to talk to Juniper, or Ivy?

He headed in the direction of the library.

I don't know why that spur-of-the-moment decision of his gave my heart such a lift, but it did.

A bell tinkled overhead when I pushed open the florist's door. Flock emerged from the back room, an expectant smile on his face. It evaporated when he saw me.

"Is there something I can help you with, Mrs. Claus?"

"Yes—I just have a few questions."

"Of course," he said petulantly. "You wouldn't be here to *buy* anything. There hasn't been a customer here all the livelong day. There's a whisper campaign against us now. I guess everyone thinks our flowers will kill them. Ivy was so depressed, she took the afternoon off."

She'd seemed more angry than depressed. Then again, I'd seen other elves shunning her with my own eyes. If she *wasn't* guilty, that would be hard to take.

"I don't have any flowers to order, but the castle has done quite a bit of business with you this month. I hope that will keep you going until this is all cleared up."

He ducked his head. "Of course—we're very grateful for the castle business. We'll have the bouquets and boutonnieres delivered to you the day after tomorrow." His mouth twitched anxiously. "But I thought we'd answered all the questions we could."

"When the constable was here last night, Ivy did a lot of the talking. I was curious if you had anything you wanted to say."

He looked beyond me to the door, as if he worried Ivy would step through it. But he knew she was at the salon—he'd just told Smudge that she was there. So maybe he only wished she'd walk in the door and rescue him from having to speak to me.

What was he afraid of?

"Flock, I get the sense that there's something you're holding back. Maybe something that you're even afraid to say."

"Afraid?" His voice looped up in alarm. "Why should I be afraid?"

"Because Ivy is a very strong personality, and she's your business partner. I assume that you don't want to lose her."

He shook his head. "I assure you, Ivy had nothing whatsoever to do with these terrible things that have happened. The poison-pen poem was a shock to both of us, and you should have seen how upset Ivy was over Sterling Redwinkle's death."

"Why would that be?"

He blinked, as if he worried he'd fallen into a trap. "She didn't confide in me, but I assume she felt as anyone would who had been involved with a murder victim. It was all over between them—long ago—but naturally she was upset that he would meet such a terrible end."

Or maybe her feelings were stronger than she would admit, and always had been. But would she have been jealous enough of Juniper to kill? Even if she was, would she poison a corsage when she knew there was a good chance that it would go through Sterling's hands?

First things first, I thought. It would be helpful to get real proof that the corsage came from here. "I assume that you keep an order book," I said. "Would you mind if I took a look at it?"

He swallowed so hard, his Adam's apple bobbed visibly.

At least he wasn't telling me categorically to mind my own beeswax.

"I just want to glance at it to assure myself that Ivy was right and hadn't forgotten about sending deliveries up to the Order of Elven Seamstresses."

"I don't think Ivy would want me to—"

"Is that it?" I pointed to a fat binder on the glass counter. Taking the initiative, I crossed to it and opened it before he could stop me.

"Ivy's going to kill me," he lamented.

The pages covering the two days of the two incidents—the poem and poisoning—weren't there.

I looked up at Flock. "Why were those two days' pages torn out?"

He gulped. "I-I-I don't know. I'm not even sure that is two pages missing. Our days aren't separated on unique pages. There might have been two days of orders on one page."

I wanted to laugh. "Okay, but why would even one page have been torn out except to hide the truth?"

"I didn't tear anything out." He looked genuinely confused. "I don't understand it."

I was pretty sure I did.

"Nobody touched the books while I was here," he insisted.

"Was anyone here when you weren't present?"

"No one." He frowned. "Except . . ."

When it became clear that he wasn't going to finish, I prompted, "Except?"

His mouth flattened into a displeased line. "Madame Neige was here this morning to speak to Ivy, but I hardly think that *she* would have taken anything."

No, Madame Neige wouldn't have torn a sheet from the order book. But Ivy, knowing that her biggest artificial flower supplier would be coming by to question her, might have. Madame Neige wouldn't want any sign that her distributor was involved with what had happened to Sterling Redwinkle at the Order of Elven Seamstresses. She was all about appearances, and apprentices and workers were devoted to working for her, not only because of the high quality of the clothes and accessories they produced, but also because of the reputation of Madame Neige herself.

Having her reputation besmirched by Ivy, a business associate, would cause her no end of displeasure.

Ivy seemed guiltier by the second. But was the absence of proof enough proof? I wanted something more definitive. "Didn't you mention a delivery elf?" I asked Flock.

It took a moment for my question to register. He frowned. "Flit?"

"He has his own delivery sleigh, right?"

"Yes. He works for us when we're too busy to do our own deliveries, like this week."

I nodded. "So as an independent contractor, he'll probably have his own records."

"Oh." Flock frowned. "Right."

"I'll just check with Flit." I smiled. "Thanks for all your help."

As I left Flock, his glum, worried gaze was trained on that order book.

Tracking down a delivery elf wasn't as easy as it seemed. Flit's Messenger and Delivery Service was located on a Christmastown side street. The office was on the second floor of what we called a carriage house where I came from. Here, they were called sleigh sheds, but that unglamorous name didn't do justice to the beautiful brick buildings.

I climbed the iron stairs up to the second-floor landing and knocked.

"He's out," a voice called up to me.

I leaned over the railing at the reindeer who'd called up to me. He was harnessed to a sleigh that had *Flit's Messenger and Delivery* written in fancy cursive across the side. Beneath was the store tag line *"We're Fleet of Foot."*

"Out to lunch?" I guessed.

The reindeer snuffled incredulously. "Lunch?" he repeated, sounding offended. "Flit's Messenger and Delivery service doesn't stop for lunch."

That was puzzling, because this reindeer was harnessed to the store's sleigh.

"He must have stopped for something—or you wouldn't be here," I pointed out.

The reindeer tossed his head contemptuously. "I'm the *backup* sleigh."

"Oh." I sighed. Apparently that's what *I* needed these days. "Do you know when Flit will be back? I need to speak to him."

"He's had to make a delivery at Kringle Heights. You're from up there, aren't you?"

He could judge from my height alone that I wasn't an elf, and most of the Claus family and the humans attached to them lived in the neighborhood around the castle called Kringle Heights. "I live at the castle," I told him. "I'm Mrs. Claus."

The reindeer blinked, then stood at attention. "Mrs. Claus! I'm so very sorry—I didn't recognize you." His head turned as he watched me. "Have you always had bangs?"

"No, they're new."

"Very becoming!"

"Thanks." A ripple of pleasure shot through me at the unexpected compliment. I'd been so focused on getting out of the salon quickly, I'd barely stopped to consider whether I really liked the haircut. I wondered what Nick would think of the change.

"Hop in, ma'am," the reindeer said. "I will find Flit for you."

"You could just give me his number."

"I don't do numbers," the reindeer said. "Besides, Flit would never forgive me if I left Mrs. Claus standing out in the cold."

It was too good an offer to refuse. I hopped into the sleigh.

"What's your name?" I asked him.

"Bolter."

"Pleased to meet you." The reins were tied down. "Should I take the reins?"

"No, ma'am. Just hold on."

I soon understood the advice. Flit's Messenger and Delivery Service wasn't joking about being fleet of foot. No speed limits were posted around Christmastown—traditional sleighs didn't come equipped with speedometers—but the heart-in-throat feeling I had as I gripped the bench seat of the sleigh told me that we were careening through the snowy streets at breakneck speed. The elves diving out of our way as they crossed the street was another indication.

"Maybe we should slow down," I called forward. "You could hurt someone on the street."

"You're right—I'll fix that."

We turned onto Celebration Boulevard and the reindeer really opened up the throttle then—and to my dismay he began that bounding motion that was the precursor to taking flight.

My insides lurched along with the sleigh and I squeezed my eyes shut. I hated flying. It's one thing to lift off when you're strapped into a seat on an airliner, but when you're perched uneasily on a bench seat in an open sleigh, it feels as if a deadly plunge is just one gust of wind away. The trouble was, once you were airborne, about the only thing to do was grit your teeth and hang on tight.

Even while scared out of my wits, the vista a flying sleigh afforded—of endless miles of wintry landscape dotted by brilliantly lit houses, trees with twinkle lights, and stunning Castle Kringle glowing like a beacon in the dim February daylight—made me feel lucky to have such a vantage. Not many people in the world got to experience this.

Bolter lived up to his name. Before I knew it, the sleigh was skimming close to the evergreens and headed back down to Sugarplum Mountain's snow path about halfway between Castle Kringle and the chateau belonging to siblings Clement and Carlotta Claus. Once we landed with a bump, I could see why he'd chosen this location. Just ahead of us was an identical sleigh to the one I was in. The driver—Flit, I presumed—twisted in surprise at being nearly overtaken by his own backup sleigh. He reined to a stop.

When he hopped down and saw me sitting on the bench seat behind Bolter, his eyes bugged. "Mrs. Claus!"

"Your reindeer was kind enough to bring me to speak to you."

He rounded on Bolter, who even after his wild exertions was barely out of breath. "Have you lost your mind to bring Mrs. Claus all this way?"

"Actually, 'all this way' is just a short ride from my home," I said. "Bolter probably saved me a sleigh-bus trip."

"I mean—*flying* all this way. And he didn't even offer you a lap robe, I'll be bound."

"I was fine," I assured him, blotting out my terror on the ride over. "I'm very grateful to him for his help. I wanted to ask you about Flock and Ivy."

Flit's expression became a mixture of annoyance and dread. I'd seen that look before. When I start asking questions, I tend to have that effect on people.

"They seem to be missing their delivery records from the past two days," I continued.

"Oh?" The thick scarf wound around his neck rippled along with the movement of his Adam's apple as he gulped. He was nervous about something, and I hadn't asked him anything yet.

"I was wondering if you remembered delivering packages from Flock and Ivy's to the Order of Elven Seamstresses yesterday and the day before."

The elf reached a gloved hand to scratch his scalp where it met the faux fur trim of his cap. "Did Constable Crinkles send you to interrogate me?"

"Not exactly," I admitted.

His face drooped as if this were bad news. "Then it was Santa who sent you, wasn't it?"

"Well . . ." I didn't want to lie to him, but the power of Santa's name packed a big moral punch here in Santaland. No one wanted to land on Santa's naughty list.

He didn't wait for me to say more. "All right!" he cried out, as if I'd really put the screws on him. "Yes! I did. I delivered a package for them yesterday morning."

"And Ivy told you not to mention it?"

His face slackened again in shock. "How did you guess?"

"There's no other reason a page would be missing from the order book. What did you take to the Order of Elven Seamstresses?"

He drew back. "Nothing."

"You didn't deliver anything to them yesterday morning?"

He looked befuddled. "I haven't been to the Order this whole week."

"Really?" That surprised me.

"No, ma'am. Yesterday I had to go all the way out to Tinkertown."

"To deliver flowers to the Redwinkle house?" I guessed.

He nodded slowly. Tears stood in his eyes. "That poor fireman. I didn't know it was a deadly delivery, I swear I didn't. I'm an honest elf."

"Then why did you agree to lie for Ivy?"

"First off, she swore it was all a big mistake. We've been working together for a while now, and she sends a lot of business my way. You should know that—I've been delivering a lot of stuff for the big wedding to the castle this week."

"Yes, I know."

"I trusted her. And maybe someone else did poison that corsage. Why would *she* have done such a thing? Everyone in town is saying she's not to be trusted, but if she really killed Sterling with her own flowers, that was really stupid."

"Criminals aren't always smart," I said.

"Maybe she's covering up for someone," he said.

Who would that be, though? She didn't seem close to anyone except Sterling. And Flock, maybe. "Did you speak to Flock about any of this?" I asked Flit.

His head swung back and forth in the negative. "Not once. He wasn't even in the front of the store when I was speaking to Ivy."

"You'll need to tell all of this to Constable Crinkles," I said.

"Ivy'll kill me when she finds out I blabbed," he lamented.

Flock had said something similar. A lot of elves seemed terrified of Ivy. Of course, Ivy had looked at me today as if she would happily have seen me get pricked by a poisoned thorn just because I'd made her wait a few extra minutes for a haircut.

"If we confront Ivy with the fact that we know that a corsage went from her to Sterling, we'll try to keep your name out of it," I said.

"Thank you!" Flit said.

"But won't she know?" Bolter asked.

I swung around to the reindeer.

"Ivy's not a fool. She can put two and two together—and then maybe we'll be next on the poison list!"

"You're right." Flit threw himself down to the snowy ground in full-blown despair. "I'm doomed! She'll have me killed, just like she killed Sterling Redwinkle."

For pity's sake. I couldn't help contrasting this little elf's panic with Juniper's stoicism in the face of threats and murder that were apparently intended for her.

"She's a suspect," I said. "Nothing's proven yet."

"But if she *is* guilty, I could be in grave danger. Who will protect me?"

"You could probably stay at the constabulary for a while," I said. As far as I knew, their bedroom cell was empty right now.

"And be there when they bring Ivy in? No, thank you!" He sighed in despair. "Please—just forget that you talked to me. I didn't see any poison on those flowers."

I was losing him. "You can stay at the castle," I blurted out.

His eyes widened. "Seriously?"

"Of course—there's plenty of room."

"Hey, what about us?" Bolter called out.

Flit eyed me hopefully. "Can Bolter and Furry come, too?"

I looked from the reindeer who'd brought me here, to the animal harnessed to Flit's primary sleigh. His shaggy winter coat made the name Furry seem apt.

"The more the merrier," I said.

I wasn't sure my mother-in-law would agree, however.

Chapter 13

Salty looked extremely puzzled when I pulled up with two delivery sleighs instead of my own. "What happened to Wobbler and Cannonball?"

"They got sidetracked by a certain doe."

Salty looked incensed. "Reindeer in love have one-track minds."

I didn't want to get into the details of my reindeers' personal issues when there were strangers listening in. "The good news is that we have guests." I gestured toward Flit's reindeer. "This is Bolter and Furry. I know you'll make them feel welcome here."

"Of course,' Salty said, remembering his manners. I felt a pang for springing unexpected guests on him. I'd be feeling more than a pang in a few minutes when I would have to announce to Pamela that Flit would be visiting. My stomach churned in dread.

I really needed to start thinking things through before I blurted out invitations.

But there was no sense putting off the inevitable. I led Flit inside the house, wondering if I should ask Jingles to find our guest elf accommodations among the other castle elves, or if Flit would feel insulted at being relegated to the servants' quarters.

My worries that the delivery elf might receive a frosty welcome were borne out when Jingles greeted us in the foyer and looked down in confusion at our visitor. It was obvious that he recognized

Flit—the castle received more than its share of deliveries—but he clearly had no idea why I'd brought a trades-elf home with me.

Luckily, Flit didn't notice Jingles's cool reaction. He'd removed his cap and stood twisting it in his hands, gaping around him. And no wonder. Not only was the grandeur of the castle's interior probably new to him, but the foyer was a hive of activity. We had to step aside to make way for six harps being wheeled past.

"Still missing one?" I wondered aloud.

"We've found another one outside Tinkertown," Jingles said, dodging an elf maid lugging a mop and pail. "We just need to get it here."

Elves stood on high ladders, stringing ribbon swags twined with twinkle lights around the ceiling. More elves were dusting and polishing the grand staircase and the great chandelier that held a hundred candles. Mostly, Flit had his eye on the multitiered, gilt-painted gift display, which already had a few select gifts on it.

"What gorgeous toasting tongs!" he exclaimed. He walked over to the object as if mesmerized. Then he frowned. "Is that walrus tusk?"

"Reindeer antler," I said. "Harvested post-shed."

"Naturally," he agreed.

Just then, my mother-in-law swept into the room. Pamela was a regal vision in an ice-blue wool dress trimmed in white. Her round figure and gray hair made her immediately recognizable as the Dowager Mrs. Claus, a combination of caring grandmother and domestic despot.

I wondered if I would ever be able to pull off that look.

She held a gorgeous cut-crystal bowl with both hands. "Another candy dish," she announced. "Isn't it lovely?"

Candy dishes were second only to toaster tongs as most-given wedding presents.

"A vision!" Flit exclaimed.

Pamela turned her attention on the elf, and I held my breath.

"Aren't you Flit, of the delivery service?"

"Yes, ma'am." He squeezed his hat anxiously, then observed,

"I never realized what lovely things I was bringing up to the castle until now."

Pamela, setting down the candy dish, bestowed her noblesse-oblige smile at him.

I cleared my throat. "I've asked Flit to stay with us this week."

"Did you?"

"Him, and his two delivery sleighs and two reindeer. You see—"

But she didn't even wait for me to stammer out more of an explanation. She clapped her hands together with a gasp, causing me, Flit, and even Jingles to hop nervously.

"What a wonderful idea!" Pamela exclaimed.

I tilted my head in surprise.

"I can't believe you thought of it, April," she went on. "Having Flit here this week is *just* what we need." She turned to Jingles. "Please prepare the bedroom adjacent to mine for our guest."

Jingles—almost as surprised as I was—bowed low. "Yes, ma'am."

Pamela took Flit by the arm. "There's so much you can do for us this week."

Flit was catching on, but he was still awed to be inside the castle and schmoozed by the Dowager Mrs. Claus, no less. "Mrs. Claus—Mrs. April Claus, I mean—invited me because I needed a place to stay that was safe."

"Yes, it's safe—we wouldn't insult you by expecting you to be idle. I know that's not your way. And I have so many little errands you could run. What do you know about transporting concert grand harps?"

"Not a lot, but I'm willing to give it a shot," he said.

She beamed at him, then cast a glance at me. Now that Jingles was off doing her bidding, she had little errands for me. "April, have the kitchen prepare hot chocolate and scones for our guest. We'll be in the family salon."

I nodded.

She suddenly focused on my face with a concerned expression. "What did you do to yourself?"

"Bangs." I waited, but no compliment was incoming.

"I thought I noticed something peculiar." She turned and led Flit away, no doubt to ply him with goodies and to school him on his guestly duties.

I made my way to the kitchen through hallways brightened by more twinkle lights, ribbons, and decorative foliage than we saw in the castle even at Christmastime. Above the doorways were hung double hearts fashioned from artificial roses—made by the Order, purchased through Flock and Ivy's. The florist bill was going to be a fortune. I wasn't kidding when I'd reminded Flock that the castle had thrown a lot of business his way.

The kitchen was buzzing with activity—not only of Chef Felice and her battalion of kitchen elves making dinner for us and all the castle denizens, but also an unfamiliar pastry chef hard at work preparing for the wedding day dessert spread. Just having a wedding cake wouldn't do for this shindig. Pamela had informed me that every guest would have an assortment of little dainties at their place at the table.

Typically when I walked into the castle kitchen while it was full of elves, some would drop what they were doing to ask what I needed. Today all the elves were sufficiently stressed that they were happy to give me room to go about my business unaided. I set a pot of milk on the stove to warm, pouring in a little extra to make a pot of cocoa for me and Nick, too. I could do with a little downtime with my husband before dinner and then having to rush off to Night Three of the Tournament of Chocolate. Sometimes it seemed a Claus's work was never done.

Jingles pushed through the kitchen's swinging door and took over cocoa prep from me.

"I apologize for dragging home unexpected guests."

"No matter—having another minion on site has made Pamela happy." He arched a brow. "By the way, what is Flit doing here?"

"He was worried that talking to me would cause whoever killed Sterling to go after him, too."

The elfman was all alertness. "You think he'll be the next to be murdered?" He gasped. "What if the killer comes here to finish him off?"

I shook my head. "I hope there won't be another murder. But he seemed so frightened."

"And so would I be," Jingles said. "Who does he think the murderer is?"

"Who else? Everyone suspects Ivy. I'm beginning to suspect her, too, even if she does seem too obvious. And frankly, if I were a murderer, I'd make myself be a little nicer to people."

Jingles drummed his gloved fingers on a nearby counter. "Some of the elves from town have mentioned something about Poison Ivy—and one of the elf maids refused to move a floral arrangement that was sent up from Flock and Ivy's for the wedding." Though none of the busy elves nearby seemed to be eavesdropping on us, he dropped his voice. "Is there any truth to the rumors?"

"She's definitely lying—and has asked others like Flit to lie for her. Why would she do that?"

Jingles waved a hand knowingly. "I've been supervising personnel in this castle for over a decade, and believe me, elves lie and wheedle for all sorts of reasons. People, too, I imagine."

He wasn't wrong.

I had already called Crinkles and Jake—hopefully they would be able to take Ivy to the constabulary and get more answers out of her than I had managed to. In fact, I imagined that Crinkles and Ollie were dragging her out of Three French Hens for questioning right about now.

My brain felt tired. The two days since bad things had begun happening seemed like two weeks. And there was still so much to get through this week. Two more nights of chocolate judging, and Claire's shower and party. Not to mention the wedding itself.

If the wedding happened at all. Would Claire actually cancel if the Valentine killer wasn't caught? The fact that she was opening wedding gifts seemed like a positive sign that the event would take place as planned.

"When did Claire come by today?" I asked Jingles.

He frowned in confusion. "Claire?"

I laughed before jogging his memory. "My friend, the bride-to-be?"

"She hasn't been here today."

"But Pamela is putting out newly unwrapped wedding gifts that were delivered to the castle. Claire must have come by and opened them at some point."

"Pamela's been doing that for her."

"Opening Claire and Jake's wedding gifts?" I couldn't believe it.

"Pamela said that Claire asked her to."

Okay, that was strange. At the family's request, Nick and I hadn't received many wedding gifts due to the timing of our nuptials so soon after his brother's death. But if I had received wedding gifts, I wouldn't have off-loaded the fun of opening them to Pamela.

While Jingles took over readying a pot of hot chocolate for Pamela and Flit, I put together a similar tray for Nick and myself.

I tapped lightly at his office and then entered. He was in his usual spot, bent over his desk. I settled the cocoa and some scones next to him and poured out cups for both of us.

"Predinner sustenance," I told him.

"Thanks."

As I poured, I shook my hair a little, then made certain we had eye contact when I handed him his steaming mug.

"Thank you." He took a tentative sip.

Hm.

I moved to the chair opposite his desk, took a seat, and feathered my fingers through my bangs.

He looked back down at the figures in front of him and tapped his pencil distractedly.

"We have a visitor in the castle," I said.

"Wedding guest?" Nick asked.

"More like a murder refugee. It's Flit, the delivery elf."

Nick's forehead crinkled in concern. "Why is he staying here?"

"I think he believes it's the last place Ivy will look for him if she wants to poison him."

"Why would Ivy want to poison her delivery elf?"

"Snitches get stitches." From Nick's blank stare, I guessed that mobster culture didn't translate to the North Pole. "He told me some incriminating information about Ivy."

"I'm sorry to hear that." When Nick contemplated elf transgressions, he really looked like a disappointed parent. "Ivy always seemed like a nice sort. I remember when she was just a little mite of a thing at the orphan home. She won an award for an art project—she was creative even then. That was when my father was Santa."

Two Santas ago, in other words. After Nick's father died, his brother, Chris, had succeeded him. And then Nick had taken on the role when Chris died tragically young. Nick was technically Santa regent, serving until Christopher, Chris's son, came of age.

But even since our marriage, Nick had taken on more and more of a Santalike personality, growing in wisdom and patience. Donning that red suit transformed a person.

"It's pretty clear now that Ivy made the corsage that killed Sterling," I said. "And then she lied."

"I don't like to hear that." His expression turned grave. "But isn't there a chance that someone else poisoned the corsage?"

"Who?"

He leaned forward. "Anyone who touched it after it was made."

"How? According to Flit, it was delivered straight to Sterling at his—"

My words stopped abruptly.

Nick's brows rose. "Where?"

"His house in Tinkertown." Where his crazy, possessive mother lived, and where his sister was often present, too.

The sister who'd been quick to protest that she *just couldn't* believe that Ivy would do something like this.

I stood up. "I have an errand to run. I'll probably head straight to the Tournament of Chocolate after that." I crossed over and kissed him goodbye.

He held onto my hand and eyed me curiously. "Did you do something to yourself?"

Finally! "I cut my hair," I said, unable to keep a little exasperation out of my voice.

"That's it! It's been bothering me this whole time. I knew something was different."

"Your mother said I looked peculiar."

He tilted his head, considering. "Not at all. It's nice."

Nice. Apparently if I wanted flowery compliments, I'd need to visit Bolter in the reindeer shed. Luckily, that's exactly where I was headed.

I wouldn't say that Mrs. Redwinkle was glad to see me, but once I was perched on the stiffest seat in her parlor, she was eager to fill me in on all the plans being made to honor Sterling.

"The funeral will be on the fifteenth," she said. "The day after Valentine's Day. It didn't seem fitting to have the service during the time when there's pink bunting and red hearts everywhere."

I murmured my agreement. "It will give you more time to plan."

I'd harnessed up Bolter and charged over to Tinkertown, ready to question Mrs. Redwinkle and Festa like a prosecutor with a quivering defendant in the dock. But in my eagerness for answers, I'd forgotten the sad reality Mrs. Redwinkle was living with. The house, which certainly hadn't seemed cheerful before, now seemed to be marinating in gloom. Formal portraits of Sterling stood on every knickknack table, some with lace black handkerchiefs over the frames. Little towers of fruitcakes piled up everywhere—signs of the many condolence visits she'd been receiving. Mrs. Redwinkle herself looked as if she was already dressed for the funeral that was still three days away.

This was not a person I could shout questions at as if I were Perry Mason. I was intruding on her grief, and ever since I'd walked through the door, my hunch that either of the Redwinkles could have poisoned that corsage seemed infinitely less likely.

She sniffed. "The Tinkertown Station of the Santaland Fire Brigade is going to put up a plaque in Sterling's honor, and they're going to be the honor guard on Sunday at the funeral."

"That seems very fitting," I said.

Suddenly, I regretted not asking Nick to come with me. I know he didn't like to inject himself into constabulary business, but he would have known just the words to comfort this grieving mother while at the same time prying a little information out of her.

As the mantel clock ticked, I looked around awkwardly. "I suppose Festa is back at her apartment."

I should have looked up her address before I came. Maybe I could do some searching on my phone.

"Oh no, she's just out shopping." Mrs. Redwinkle sighed. "She's trying to be a help to me—heaven knows I'm appreciative—but she's very restless. Always popping out to go places on her own. Sterling never behaved that way. If he said he was going to spend a day here with me, he'd stay the whole day and we'd play cards. Or sometimes I'd play the harmonium for him."

"But Sterling actually lived here," I couldn't help pointing out.

She batted away that point with a wave of a black hanky. "Festa was always the same. She wanted to be flitting around town, or *hanging out*."

The front door opened and then closed, and I could hear the crinkling of a grocery sack as Festa called out, "I'm back, Mother!"

"We have company," her mother replied.

Festa appeared in the doorway then, her cheeks bright from walking to the grocery store and back. Her broad smile felt almost jarring. "Mrs. Claus! I saw the delivery sleigh outside and thought we might be getting a package."

"No—I just borrowed Flit's sleigh. I was on my way to judge at the Tournament of Chocolate tonight, so I thought I would stop by . . ."

Festa looked puzzled. "Isn't the Tournament of Chocolate in Christmastown?"

I nodded. "At the Municipal Hall."

She tilted her head in curiosity. "Then aren't you a little bit out of your way?"

"Yes, well . . ." I shrugged awkwardly. "I wanted to see how you were getting along."

My uneasiness leached into my voice. Festa shifted her grocery sack to her other hip and eyed me a little more cautiously now. "Let me just put these away," she said. "Can I offer you anything to drink?"

"No, thank you. I won't stay long."

When Festa came back, she took a seat next to her mother on the couch. "Was there something you wanted to tell us, Mrs. Claus? Perhaps you've heard news from the constabulary?"

Mrs. Redwinkle's lips set in a tight frown. "Everyone who's come by mentions Ivy to us. I confess I never liked her."

"But we don't think she could have murdered Sterling, do we, Mother?"

Mrs. Redwinkle made a *who knows?* gesture.

"Actually, there's been some confusion about where the corsage Sterling gave Juniper came from."

Festa frowned. "It didn't come from Flock and Ivy's?"

"Yes, it did. Ivy admits she made it, but she denies putting poison on it."

"Naturally she does!" Mrs. Redwinkle exclaimed. "Did you expect her to break down and confess? That elf is hard as lake ice in February! I had her pegged from the first moment Sterling introduced me to her."

"But we don't understand what her motive would have been," I said.

"My Sterling dumped her. She was an elf scorned."

Festa fixed me with a raised brow expression, letting me know that I would never convince her mother that it was Ivy who called off the relationship.

Mrs. Redwinkle dabbed a tear. "I told him to watch out for her, but he had a soft heart."

"I was just wondering about the corsage," I said, trying to bring them back to the real reason I'd come. "The delivery elf said it was delivered here yesterday morning."

The two elves facing me blinked. "And?"

"Were either of you here when it arrived?"

Mrs. Redwinkle shook her head. "I never heard a delivery arrive."

Festa clucked her tongue. "That's because you weren't here. I came to take you to the eye doctor, remember?"

"Oh yes—that's right."

Festa explained, "Mother was having an exam and they were going to put drops in her eyes, so I went with her to the appointment and walked her home."

"Usually Sterling would take me, but he said he was eager to go out."

"He didn't have to go to work?" I asked.

"No, he was going to work this upcoming weekend." The reminder of the shift her son wasn't going to be able to fulfill caused a tear to slip down her cheek.

"When I saw him at the Order of Elven Seamstresses, he was wearing his dress uniform."

"He wore it because he wanted to look especially nice, I'm sure," his mother said.

"He did look very handsome," I admitted, frowning. "So it sounds as if neither of you saw the corsage box when it arrived here."

"We came back as he was leaving," Festa said. "I was helping Mother up to her room."

"I could barely see," the older elf admitted, "but I saw the shiny buttons on his uniform tunic."

"And was he carrying the corsage box?"

"If he was, I didn't notice it."

"He might have picked it up off the table or something right before he left," Festa said. "I never saw it."

"Oh." That made sense, I supposed. Except it did mean that they were both in the house while the corsage box was in it. I would take their word that Mrs. Redwinkle wouldn't have been able to see, especially not to swab a rose stem with bug poison. But Festa could have.

The mood in the parlor shifted, and I looked up. Festa's sharp gaze drilled into me.

She crossed her arms. "You've got a lot of nerve."

I really needed to work on my poker face.

Her mother turned to her in shock. "What are you talking about?"

"Mrs. Claus didn't come to see how we were, Mother. She's here to figure out if either of us could have slipped poison into that corsage while Sterling wasn't looking."

Mrs. Redwinkle sucked in a shocked breath. "Surely not!"

"We just need to know where that corsage box had been," I admitted.

The older elf's face turned as red as a holly berry. "It was with Ivy. She's the guilty one. Everyone knows it."

"And she's being questioned by Constable Crinkles," I said.

"Good!"

"But she insists she's innocent, and if there's a chance that she's telling the truth, we need to find out who the real killer was."

"So you thought of us." Festa gave an incredulous laugh.

Her mother was not so kind. "Festa, show Mrs. Claus to the door."

"Yes, ma'am." Festa got up and gestured to the entrance doorway. I again made the walk down the hallway tribute to Sterling. Ahead of me, Festa plucked my coat off the peg. "This yours?"

I nodded and shrugged into it as fast as I could. I should be used to being kicked out by Mrs. Redwinkle by now, but for some reason it still seemed embarrassing the second time around.

As I was leaving, Festa stopped me. "I can tell you still have doubts, so let me repeat this for you. I didn't do it. I have no idea about poisons, and I didn't even know where Sterling was on his way to that morning. As you've probably figured out, Mother and Sterling didn't exactly treat me like a confidante."

Her words, spoken so plainly, struck me as true.

But though she and her mother obviously didn't have a close relationship while Sterling was alive, Mrs. Redwinkle would no doubt turn to her daughter more now that he was gone.

"Enjoy the Tournament of Chocolate," Festa said with a smile. Then she shut the door before I could say a word in reply.

Chapter 14

For the Tournament of Chocolate, the great room at the Christmastown Municipal Hall was even more elaborately decorated than it had been the previous evening. Balloons resembling old-fashioned candy hearts were attached to every pillar and chair, meeting the pink and red streamers that hung from the ceiling beams and light fixtures. In the center of the room stood a chocolate fountain, which was a big hit. Elves scooped up the contents in paper cups festooned with hearts.

At the back of the hall, on the side opposite where the tables of candies were set up again in a horseshoe arrangement against the wall, a dais had been erected. On top of it was a huge heart fashioned out of pink, white, and red ribbons. On the floor in front of it stood a sign that read, *GET YOUR PICTURE TAKEN AT SWEET-HEART CENTRAL. Proceeds benefit the Christmastown Little Theater.* The drama group put on shows at a theater in Kringle Heights every summer.

Nick's cousin Mildred Claus collected donations from couples wanting to be photographed inside the heart, while Mildred's elf companion, Olive, took the photographs. Enough couples were lined up to get their picture taken to make it look like the theater would be flush with cash this season.

Nearby, the Santaland String Quartet was playing "Tea for Two."

I noticed a familiar elf next to me, swaying to the music.

"Blanchette?" I asked, touching her lightly on the arm.

She turned, smiling at me in recognition. "Mrs. Claus! Isn't this fun?"

For some reason, I wouldn't have expected to see her here—and from the look on her face, she wasn't used to attending big Santaland social functions. Her life was so centered on the Order of Elven Seamstresses.

She must have read my thoughts, because she let out a little laugh. "I know, Madame Neige usually keeps me too busy to come to events like these. But I helped design the Christmastown Little Theater's big heart, so I naturally wanted to see how it turned out."

I looked up at the spectacular heart framing two elves grinning deliriously for Olive's camera. "You did that?" I asked. "I should have guessed. It's beautiful."

"Thank you. I did some of the costumes for the Players last year. It's a fun group. I don't have the nerve to join them myself . . ."

I laughed. "It sounds as if you already have."

"I mean, not to audition." She shrugged. "I would have to devote too much time to rehearsals anyway. Madame Neige probably wouldn't approve."

Another workaholic, like Nick. I felt a little sad for her then. She definitely seemed happier away from the Order. Probably the pressure of being Madame Neige's second-in-command and overseeing so many workers made it difficult for her to loosen up at work.

She was a different elf tonight—lighter, friendlier.

"I like your bangs," she said. "They're very cute on you. They make you look even younger."

"Thank you!"

That "even" won me over. I remembered the bachelorette bash we had planned for Claire tomorrow night and told Blanchette about it. "You should drop by the Mistletoe Tavern for a drink," I said.

She looked almost stunned by my words. "You want me there?"

"I think you'd enjoy yourself."

Her face broke out in another smile. "That's so nice of you.

Thank you! I'll try to make it. I guess all the bridesmaids will be there, so I'll know some other people, too."

It was odd that an elf who'd spent her entire life in Santaland would worry about not knowing anyone. But now that I thought about it, she and I were probably the same age, and lived not far from each other, and we'd rarely crossed paths outside of Madame Neige's. The elves of the Order didn't socialize too often.

I nodded. "Of course. Me, Dolly, and Juniper—" I frowned. "Have you seen Juniper?"

"Oh yes." She scanned the crowded room and seemed to have no more luck finding her than I was having. Contestants were still setting up their chocolate entries in the ten minutes before the judging was to begin, and lots of elves milled about the hall. Some were dancing to the string quartet's rendition of "The Blue Danube Waltz."

Blanchette finally spotted Juniper by the chocolate fountain. "There she is."

She was standing with another elf. An elf in a purple-and-yellow tunic . . .

Smudge?

Thanking Blanchette, I went over to say hello.

Juniper greeted me with a huge smile. The anxiety that had hovered in her eyes since Sterling's death had lifted.

"I didn't see you at first," I said. "I thought maybe you weren't coming."

Two blotches of red appeared in her cheeks. "Smudge and I lost track of time."

He nodded. "We went over to the Midnight Clear diner for a bite to eat before coming over here."

My brain did a few calculations. I'd last seen Smudge heading over to the library over five hours ago. In a way, it seemed even longer. This day already felt like it had gone on for a week.

Juniper cleared her throat. "You know how we had to punt the idea of going to the Midnight Clear yesterday? I'd been craving it ever since."

Smudge added, "Sometimes you just need a Glorious Sandwich of Old."

They laughed together. I was smiling, too—half in wonder that these two couldn't seem to stick together when they had such deep history—when a streak of red barreled toward us.

Ivy.

"Uh-oh," I said.

"Avalanche incoming," Juniper muttered.

We all braced for impact.

"I should have known I'd find you all here," Ivy said angrily.

What was she doing here? I'd thought that Crinkles would keep her at the constabulary overnight, at least.

From the looks of things, I wasn't the only one to be shocked to see her on the loose again. Elves had parted to give her a wide berth as she'd steamed toward us, and now they kept their distance but stared openly.

Ivy rounded on Smudge. "Thanks for coming to visit me at the constabulary. I guess it's good to know that you'd just let me rot in jail."

"I didn't know you were at the constabulary." He frowned. "Somebody told me you were getting your hair done."

"I was until the SWAT team arrived and dragged me out from under the hair dryer." She rounded on me. "I suppose I have *you* to thank for that."

"New information came to light," I said.

"I can just imagine how. You've evidently been running around interrogating half the town."

I could hardly deny it. I leaned forward. "How is it that they let you go?" I asked. Did she come up with an alibi or something that would prove her innocence?

"You're not the only one with friends in high places." She crossed her arms and nodded toward the chocolate contest tables. Constable Crinkles was there with Ollie. "Besides, Crinkles didn't want to miss the contest."

Great. Our constable was letting suspects go because he wanted to attend the Tournament of Chocolate. He couldn't have done that if he was watching over a prisoner.

Ivy shook her head at me. "What did I ever do to you?"

"Don't blame April," Juniper said. "She's just trying to find out the truth. If you didn't do anything wrong, you have nothing to fear."

Ivy practically brayed with laughter at that statement. "How naive can an elf be?" she wondered aloud, and then gestured around the hall. As she did so, elves in our vicinity recoiled from the sweep of her arm in a perfect wave. "Do you think these people are concerned with whether I'm innocent or not? No. On next to no evidence at all, they're canceling their Valentine's orders and calling me Poison Ivy." She pinned Smudge with an angry gaze. "And even you won't stand up for me."

"I didn't know what had happened," he repeated. "And I was worried about Juniper. They think she was the intended target of the attack that killed Sterling."

"Useful to find out who you *really* care about," Ivy said.

I'd never been good at dealing with heated arguments. I made the mistake of trying to hop in and play peacemaker. "I ran into Smudge at the florist today while you were in the salon, Ivy. He was there to see you."

"And who were *you* there to see?" she asked, turning back to me. "Oh, that's right. You were there to interrogate Flock about who I'd killed lately."

"Ivy . . ." Smudge said.

"I guess you convinced Smudge that I intended to have another go at Juniper, is that it?"

"I didn't say anything about you except that I'd just seen you at the salon," I told her.

"Well, thanks." She glared at Smudge. "I could've used some moral support from my boyfriend. I guess that was too much to hope for."

Juniper tried to keep her voice down. "If you want to convince the world that you didn't kill anyone, yelling at us like a lunatic in public isn't a great way to go about it."

Ivy's gaze shot daggers back at her. "You think you'll get what you want from this?" she said, jabbing her thumb in Smudge's direction as her voice looped up to higher volume. "You won't, you know. And you'll be sorry."

She spun on her heel and stomped out as suddenly as she'd descended upon us. Elves nearby who'd witnessed the scene parted for her like the Red Sea in *The Ten Commandments*.

Juniper, Smudge, and I stared at each in shock.

"What did she mean by that?" Juniper asked.

"It sounded like a threat," I said.

Smudge took Juniper's hand in his. "I should take you home."

"I can go on my own."

"No," I said. "Let Smudge take you."

To be honest, I was a little worried about both of them—and I was glad Juniper's apartment had new locks. Ivy seemed unglued.

Mrs. Firlog grabbed my arm, causing me to jump in surprise. "What's going on?" She nodded at the exit Ivy had disappeared through. "What was *she* doing here?"

"Just an argument . . ." I wasn't going to cause Ivy more trouble tonight. I'd angered enough elves for one day.

Her suspicious look took in the three of us. "Well, it's time for the judging to begin." She lowered her voice. "Don't worry—I had elves watching the tables as soon as I saw Ivy come in."

So I was safe from being poisoned. Presumably.

For some reason, the thought of any of the chocolate contest entries being poisoned had never entered my mind.

She dragged me away from Smudge and Juniper over to the contest tables. The candy all looked incredible, and the smell of cocoa and sugar drove away fleeting thoughts of thallium. Piles of nut clusters spread before me, followed by a table of chocolate-covered caramels. Turtles were also included in this evening's competition, but I couldn't tell the difference between a turtle and nut cluster just by looking. It was surprising when I picked up a dark chocolate nut cluster and bit into it, only to discover that it was filled with the most delicious liquid caramel filling, slightly salty and amazingly good. I looked up at the elf behind these marvels that bore a sign designating them to be "Happy Turtles."

It was Happy Greenberry.

I could have cried with gladness. Here was a chance to right the wrong of the previous evening. Which hadn't been a wrong, exactly. Just a very unfortunate judged-contest conundrum.

"These are excellent," I told him.

He puffed up proudly, but his expression remained wary. "I've heard that song before."

"*Really* excellent," I said.

I didn't see how a plain chocolate-covered caramel could beat a Happy Turtle.

If I could have done so, I would have just awarded the Happy Turtles the blue ribbon for the whole tournament right then and there.

But alas, I had Mrs. Firlog at my elbow, telling me to move along to caramels. And I hadn't reckoned on local caramel wizard Flake Butternut's joining the competition. Flake specialized in caramels that he sold out of a cart on the streets of Christmastown. I had been addicted to his caramels for a while.

In fact, my heart sank to see him. The only thing that made me think that I wouldn't really have a conflict here was when I noted that he had entered an entirely new product for the competition: Cinnamon Caramel Hearts.

To be honest, the concept of cinnamon caramel didn't appeal to me. And just because it was heart-shaped . . . This tournament was about taste, not cutesy presentation.

Except sometimes the very thing you think won't be good absolutely surprises you. And that caramel was the most delicious thing I'd put in my mouth since . . . well, since Ollie's Constable Creams.

My heart sank.

I once again dawdled my way through the rest of the table's offerings, nibbling overly waxy chocolate-covered caramels, slightly grainy chocolate caramels, chocolate caramels with lackluster flavor. Each one just made me want to run back and sample another Cinnamon Caramel Heart. Even the constabulary's offering of white chocolate–covered caramels didn't impress me. In fact, I wanted to berate Crinkles. *For this, you let Ivy go?*

But she'd also mentioned something about friends in high places. Maybe that was the real reason he'd released her. Either way, the middle of a chocolate judging was not the time to discuss a murder investigation.

Finally, I had to present the ribbons. Part of me would have done anything not to present that red ribbon to Happy, whose face went crimson when he saw me coming.

"This is outrageous!" he said, refusing to take the red ribbon from me. "You know my Happy Turtles are the best thing on this table."

Guiltily, I left the red ribbon by the plate of Happy Turtles and made haste to award the blue ribbon to Flake Butternut.

"That elf is a professional candymaker," Happy protested. "This is unfair."

Part of me agreed with him. Flake Butternut made his living selling caramels. It was a little like watching American pro basketball players beat amateur players from Lithuania at the Olympic Games.

"You'll be sorry!" Happy said, gathering up his turtles and stomping out of the room.

It was the second time I'd heard that threat uttered tonight.

The constables appeared by my side. "Talk about a sore loser!" Ollie said.

Crinkles shook his head in pity. "It's embarrassing to see grown elves get so emotionally invested in a candy contest."

I planted my hands on my hips. "How was it that Ivy wasn't kept at the constabulary? She came here mad as a hornet, yelled at Juniper, Smudge, and me, and then left."

"I had to let her go. Puddin' Bayberry came to the constabulary. She said we didn't have enough evidence to keep Ivy."

"Puddin' Bayberry is a lawyer, I take it?"

Crinkles scratched his chin. "We don't really have lawyers here, exactly. Just counselor-arbitrators."

Another reason to love Santaland.

"She must have been very persuasive."

Crinkles nodded.

"Ivy mentioned friends in high places, too," I said. "Do you know who that was?"

Crinkles blinked. "I don't know—but I imagine someone's paying Puddin'."

Who, though?

"What happened to Jake?" I asked. "Wasn't he with you when you questioned Ivy?"

Crinkles nodded. "He had to leave to go see Claire. He's worried she might be sick."

That sounded bad. "Did he say what's wrong with her?"

He shrugged. "Just said she looked peaked."

I needed to call Claire and check in. I'd assumed what was bugging her was stress-related.

My job finished, I was ready to retrieve my coat and go home—and to get away from the competition tables. Happy hadn't been the only disappointed elf, just the most vocal. I wanted to escape the doleful expressions of the other losers.

"Hi, April! Did I miss anything?" a bright voice asked.

I looked over at Dolly Frost. "Where did you come from?"

"I've been around." She smiled. "We newcomers have to watch everything from the sidelines."

She sighed, then gestured up at the giant heart on the dais, inside which two people were huddled in an embrace. I drew in a breath. It was Amory Claus and his wife, Midge. The two of them looked so happy.

As I glanced at the blissful tableaux, I felt a pang. I wish Nick were here to take a picture. But of course Nick was adamant that he shouldn't be influenced by the early rounds of the Tournament of Chocolate, since he would be judging the finals on the morning of Valentine's Day.

I gave myself a shake. How pathetic to feel jealous of Midge and Amory.

"Do you know I get jealous sometimes?" Dolly looked up at me anxiously. "Do you think that's weird? I look at happy, smiling couples sometimes and think, why can't *I* have that?"

"It's not weird," I admitted.

"But *you'd* never feel that way." A little smile tilted at the corners of her mouth.

Was she trolling me? That was literally what I'd just been thinking.

It was unnerving.

I shifted uncomfortably, taking my gaze off Midge and Amory. "I'm happy to see other people happy," I said, tapping into my inner Goody Two-shoes.

"That's *such* a healthy attitude to have," Dolly said. "But of course you would feel that way. You're married to Santa. It must be such a thrill just to be Mrs. Claus."

Right. But Mrs. Claus wanted a little Valentine romance, too, darn it.

Unfortunately, it looked as if I'd have to make do with solving murders instead.

"Sometimes it really does seem as if the whole world's part of a couple," she prattled on. "Jake and Claire, Smudge and Ivy, Juniper and Sterling . . ."

I glanced over at her. She was still eyeing that oversized heart on the dais as if it was the world's biggest prize. "Sterling's dead," I reminded her.

She looked back at me, her cheeks stained with red. "I know. I don't know why his name slipped out."

I bit my lip. The words *slipped out* jarred something in my brain. Dolly had slipped out of the viewing room to look for her purse just before Sterling had come in. Button had seen her. But would Dolly have had enough time there with the corsage box to do the poisoning?

We were all so focused on Poison Ivy. Should we also be considering Poison Dolly?

Chapter 15

"I'll sure be glad when this wedding is over with," Christopher said.

I could see where he was coming from. Nick's teenaged nephew was doing homework in the breakfast room because his room shared a wall with the Old Keep, where elves were working tirelessly—and noisily—to get it ready in time to be the alternate great hall for Claire and Jake's big day.

Just two days away now. Even I was starting to feel jittery. This evening, Juniper and I were hosting the wedding shower-bachelorette party. I needed to make calls to make sure everything would run smoothly.

"No one made this amount of fuss when you and Uncle Nick got married," Christopher observed.

His mother, Tiffany, eyed me over a plate of scrambled eggs. Tiffany, who had been a competitive ice-skater before she moved to Santaland to marry Nick's late brother, the former Santa, had not fallen into the carb habit. She was almost as tiny as she'd been when she'd skimmed across the ice in her youth, performing elegant spirals and double axels.

"Nick and April had a lovely wedding," she admonished her son. "You remember that day. You were a ring bearer."

He groaned at the reminder. "I had to wear the itchiest wool suit ever."

"That's nothing," I said. "You should have tried on my shoes." My wedding had been my first experience wearing elf-style shoes with curling toes, even if just as a ceremonial show of Santaland solidarity. I'd been sorely tempted to kick them off and walk around in my stockings. But at that point my body hadn't acclimatized to the cold. I was a bride with cold feet—in the literal sense, not figurative.

"It doesn't seem worth it." Christopher tapped his pencil against his notebook in a way that made me think of Nick. Maybe it was just my imagination, but as he grew older, Christopher seemed to be watching his uncle more closely and taking on a few of his habits. "I like the idea of getting a lot of presents," he continued. "The trouble is, most of them seem really lame. How many candy dishes does a couple need?"

"That's a strange question coming from someone who's practically eighty percent gumdrop," I said.

He laughed, which turned to a bleat of alarm when the grandfather clock in the corner chimed the hour. "Golly doodle—I need to get going." He snatched up his books and dashed for the door, nearly knocking over Jingles. The elfman, who was holding a beautiful flower arrangement, gingerly sidestepped at the last moment.

The smell of lilies hit me full force. "Hothouse flowers," I said with awe.

Someone must have spent a king's ransom for those. My cheeks heated as I thought of Nick making such an extravagant gesture.

I probably reddened even more when Jingles presented the bouquet to Tiffany.

"How beautiful!" she exclaimed.

"They are," I agreed, careful to keep smiling. Now I knew how Happy Greenberry felt. "Who sent them?"

"Flock of Flock and Ivy drove them all the way up here," Jingles said. "He apparently doesn't know that his delivery person is holed up in the castle, afraid for his life."

"No one said anything to Flock about Flit's being here, did they?" I asked.

"Of course not." Jingles drew up, offended. "Charging polar bears couldn't get it out of me."

While Jingles and I talked, Tiffany had been reading her note. Her cheeks turned scarlet.

"A secret admirer?" I asked.

"He's not being very secret, sending a gift like that," Jingles said.

Tiffany smiled. "It's just from Burl Silvertree. He's been helping me with my Tiny Gliders group. You know—getting the little elf boys involved."

Tiffany not only ran a tea shop in town—Tea-piphany—she also taught figure skating to young elves. Burl, a renowned iceball player in Santaland, was a natural on the ice, like Tiffany. I could see how his involvement would have little elf boys flocking to Tiny Gliders.

"Those flowers don't look like a 'thanks for letting me help out' kind of gift," Jingles observed.

She flushed a little deeper. "Well, he did ask me out for a date on Valentine's."

This was such great news. Tiffany had been alone since she was widowed four years ago. "What did you say?"

"I said no, of course."

My heart sank. Burl was a handsome elf, and it seemed that they had a lot in common. "Why?"

She blinked. "Because I'm attending Claire's wedding on Valentine's Day."

"So? Invite Burl. Five hundred and forty-three guests or five hundred and forty-four—what's the difference?"

She'd thought this through. "You wouldn't want your first official date to be at a wedding, would you? It's not exactly an intimate atmosphere."

"With so many people and elves milling around this place, it might be easy to get lost in the crowd."

"The key word there is *crowd*," she said. "So we're going out tonight instead."

I straightened. "That's great."

Worry lines appeared in her brow. "You don't think Claire will mind if I skip the bachelorette party and just attend the shower, do you?"

"Of course not." I couldn't contain my curiosity. "Where are you going?"

"Burl made reservations at Twelve-Twenty-Five."

Jingles and I sucked in our breaths. Twelve-Twenty-Five was the ultimate in haute cuisine in Christmastown. Nick and I hadn't been yet. "I was just reading a review of it in *Elf Life* magazine," I said.

Jingles nodded. "It received five gold rings."

"Then we're going dancing at the Twinkle Ballroom," Tiffany said.

Dinner and dancing. It sounded like a dream.

Jingles sighed. "And I thought romance was dead here at the castle."

I bristled inwardly at his insinuation that Nick and I weren't very romantic. Not that he seemed to be far from wrong. I could hardly tout last year's concert band cymbal donation when Tiffany was being swept off her feet like a starlet in an old MGM musical.

Jingles sent me a wry look. "Speaking of adoration, you're certainly not getting any love from the elves in the Tournament of Chocolate."

The mood in the room turned almost funereal.

Tiffany sighed. "Poor Happy Greenberry."

I looked from one sad face to the other. "It's a tournament," I said in my own defense. "I can't hand out blue ribbons to everybody."

From the look in her eye, Tiffany was sympathetic to that argument. She'd spent her formative years enduring the heartaches of judged competition.

"Juniper told me that Happy Greenberry's a hothead." I could hear the defensiveness in my own voice. "He blew up at her over library fines."

"He doesn't have any family," Jingles said sadly.

I frowned. "You mean he grew up in the Home for Orphaned Elves?"

Tiffany and Jingles nodded as if this were common knowledge. Was everyone aware of this except for me?

"After his Granny Greenberry died," Jingles said. "She'd been raising him."

I sank a little in my chair. "Maybe he'll win a prize for fudge this evening," I said. "Mrs. Firlog is the judge for that."

"He's not entering in fudge," Jingles countered.

I couldn't hold back my astonishment. "How do you know?"

He shrugged. "Just heard it through the bearberry vine."

I needed to pay more attention. Not that it mattered. The purpose of the tournament was to judge chocolate, not misfortune.

I stood. "I should probably get going—I have a hundred things to do today."

"And I need to get to the tea shop." Tiffany took her magnificent flowers with her to her room.

I wasn't kidding about having a lot to do. I needed to get to Santaland Graphics to pick up game cards Juniper and I had dreamed up for the wedding shower. Then I was going to make sure everything was lined up for tonight, and head over to We Three Beans to decorate. Finally, it was my job to lure Claire to the coffee shop. She was expecting tonight to be her bachelorette party. The wedding shower beforehand would be a surprise.

Unless someone had blabbed. Always a danger in a hive of gossip like Santaland, where news traveled faster than flying reindeer.

I asked Jingles to order my sleigh and hurried to get ready for the day, changing into a red wool dress that would transition easily from daytime errands to nighttime party wear. I wouldn't have time to come back to the castle to change outfits.

When I arrived at the side portico to pick up my sleigh, I found Bolter waiting with Salty. "Good morning, Mrs. Claus," the reindeer said, bright as a button.

I looked in confusion and a little alarm at Salty. "Didn't Cannonball and Wobbler come back last night?"

On second thought, they must have, because Bolter was harnessed to my hybrid sleigh. There weren't many like it in Santaland.

"They came back, but I had to call in the veterinarian. Our love-struck reindeer got into another scrap."

I always worried about this. Wobbler and Cannonball were both misfits, which could cause tension with reindeer who lived in their regular herds. "Who were they fighting with?"

"Each other," Salty explained. "Wobbler even had a bite mark."

My jaw dropped. "They were physically fighting?"

Bolter shook his head. "Springtime's just around the corner. Reindeer can really run amok." He lowered his voice. "Last year two other reindeer got into a fracas over Flouncy. One of them lost an eye."

I gasped. "That's terrible."

"You've never run across Pirate Prancer?"

I shook my head.

"Very unlucky in love," Bolter said, shaking his head. "But that's spring for you. It turns some reindeer into animals."

With Bolter in harness—and blessedly staying on the ground today—I managed to get all my errands accomplished in good time. After picking up everything from the printer, I checked up on Dazzle Winterbright at his apartment. Days of hot tea with lemon and honey had worked their magic on his throat, and Doc Honeytree had greenlighted Dazzle to sing tonight at the Mistletoe Tavern.

Juniper and I spent part of the afternoon getting the decorations up at the We Three Beans coffeehouse. The chore took a little longer than expected because Dolly, our fellow bridesmaid, was AWOL.

Her absence gave me an uneasy feeling. Last night, I had convinced myself that I was overreaching to a few remarks she'd made. And I really didn't think she'd been out of the room long enough to switch out the corsage Sterling had brought with him to the Order of Elven Seamstresses for a different, poisoned one.

Where would the poisoned corsage have come from? Her handbag?

It was ridiculous. Why would she want to kill Sterling, or Juniper?

When I finally swung by the Santaland Scoop to lure Claire to the surprise bridal shower, I found her leaning back in a chair, eating a parfait glass full of lemon sorbet.

"Why don't you get dressed for tonight, and then we can go grab a quick coffee before the fun begins," I suggested. "And maybe have a buttery scone or something. You know it's good to have something in your stomach before drinking."

"Ugh—I'm not in the mood for coffee, or buttery anything."

Since when was Claire not in the mood for coffee and scones? "Then come watch me drink coffee." I smiled. "You can have an eggnog."

That was supposed to be a joke. Claire and I, Santaland outsiders, both found eggnog too sweet and gluey for our taste.

Butterbean, who was polishing glasses, hopped out from behind the counter. The elf was in on the plans for tonight. He also was aware that the bridal shower was supposed to be a surprise. He assured Claire brightly, "I can handle things here while you're having your sh—"

I tossed him a warning look.

"—shhhhot of eggnog," he finished.

At the suggestion, Claire visibly paled. For some reason, I hadn't anticipated having trouble coaxing her over to We Three Beans. Usually it took the slightest suggestion to make her drop everything and head over to our favorite hangout.

"Anyway," I said, "I already told Juniper that we'd meet her there."

She sighed and stood. "Okay—give me ten minutes."

Claire was quick to get dressed for the evening, but she slowed down when we were out on the sidewalk and headed for We Three Beans. She seemed to hold herself stiffly and carefully, as if she weren't certain of her movements. I'd been concerned about her lack of energy all week, but now I really started to worry.

I remembered that Jake had been worried about her health.

"Are you feeling okay, Claire?"

She glanced at me sharply. "Why are you asking?"

"You're critching along like an old lady. No—actually, I've seen octogenarians with more vitality."

She straightened. "It's hard to feel perky when there seems to be a crazed killer targeting my wedding party."

"But I noticed the change in you before that," I said. "I was worried about you starting last week. You've seemed distant and distracted."

"I'm fine."

I wanted to believe that, but I wasn't imagining the change in her. "Juniper was wondering earlier if a snow witch might have hexed you."

Claire laughed. "Not that I know of."

It was good to hear her laughing, at least. Maybe this was what she needed—getting out and socializing. I'd been so busy with the chocolate tournament, the murder, and wedding party prep that I hadn't been doing that thing I loved almost more than anything in the world—hanging out with my friends. Hanging out with Nick was probably the only thing I enjoyed more. I hadn't been doing enough of that.

"You know, I've been so focused on ridiculous things this week, I think I'm losing sight of what really matters."

Claire sent me a sidewise glance. "What kind of ridiculous things?"

"I've been focused on everyone else's new romances so much that my four-year-old marriage looks boring in comparison. That's not really an attitude of gratitude."

We approached the We Three Beans entrance. Claire reached out to push against the door. "Believe me, I would give anything for Jake and I to be an old married couple right now and have all this wedding nonsense behind us."

Just as she finished that last sentence, we stepped inside We

Three Beans and an entire coffee shop full of elves hopped up out of their chairs to yell, "Surprise!"

Claire's jaw dropped. She really hadn't expected this.

A big banner reading CONGRATULATIONS, CLAIRE AND JAKE! swagged over the counter where Trumpet, the proprietor, stood wearing a pink party hat. It wasn't really that much more fanciful than his usual elf cap, but all the elves were wearing pointy paper cones on their heads and seemed to think they were hilarious.

Even Smudge was there—in his old, non-Ivy-influenced clothes—wearing a goofy hat and getting into the spirit of things. Mostly, I think he wanted to make sure Juniper remained safe. Not that I expected that anything could happen to Juniper here.

Claire looked around. "Is Jake coming?"

"I couldn't convince him that a bridal shower wasn't just a party for the bride. He definitely plans on coming to the Mistletoe Tavern later, though."

Her reaction was lost as Tiffany and Butterbean scampered over and, like a fairy godmother and her elfin minion, tossed a shower of confetti over Claire and me.

Claire laughed. She got even more into the spirit of things when she saw that all of Christmastown had pitched in on the surprise. Trumpet was offering mugs of eggnog, punch, or coffee to everyone, and alongside a counter stood a table laden with offerings from all of our favorite hangouts in town: Merry Muffins, Puffy's All-Day Donuts, Chestnut's Cake Shop, and assortment of appetizers from the menu at the Midnight Clear diner.

"Oh my," Claire said, taking in the spread. "Did you and Juniper plan all of this?"

"We planned," I said, "but you wouldn't believe how eager all the merchants in town were to pitch in. Sparkletoe's Mercantile donated the bunting material."

Just then, Trumpet turned on some music. It was excerpts from *The Nutcracker*, but hey, it was Santaland. The opening bars of that music were like putting a match to a flame. Elves started line-dancing around the coffee shop's cozy, low-ceilinged main room. Someone grabbed Claire, and she joined in.

I looked at the merry mayhem around me and loaded up a plate with a donut and a piece of double chocolate cake. Juniper sidled up next to me. It was hard to miss that Smudge watching her intently, like her own Secret Service protection. "He's still nervous about Ivy," she said.

"I doubt we'll have to worry about her tonight." Although I couldn't help scanning the room. I frowned. "Where's Dolly?"

Juniper's brow puckered. "Do you think she forgot?"

"I doubt that." My uneasiness about Dolly returned. I wanted to believe she was harmless and suffered from a hopeless case of foot-in-mouth disease, but . . . "Does Dolly ever give you psychotic vibes?"

Juniper sent me a hard stare. "What do you mean?"

"She's made some weird remarks to me, and I keep remembering that she got up and left just before Sterling came into the room that morning."

Juniper shook her head. "Because she'd mislaid her purse. That could have been happenstance."

"That's true . . ." A carefully planned coincidence, maybe?

"And why would she have any animus toward Sterling, or me?"

"I don't know."

"I just can't see her as a calculating, cold-blooded killer, April." She was right. My imagination was going haywire.

It was a full half hour before the elves needed to stop dancing and carb up again. At that point, we all sat down to play the games Juniper and I had concocted for the evening. According to Juniper, a staple of every child's party in Santaland was "Pin the Hat on the Snowman," so we'd had a life-size cardboard cut-out of Jake Frost made, and now the elves were pinning the hat on Jake. Naturally, miniature cut-out hats of all descriptions were ending up everywhere.

"I'm glad we decided to play this game here and not at the Mistletoe Tavern," I said. "Those pins are dangerous enough in the hands of elves who are merely drunk on cake. With a little grog added to the mix, this could have been a bloodbath."

After the first game, some of the elves presented gifts to Claire, and she spent another half hour oohing and ahhing over an assortment of toaster tongs, candy dishes, and other traditional wedding offerings. Claire treated each like a priceless treasure.

After the last one was opened, Juniper said, "Now for real fun. Everyone gets a card. We're going to play take a quiz called 'Jake or Claire?'" She started handing out the cards that we'd had printed up on heavy card stock. "We're all going to take a few minutes to answer the questions on these cards, and then Claire's going to give us the answers." She smiled. "Whoever has the most correct answers will win a cake sampler from Chestnut's Cake Shop."

I was surprised to see Claire hadn't had anything to eat yet. "You might need cake for this," I said. I fetched her a piece. To my mind, cake was always a good idea.

Everyone sat down at the tables with the detritus of their refreshments and labored to answer the questions on the cards with the short pencils we'd provided. Judging from the intense concentration on the faces beneath those party hats, you would have thought the guests were taking the SAT.

When they were done, Juniper started reading the questions aloud to get Claire's verdict on the correct answer.

"Who puts their Christmas tree up first?" Juniper asked her. "Claire or Jake?"

Elves tended to have one-track minds—the Christmas track—and I hadn't been able to convince Juniper that the questions in this bridal shower quiz didn't have to be holiday-centric.

Everyone turned to Claire, waiting for her verdict.

She swallowed down a forkful of cake, giving the matter some thought. "Jake," she announced.

A good number of the elves groaned, while a few pumped their little fists.

Questions followed about who made the best Christmas pudding, who was the best at untangling strings of lights, and who was the best singer of Christmas carols. According to Claire, Jake was the correct answer on all of them.

Standing in front of the room, Juniper blushed as she read the next question. "Who made the first move, Jake or Claire?" She glanced apologetically at Claire. "I did not come up with that question."

"I guess I know who did," Claire said, eyeing me with amused resentment.

Guilty.

She took a last swallow of the cake and pushed the plate away from her.

Unfortunately, I hadn't known that the wording would puzzle some of the elves.

"Move where?" one called out.

"Claire moved from Cloudberry Bay," another said. "Is that what you meant?"

"I think she meant who was responsible for the first kiss," Juniper said, blushing.

Several elves got busy with their erasers to change their responses before Claire gave the definitive answer. "I did," she said.

She wasn't smiling.

The final question, "Who wants more kids?" seemed like a garden-variety bridal shower question when Juniper thought of it. But as Juniper read it aloud, Claire looked stonily at the table in front of her.

"April, Claire's turning green," Tiffany warned.

I turned just as Claire was jumping up. She bolted for the washroom.

The room watched her mad dash in astonishment. Juniper and I exchanged puzzled glances—and then tilted our heads back toward the washroom door as an astonishing idea occurred to both of us.

Tiffany leaned toward me and confided, "Back when I was expecting Christopher, I couldn't stand chocolate cake, either."

Chapter 16

"I'm fine," Claire assured Juniper and me through the bathroom stall.

"You keep saying that," I said, "but I'm not convinced."

A hand—Tiffany's—jutted through the washroom's main door. The hand was holding a snow cone, the only thing Claire had asked for.

"Special delivery from Snappy's," she announced.

Juniper, who was standing closest to the door, took it.

"Thanks, Tiff," I said. I knew she was eager to get ready for her date with Burl.

Claire finally emerged from the stall, her face looking better but still pale. She staggered toward the sink to wash her hands and face. "I meant that I'm fine for a pregnant person with twenty-four-hour morning sickness."

Juniper gasped. "Omigosh! I knew it!"

I was surprised. "You did?"

"Yes—I suspected it just now. I couldn't think of any other explanation of why Claire could resist that platter of Puffy's polar bear claws."

Claire held her stomach as if just the thought of a donut might make her about-face back into the stall. Then she shook her head. "The ice child doesn't like sweets—except frozen ones." Once she'd cleaned up, she turned and took the snow cone from Juniper and downed it like it was medicine. "He-she is already taking after Jake."

For some reason, in my concern for Claire, I'd forgotten about the other parental unit. "Is Jake happy?" I asked.

"He must be over the moon!" Juniper exclaimed.

"He doesn't know," Claire confessed.

The joy on my face and Juniper's faded at once. "You haven't told him?" I asked.

"I can't make myself do it," Claire explained. "First I wanted to verify with Doc Honeytree. And then I just couldn't find the right moment. Jake's already been through so much upheaval for me. He left his home in the Farthest Frozen Reaches . . ."

"*You* left Oregon to be with him," I pointed out. "That's an even bigger change."

And it was a change I was familiar with. I'd also left Oregon to be with Nick.

"And that's part of the problem, too," she said. "I've been driving this bus all along—after visiting you and meeting Jake, I wanted to move here permanently to be with him, and so I did. And then I wanted him to be around more, so he moved to Christmastown, too."

"He moved because he loves you," Juniper said. "Anyone with the eyesight of a narwhal could see that."

"You guys are about to be married," I reminded her.

"But he was always a carefree bachelor," she said. "How old is he? Even he doesn't seem to know—the ice in his veins is some kind of preservative, I think. Anyway, I do know that he said he never had thought to get married until I came along."

I tossed up my hands. "Precisely, until you."

"But what if I hadn't? He could have been happily gliding along his frigid way." She frowned. "That's why I started wondering if what's been happening surrounding the wedding is some kind of omen that I should put the brakes on the whole thing."

"If anything, it should make you want to accelerate," Juniper said. "What are you waiting for?"

"Certainty that I'm not chaining Jake down to a life he didn't want? A month when I don't feel as if the only way to keep my stomach from exploding like Krakatoa is to suck on icy things?"

"I can see now why you made peace with Snappy and his snow cone cart," I said.

She nodded. "I even asked Madame Neige to design a veil that would cover up the fact that a bride would be sucking on ice."

I laughed. "I thought you were going for the ghost look. What accounts for the weird ruffles on the dress?"

Claire's smile evaporated. "You think the ruffles are weird?"

"Well . . ." Now I'd stepped in it. "Unusual."

"You don't like my dress?" she asked.

"I love it," Juniper said, trying to rescue me. "I bet Jake will, too."

"If he hasn't run back to the icy hills by then," Claire said wryly.

"You're selling him short. He's going to be thrilled that he's going to get a whole family sooner than he thought."

"That's what I think," Juniper said. "Just imagine how you'd feel if the only family you had around you was Dolly Frost."

We all laughed.

And then, just as suddenly, we weren't laughing. "Where *is* Dolly?" I asked.

Claire brushed the subject away with a wave of her hand. "She's probably out chasing after Jake. She follows him around like a puppy."

Juniper crossed her arms. "Aren't you worried about that?"

Claire shook her. "I trust Jake."

Except in the matter of telling him that he was going to be a father.

A knock sounded on the washroom door. "Mrs. Claus?" Trumpet asked through the thick wood. "Is everything okay in there?"

I'd forgotten we'd left a coffeehouse full of elves wondering what had happened to us.

"Everything's fine," I singsonged back.

"We're still waiting for the answer so we can figure out who won the cupcakes."

Claire bit her lip. "The answer's both of us."

As Trumpet relayed the information to the crowd, Claire looked from me to Juniper and assured us, "I'll tell him tonight. After the bachelorette party."

"You could tell him at the party, probably," Juniper said.

Claire frowned. "Jake's coming to our hen night?"

"I hate to burst your bubble, but half of Santaland is coming to your hen night—and it's not just the hens."

Claire and Jake were popular in Christmastown, but I suspected most of the reason so many elves and people of Santaland crowded into the Mistletoe Tavern was to see Dazzle Winterbright. When we arrived, the Tavern was already full to the gills. Even a few snowmen had made their slow way over to the street so they could stand outside and hear the North Pole's favorite crooner.

Dazzle had a flair for the dramatic, and tonight he didn't disappoint. As Claire walked in, as if on cue he turned his bedroom eyes on her and sang a dreamy version of "My Funny Valentine" as if he were singing to her and her alone. Claire wasn't one to go all swoony over entertainers, but I could tell even she was feeling a little wobbly about the knees during that song.

Dazzle's smooth, husky voice had a way of wrapping you in a warm hug. When he was crooning that each day was Valentine's Day, gooseflesh broke out on my arms. Juniper, Smudge, and I found a table just beyond the bar with a couple of stools free. I looked around, hoping to spot Nick somewhere in the Tavern. He said he would try to join me when he'd finished work.

Dazzle ended his first set, and the band broke into a jazzy version of "We Wish You a Merry Christmas." Valentine's Week in Santaland made for strange musical bedfellows, but the elves loved it. The crowd danced and bobbed and sang the words.

"Hi, April!" I'd been longing for Nick, but I was out of luck. The voice at my elbow belonged to Dolly. "Isn't this fun? I never thought I'd be at a big party in Christmastown like this."

"We were surprised that you skipped the bridal shower."

"Was I absolutely supposed to go to that?" Dolly asked, eyes wide. "Jake wasn't going, so I felt it wouldn't be fair if *all* of us went."

"Bridal shower," I repeated. "Usually includes the bridal party."

A flush of red climbed into her cheeks. "I'm sorry, I'm not from here. We don't have weddings like this in the Farthest Frozen Reaches."

"What do you have?"

"Elopements." She frowned. "Or abductions, if you're talking snow monsters."

"What a place."

Tears stood in her eyes. "Maybe I should just go back there, because I certainly don't seem to fit in here."

I bit back a sigh. "I didn't mean it as criticism of you."

"No, it's true—I'm different from elves here," she insisted. "Jake's the only one who understands what I'm going through."

Juniper, listening in, responded with a subtle eye roll.

It was probably a good thing that Dolly did skip the bridal shower. If she had heard that Claire was pregnant, she probably would've blurted it out to the entire Tavern by now.

"Never mind," I said. "You just missed a lot of fun."

Her gloom lifted immediately. "Oh, I had plenty of fun on my own. Jake and I went to the fudge contest. You would have been amazed at how smoothly the contest went this evening, April. Mrs. Firlog got it all done with no fuss at all."

My smile tightened. "Of course she did."

"And no one threw a tantrum over the judging results, which was a nice switch. Not that it was *your* fault that elf kept losing." Her face twisted into a puzzled frown. "Except I guess it was, technically."

"I heard Happy didn't enter tonight anyway," Juniper said.

"And fudge is pretty straightforward," I added, hoping I didn't sound as defensive as I felt. "Who won?"

"An elf named Dash."

"Good for him." I wasn't a frequent fudger at Dash's Candy and Nut Shoppe for nothing.

"Speaking of Jake, I should probably go find him." Dolly peered around the room. "He disappeared right after we got here."

I knew where he'd disappeared to. I doubted he and Claire needed Dolly around at this moment.

"You should get yourself something to drink," I suggested to distract her from intruding on their privacy. "The grog here is Christmastown's finest."

"Really?" she asked.

"It's a must for any newcomer," Juniper said.

Dolly's gaze moved to the bar, where elves were lined up two- and three-deep. She bravely hopped off her stool. "Save my spot— I'm going in!"

Juniper, Smudge, and I watched her go, shaking our heads.

"I wonder if Claire trusts Jake too much," Juniper said.

"She knows him better than we do," I said.

Her face broke out in a joyous smile. "I can't wait till we're aunties!"

She seemed so delighted, I almost hated to burst her bubble. I had Christopher, and she had multiple nieces and nephews from her own siblings. "We already are aunts."

"I know, but this will be more fun, because it's Claire. I hope it's a girl!" She tilted her head. "Or a boy."

I laughed. "I just hope Claire will feel better when Jake knows."

"Of course she will. Imagine—" Juniper's words cut off abruptly and she blinked at Festa Redwinkle, who was leaning against the bar just next to us.

"What's *she* doing here?" I asked.

Smudge answered dryly, "Drinking, by the looks of things."

I glanced back at Juniper. "Did you invite her?"

"Golly doodle, no. She's in mourning—I wouldn't expect her to want to show up at a wedding shower. But she probably doesn't think I should be out on the town days after her brother died."

Something told me that shaming Juniper for having a good time was the last thing on Festa's mind. I recalled hauling liquor down from the cabinet for her at her mother's place. "It's a public tavern. Maybe she just needed a drink, and to escape."

"I suppose I should go say hello to her."

After my last encounter with her, I was hesitant, but I followed Juniper.

Festa raised a tankard of grog to us. "Word has it that you two are responsible for this celebration."

"It's for Claire and Jake's wedding." Juniper couldn't help adding, "We've been planning it for weeks."

"Nice." She looked at me. "Hello, Mrs. Claus."

"Hi. I'm surprised to see you here."

She laughed at my sheepishness. "I'm not a big one for holding grudges—unlike my mom. I know you were just asking questions." She looked over and took in the sheepish flush in Juniper's cheeks. "And don't worry, I won't tell Mother you're out partying"—she glanced over at Smudge at our table—"with another guy. I needed to escape the gloom of home myself."

"I'm so sorry," Juniper said. "I should have gone back to see Mrs. Redwinkle."

"No, you shouldn't. She's got a whole circle of cronies to mourn with her." She sighed. "They've all heard about how Sterling got the poison meant for you."

Juniper cringed.

Festa's lips twisted. "Most people seem to think Ivy did it." She shook her head. "I used to like her."

I glanced at Juniper to see if she was having any thoughts about suspects, but her face had gone as white as a snowman's. I tracked her gaze to another elf standing at the bar. No wonder she looked alarmed. Ivy was here.

From the stage, Dazzle was back for another set, and launched into a heartfelt rendition of "Hello, Young Lovers."

Festa tracked our gazes. "Speak of the devil."

Juniper's hand tightened around the handle of her grog mug. "What's she doing here?"

"Half of Santaland's here to see Dazzle," Festa said. "Why not my brother's killer?"

I shook my head, fighting to retain some vestige of impartiality. "We don't know that."

"I know that Madame Neige went over to Ivy's place to cut off business relations with her," a voice said at my elbow.

"Blanchette," Juniper said, surprised to see Madame's star seamstress at our gathering.

I'd forgotten to tell Juniper—or anyone else—that I'd told Blanchette to come tonight. To be honest, I hadn't given her a thought all day.

Blanchette sent a scowl Ivy's way. "If I were you, Mrs. Claus, I'd get rid of her."

"How? It's a public tavern."

"Don't look now, but she's headed this way," Festa said.

As Ivy approached from one direction, a wary Smudge closed in from the other. Last night Ivy had told Juniper, "You'll be sorry." Small wonder that her sudden reappearance put him on high alert.

Ivy greeted us all with a big smile. "Am I crashing your party?" She barely spared Juniper and Smudge a glance. It wouldn't have mattered. Those two were having an entire conversation with their eyes.

"It's a public tavern." I was beginning to sound like a broken record.

"Why did you come here?" Smudge asked her.

"Why do you care?" she shot back. "Is Poison Ivy harshing everyone's mellow?"

Smudge lowered his voice. "You knew this was going to be a party for Claire and Jake."

"And you know I'm a big fan of Dazzle Winterbright. Why should I hide myself away?" For the benefit of the elves around us staring at her, she announced, "I didn't do anything wrong."

"Are you sure about that?" Festa asked her in a deadpan voice.

Ivy's color deepened. "Hello, Festa. I was sorry to hear about Sterling. I've been thinking of you ever since."

The condolences didn't impress Festa. "Phones exist."

"I know," Ivy said. "I'm so sorry. It's been a busy week."

"What with the wedding and the murder and all," Festa said.

Ivy took in our hostile faces and shook her head. "Tough crowd."

"You threatened Juniper last night."

"Okay, I probably shouldn't have done that," she admitted. "Let me make amends and buy you all a round."

"No thanks," I said. I wasn't ready to make nice quite yet. Nobody else seemed inclined to, either.

Ivy looked over at Smudge, and something in her face shifted. "Smudge? A grog for old times' sake to show that there aren't any hard feelings?"

He hesitated.

She sputtered impatiently. "This is ridiculous. We all live in the same town. I'm willing to bury the hatchet, why not you?"

"Okay, Ivy," Smudge said. "I'll have a grog. Thank you."

She stepped away to talk to the elf behind the bar.

"That was awkward," Blanchette said, bringing nervous chuckles from the rest of us. "I could use a drink myself." She edged down the bar.

"Where is Claire?" Dolly asked. "She's missing a lot of Dazzle."

My guess was that either she and Jake had found some quiet corner to celebrate their joyful news, or else morning sickness had sent her darting back to the ladies' room.

"Grog incoming!" Ivy called out.

The tankard of grog she'd ordered for Smudge was passed elf-to-elf down the bar to him. Festa pushed it down the bar to Blanchette, who inspected the dark contents from all angles. "This is a beverage?" she asked with a delicate shudder.

I guessed the Order of Elven Seamstresses didn't imbibe a lot of grog. Madame Neige was more of a wine type.

She passed the tankard to Dolly, who seemed confused. "Whose is this?"

"It's for Smudge," Juniper said, taking it from her and giving it to him.

"I still can't believe she's here," Dolly said. "What possessed her?"

"She hasn't done anything wrong, and she doesn't want people to think she has anything to feel guilty about," Smudge said, taking a sip.

If I were Juniper, I wouldn't have been happy to hear him defending Ivy, but Juniper was fair-minded. "I can see how she wouldn't want to turn tail and flee," she said.

Ivy was still waiting for Perk, the bar elf, to mix some elaborate cocktail in a shaker, but she looked over and gave a gesture to go ahead and enjoy his grog. He took another drink.

"I still say she has a nerve," Festa remarked.

"I'm going to find Claire," I said. Dazzle had moved on to singing the love theme from *Titanic*, which always made me a little twitchy.

Apparently I wasn't the only one the song had that effect on, because Smudge's hand shook so hard that he splashed grog on several nearby elves. They jumped away from him, which left him more exposed as it became clear that something was very wrong.

Juniper reached out for him. "Smudge?"

He dropped the tankard and then, as if boneless, collapsed to his knees.

"Oh no." Juniper held his arms as if wanting to jack-in-the-box him right back up. But his weight was too much for her and she ended up joining him on the floor.

It was a strange echo of what had happened just two days before. A roiling sensation ginned up in the pit of my stomach.

And just like Sterling had two days before, Smudge fell into Juniper's arms as the life seemed to seep out of him.

"Help!" Juniper called. Dazzle's rendition of "My Heart Will Go On" reached a crescendo and then suddenly stopped altogether.

"Call the Infirmary!" I shouted at Perk behind the bar.

The shocked faces of elves all around me seemed like a horror movie reflection of what my own expression must have been. A hundred thoughts flew through my mind as I looked from Juniper to Blanchette to Festa and finally to Ivy. But it wasn't until I heard Claire's voice that I realized what the uppermost question in my mind was.

"How can this be happening again?"

"It was Ivy!" An elf near the bar pointed to her. "I heard her at the tournament last night. Everybody did. She said 'you'll be sorry!' to Smudge."

Heads bobbed, and along with them caps with jingle bells created a tinkling of agreement. Ivy crossed her arms, her lips tight. She couldn't deny the threat.

"And now he's been poisoned!"

I was too focused on Juniper and Smudge and listening for the klaxon of an approaching ambulance sleigh to pay much attention to the name "Poison Ivy" rippling through the crowd. Or to the intensely hostile looks being thrown at Ivy.

"Murderer!" Festa yelled at her.

Chapter 17

When the ambulance sleigh arrived, Ivy muscled her way onto it with Smudge and Juniper. I think it was more to escape the hostility in the Mistletoe Tavern than real concern for Smudge—but maybe I was selling her short. They had just been a couple yesterday.

Claire, Jake, and I followed on foot to the Santaland Infirmary a few blocks away. We didn't have to whisper.

"Did Ivy really threaten Smudge at the Tournament of Chocolate?" Jake asked.

I nodded. "It was just before the Caramels and Nuts judging. She seemed angry because Juniper and Smudge had arrived together— and had spent part of the afternoon together at the Midnight Clear diner."

Claire shook her head. "Poisoning someone's an extreme reaction to two elves having a snack."

But we both knew there was more to Smudge and Juniper's relationship than that.

"Jealousy twists people's minds," I said.

At the Infirmary, Nurse Cinnamon, an elfin dervish in sensible, rubber-soled booties, stopped us. "Doc Honeytree will be examining Smudge. You'll have to wait outside the room with them."

She indicated Ivy and Juniper, who were already seated on

benches on opposite sides of the hallway. Tears streaked Juniper's cheeks. Ivy was stone-faced.

Even Nurse Cinnamon was giving Ivy the stink eye.

"Any word on how Smudge is?" I asked Juniper.

She heaved in a ragged breath. "Not yet."

Jake turned to Claire. "I want to go back and have a word with the constable when he arrives at the tavern," he said. "Let me know if there's any word about Smudge's condition."

Claire and I sank down on either side of Juniper.

We didn't say anything more. The tension in that hallway was uncomfortable enough even in silence. One wrong word was liable to set everyone off. In addition to anxiety about Smudge, Claire clearly worried her wedding was cursed. And Juniper, who had been unlucky in love many times, was coping with the possibility that two elves she was involved with might both die within days of each other.

I couldn't guess what Ivy was thinking.

Why had Ivy come here? She didn't look heartbroken—or guilty, either. Her demeanor seemed more like a sullen teenager. After she'd left the Mistletoe Tavern, she could have just gone home.

After about twenty minutes, the Candymints, Smudge's parents, arrived from Tinkertown. Juniper stood, with Claire and I following suit. Mr. Candymint must have been working the night shift, because he was still in his red-and-white-striped coveralls from his job at the Candy Cane Factory.

Juniper gave them both a hug. "He's still breathing—Doc's with him now. Nurse Cinnamon told us to wait here."

"Can't we see him?" Mrs. Candymint said, eyeing the hallway benches unhappily.

"They have to let us see him," her husband said.

"I think Doc's worried because of what happened the other day," Juniper told them. "He didn't want any of us in the room for some reason."

Despite all our best efforts, we all flicked glances Ivy's way.

Ivy let out a breath.

Smudge's mother's face tensed in confusion. "You mean they're worried what happened to Sterling this week had something to do with poor Smudgie's collapse tonight?"

Juniper nodded miserably. "I'm so sorry."

"But Sterling *died*," Mr. Candymint said.

His wife nodded. "Everyone said it was because of some flowers from—"

Her words cut off as the dots finally connected.

Ivy darted a resentful glance at us. "I swear to you that I had nothing to do with what happened, either to Sterling or Smudge. I bought him a drink, to be friendly. I did not poison it."

Her protestations did nothing to soothe the anxious parents, who evidently hadn't heard the possibility that he'd been poisoned by a tankard of grog. Mrs. Candymint's throat caught in a sob of despair, and her husband pulled her into a comforting embrace.

The door next to us opened and Doc Honeytree appeared. He looked relieved to see Smudge's parents, and to be able to give them some hope to cling to. "Smudge is stable, but not conscious. Why don't you come see him?"

We all stood, ready to fall in behind the older elves, but Nurse Cinnamon inserted herself as gatekeeper. "Two at a time, please." The two she waved through were the Candymints.

After the door shut behind them, we all sank back onto our benches again.

"Thank goodness he's okay," Juniper said.

"Doc didn't say *okay*." Ivy's voice bristled with scorn. "He said stable. That's one of those things doctors say when they don't have good news."

Her grim pronouncement unsettled us.

"He's just got to pull out of this," Juniper said.

"Okay, Pollyanna," Ivy said under her breath.

I felt incensed, and I wasn't the only one. "It almost sounds as if you don't want him to improve," Claire told Ivy.

"I'm just being a realist." She nodded toward the door. "Mrs. Candymint added one plus one fast enough—what happened tonight is just like what happened to Sterling. And Sterling died."

"That doesn't mean that this incident will have the same outcome," I said. "And how would you know that what happened to Smudge was exactly what happened to Sterling? You weren't at the Order of Elven Seamstresses the morning Sterling collapsed."

Ivy blew out a breath. "Okay, I *assume* it was the same. Poison. But as you say, I wasn't there when Sterling died, so I don't see why everyone is pointing the finger at me. For that matter, I wasn't near Smudge, either."

Claire was having none of this. "You didn't need to be near him. You just needed to spike his drink, and you were the first elf who touched it."

"But not the last," she reminded us. "I just took the tankard from Perk and passed it down."

"You could have spiked it before you passed it," I said.

"So could anyone," she argued. "Who were the elves closest to him?" She stared pointedly at Juniper. "For that matter, who was right next to both victims when they died?"

I hopped to my feet. "Don't go trying to deflect suspicion by blaming Juniper. Can't you see she's devastated?"

Ivy shook her head. "She was so devastated by Sterling's death that she immediately sought out Smudge for consolation."

Juniper's voice rose above ours. "It's wrong to sit here arguing like this when Smudge could be dying right on the other side of that door."

I shut my mouth and leaned back in my chair.

Ivy folded her arms and glared at me. If looks could kill, she wouldn't have even needed poison. "The bar elf saw me take the tankard," she muttered. "Talk to Perk."

"We did."

At the sound of Jake Frost's voice we all looked up. Jake and Constable Crinkles were standing together, and behind them was Nick, wearing his everyday red Santa Suit.

The mood in the hallway shifted. Sensing that something momentous was about to happen, we all stood up. Nick sent me a concerned, comforting glance, which made me feel stronger. I'd called him, of course, to tell him what had happened at the Mistletoe Tavern. He must have dropped everything to get here from Castle Kringle in record time.

Then my gaze shifted to Constable Crinkles's face, which was set in a pout—a sure sign that he had bad news to deliver. No lawman in the world disliked unpleasantness more.

"The constable spoke to Perk," Nick announced.

It took Crinkles a moment to realize that this was his cue. "Perk remembers handing you the tankard of grog, Ivy. But he doesn't know what happened after that."

"I pushed the tankard down the bar," she said. "Someone else passed it to Smudge. I was nowhere near him."

"Perk couldn't recall how long the tankard was in your possession," Jake said.

Ivy shook her head. "No time at all. Why would I want to hang onto it? I was waiting on my own drink."

Nick, Crinkles, and Jake exchanged glances.

Crinkles shifted uncomfortably. "The thing is, several elves heard you threaten Smudge just the night before. 'You'll be sorry,' you said."

"That was just something I blurted out in the heat of the moment."

I'd been there when she said it, and it hadn't seemed like nothing to me at the time. I remembered being anxious about Juniper going home, and the relief I felt when Smudge offered to escort her.

"I didn't mean I was going to kill him," she insisted.

"And then there's the matter of Sterling Redwinkle," Jake continued. "He was killed by a corsage made at your shop."

She crossed her arms. "I deny that."

"I talked to Flit," I said. "He told me that he delivered a small box from your store to Sterling's house in Tinkertown. A delivery you asked him to deny, and erased any record of."

Her chin jutted forward, and for a moment she couldn't seem to think of a response. "What's going on here? You're like orcas circling a seal, and I'm the seal. Am I being arrested?"

Crinkles waved his hands, a look of dread on his face. "It would be good if you stayed at the constabulary for a little while. Just till we have some answers to all our questions."

"You have the answers already," Ivy told him. "You just want to convince me to tell you what you want to hear. But that would be a lie."

Crinkles looked uneasy until he hit upon a way to sweeten this non-arrest. "Ollie just put out a batch of cinnamon rolls to rise. They'll be piping hot and fresh from the oven tomorrow morning."

She laughed dryly. "I guess if I'm going to be unjustly incarcerated, I might as well have yummy baked goods." She picked up her purse. "Lead the way, Constable."

Before she followed Crinkles down the hallway, Ivy turned back to us. "If Smudge wakes up, tell him I was here but I was forced to leave. *He'll* know I didn't try to kill him."

But how would he know? He'd probably seen even less than Perk the bartender.

After they left, Doc Honeytree emerged from Smudge's room. He took in the empty bench where Ivy had been sitting, and then he flicked a gaze up and down the corridor. "Ivy's gone?"

"Constable Crinkles is escorting her to the constabulary," Nick said.

"Well, you can all come in, then. I just didn't want to risk letting Smudge's possible poisoner into the room with him."

He'd made up his mind about Ivy awfully quickly. "Why do you think she did it?"

"This discoloration on Smudge's tongue is just what Sterling's was—only not quite so severe."

"Poison Ivy strikes again," Claire muttered.

Something about that moniker didn't seem right to me. "Innocent until proven guilty."

She raised a brow at me. "Would you drink something she passed to you?"

Nope.

Point taken.

We filed in and stood around Smudge's bed. The rooms of the Santaland Infirmary were more like the rooms at a B&B than a hospital. The adjustable bed had a wooden headboard, and next to it was a tall, narrow drop-leaf table that I would have considered myself lucky to have found in a high-end antique store. The curtains, which had Currier & Ives–like winter scenes embroidered on them, stood open, allowing a look at brightly lit Christmastown and even a glimpse of Castle Kringle in the distance, midway up Sugarplum Mountain.

Nick put his arm around mine. We hung back, as did Jake and Claire, allowing Smudge's family and Juniper to stay closer to him.

Juniper held his hand. "We're here, Smudge," she said. "Me, and your mom and dad."

Part of me was expecting to hear the patient reply in his gruff voice. But he remained unresponsive, and the silence was heartbreaking.

After a few minutes, Nick and I ducked out. "I'm going back to the castle," he said. "Ride with me?"

It was tempting. After the scene we'd just come from, I wanted to hold Nick close. But that would have to wait.

"I have my sleigh here," I said.

He looked disappointed, but nodded. "Bundle up on the way home. There's supposed to be snow tonight."

Snow was a regular occurrence, so I surmised that he meant more snow than usual was expected. "I'll be right behind you," I said.

He gave me a quick kiss. "Be careful."

"So you don't think taking Ivy into custody has made the streets of Christmastown safe again?"

"I'm not sure."

I wasn't either. I still couldn't shake off my first impression after what happened to Sterling. Why would a person place threats—and then an actual murder weapon—in a box bearing the name of her business? She might as well have left a series of neon arrows pointing to Flock and Ivy's.

"I'll be careful," I assured Nick.

Maybe it was this short exchange with him that made me feel jumpy as I walked to my sleigh. I could see Bolter waiting for me just at the end of the street, but as I walked toward him, shadows jumped out at me, making my breath catch. Once I spun around, terrified by the sound of an ice rat scampering across the snow. That little rodent nearly gave me a heart attack.

Get a grip, April. This was Christmastown. All around me, the world looked like one of those decorative snow villages people put out at Christmastime when I was growing up, except this one was decked out in red, pink, and white, with shiny hearts hanging from lampposts. I walked past a big goofy inflatable of two hugging polar bears. Yet I was as jumpy as if I were walking through the mean streets of some metropolis.

I hunched more stiffly in my puffy coat, but I couldn't completely shake off the anxiety, even when I climbed on the sleigh. I wished I could accept that Ivy was really Poison Ivy, the Valentine poisoner. But I just couldn't.

"Back to the castle?" Bolter seemed uneasy, too. Probably because I was sitting frozen behind him, trying to sift through the many questions I had. *Was Ivy devious enough to make it so obvious that she was the killer that we would assume she wouldn't be?* If so, that strategy hadn't entirely worked out for her.

"Mrs. Claus?" Bolter asked. "Is everything okay? You're as still as a snowman."

Snowman!

I jerked back to my senses. "We need to go around to Flock and Ivy's."

He pawed the ground doubtfully. "I think they'll be closed at this hour."

"I know—I need to talk to someone outside the florist."

"Whatever you say."

He took off so quickly that I fell against the backrest before righting myself again. It was just as well that he was in a hurry. I'd told Nick that I would be right behind him; I didn't want this detour to last any longer than it had to.

"Stop right here," I said when I saw Bumble on the sidewalk.

Bolter was confused. "I can take you right up to the florist's door."

"It's the snowman I need to talk to."

I hopped down and hurried over to Bumble. His eucalyptus arms were still in place, although they were drooping a little with snow tonight. With his permission, I whisked some of the accumulated snow off.

"What's going on this evening?" he asked. "There's been quite a hubbub downtown tonight—I even heard the bell of the sleigh ambulance."

"My friend Smudge collapsed at the Mistletoe Tavern and was taken to the hospital."

The snowman had some sticks arranged in a smile beneath his carrot nose, but when you got to know snowmen, you understood the subtle changes in demeanor they could project even in stillness. Right now, his expression projected sympathy. "I'm sorry to hear that," he said. "Is he okay?"

"So far he's holding his own." I tilted my head. "You know when you said you saw Sterling talking to someone in a red coat?"

"Yes."

"You're sure that wasn't Ivy?"

"Like I said, I would've recognized her."

Of course he would have. He'd been standing sentry on this street for months.

"You wouldn't try to cover up for her, would you?"

"Cover up—why?"

"The constable has her in custody. He suspects that she might have been behind Sterling's death, and now the attempt on Smudge's life."

"Oh no. That can't be!" he said. "She gave me my new arms and opened up my sinuses. She's a good elf."

I nodded. I wasn't convinced of her goodness, just of her innocence.

"I should hurry over there and talk to the constable myself," Bumble said. "I can be there in a day and a half."

"Stay right here. It's not even certain that the elf you saw in the red coat that night was connected with his death. But if the constable needs your testimony, I'll tell him to come talk to you."

"Poor Flock. No wonder he seemed distraught when he passed by this evening. Didn't even say 'Hello, Bumble,' like he usually does."

"You mean when he went home?"

"Oh no—he hasn't gone home yet."

I would have sworn that his right branch arm pointed to the florist's building, where a light shone through the plate glass window.

I stepped back to the curb and told Bolter I needed to duck into the florist's for a few minutes.

After I knocked, I stood shivering on the stoop for a full minute before the door cracked open and Flock peered up at me. "Oh, Mrs. Claus. It's you."

"Who were you expecting?"

He shook his head. "No one, really. Would you like to come in?"

The warmth and humidity of the florist shop was a welcome change from the cold outside. "Can I offer you a cocoa?" he asked. "I was just making some for myself."

I rarely say no to cocoa, especially on a cold night like this. "That would be lovely—thank you."

He turned to go back to the little hot plate in the corner, where a saucepan of milk was warming. He stirred cocoa into it. "Please believe me when I say that I had no idea what Ivy was up to."

I tilted my head. "You mean . . . ?"

"First Sterling—and now Smudge. They're saying she's been arrested." He heaved a sigh. "We've already lost all our customers. I'm not going to have a business after this is all over."

"So you think she's guilty?"

"What else am I to think?"

The betrayal in his voice irritated me. "You lied when you said that the corsage that killed Sterling hadn't come from here."

"I didn't say that. I only said that *I* hadn't made it."

"You knew we assumed that meant neither of you had."

"I know, I'm sorry." He hung his head. "I lied about the delivery, too."

I waved a hand and sat down on a stool by the counter. "I've known that since yesterday."

He poured the cocoa into mugs. "How?"

I wasn't going to rat out Flit. "It was foolish of you to tear pages out of the order logs."

"I didn't! Ivy did."

"Why would she have done that, if she was innocent?"

"I don't know." He frowned. "I really don't want to believe she's guilty. Maybe she was induced to do it by someone else."

I tilted my head. "Someone like who?"

"I probably shouldn't say this, but I don't guess it matters now." He pushed a mug of cocoa toward me, then hiked himself up on a stool on the opposite side of the counter. "The golden days of Flock and Ivy are all over. Without Ivy, I'm probably nothing. She was the creative engine, and she was the one with the benefactor."

This was the first I'd heard of a benefactor. Or was it? *Friends in high places,* she'd said. "Who?"

"I don't know. She never told me. All I know is that every month, Ivy received money in the mail."

"Cash?"

"Yes, in a large envelope marked 'Ivy' that would be pushed through our mail slot. The first of every month, like clockwork."

"Ivy never told you who it was from?"

"I wasn't even sure *she* knew." His face screwed up in puzzlement. "But she must have. I asked her if she thought it might be intended for her personally, and she replied that she didn't want it for herself—almost like she was resentful. Said she would only put it into the business."

I took a long sip of cocoa. It was delicious—creamy and choco-latey, with just a hint of cinnamon. "So every month you received a large sum of money from a stranger. Did you ever worry that the person giving the money might not be on the up-and-up?"

"A criminal, you mean?" He shook his head. "Sometimes that money was the difference between making a profit or going into the red. I like to consider myself an ethical person, Mrs. Claus, but our benefactor would have to have done something very bad indeed for me to have turned down that injection of cash each month."

It sounded like a fairy tale—but fairy tales could be sinister. That last thought made me think of the money drop in a different light. I asked, "As far as you know, was there ever any demand made in exchange for the money?"

"What kind of demand?" he asked, confused.

I shrugged. "Ivy never felt this was a quid pro quo?"

"There's no service we could have offered except flowers." He slumped. "I don't see how I'm going to get along without her. And it's not just because those monthly donations will dry up. How will I get along without her creativity?"

"You really don't think you can manage on your own?"

"It's going to be difficult," he said. "Even if I do manage to put together nice arrangements, who's going to want to order anything from the store Poison Ivy ran?"

"The controversy will die down," I predicted.

"I hope so, but Sterling Redwinkle was very popular," he said gloomily. "So was Smudge, in his way."

I didn't like his use of the past tense. "Smudge could very well pull through."

He perked up at that news. "Really? That's great. I should send him flowers." His eyes took in the store's interior, as if there might be a spare Get Well bouquet lying around. "Might serve the dual purpose of letting everyone know that Flock and Ivy's is still going, even without Ivy." He frowned. "I'm going to have to change the sign. Maybe spruce up the whole place."

For an elf who'd just been worrying how he was going to get along now that his partner had been taken away, he sure seemed eager to carry on without her.

Chapter 18

"The reindeer would like to speak to you," Jingles announced the next morning before I was fully awake.

"Which ones?"

"Cannonball and Wobbler."

I yawned and sat up in bed, taking the coffee tray that he offered me. The reindeer would have to wait until I was caffeinated. "Is there any news?"

Jingles didn't have to ask what news I was referring to. "Santa phoned the hospital this morning. Smudge's condition is still the same."

Poor Juniper. I wanted to get to the hospital to see her. I had no doubt that she'd stayed with him all night. But I also needed to go to the constabulary and talk to Ivy. After last night's conversation with Flock, I had questions about the mysterious money that had been appearing at the florist doorstep every month. Money Ivy said she would only use for her business. Her reluctance to spend it on anything personal made me suspect she knew more about the provenance of that cash than she'd told her partner.

I sipped my coffee and gathered my thoughts. Sometimes this brief moment of peace—just me and my coffee cup—seemed like the most precious time in my day.

Jingles hitched his throat, reminding me that it *wasn't* just me and my coffee cup in that room.

"Reindeer?" he prompted.

"I'll speak to them first thing."

"Don't forget you have the Tournament of Chocolate this evening." He checked the schedule he kept on a clipboard. "It's Brittles and Truffles night." He looked up with a vaguely troubled expression. "Aren't truffles just a subset of creams? You already judged those."

"According to Christmastown chocolatiers, there's a huge difference." When he looked ready to press me on the subject, I said, "I just do what I'm told."

"Speaking of which . . . What are you going to do about the reindeer?"

"I'm not sure," I said. "Those animals need to get their heads on straight."

"I don't think logic has much to do with love. It's not something you can work out on paper."

"It helped Juniper," I said, smiling at the memory of the *Elf World* quiz.

Suddenly, I had an idea. "Jingles, can I borrow your clipboard?"

"Are we being replaced?" Wobbler asked, his voice bristling with barely disguised outrage.

Both his and Cannonball's anger threw me for a loop. "What?" I frowned. "Why would you ask that?"

"Two interloper reindeer are living in *our* barn," Wobbler said. "Cannonball and I were forced to sleep in the sleigh shed."

I crossed my arms. "Two nights ago you *wanted* to sleep in the sleigh shed."

"Well, sure. Because I was annoyed with Cannonball. It's different when a couple of strange reindeer turf us *both* out."

"Salty gave them the best stalls," Wobbler added resentfully.

"And my reindeer cookies!" Cannonball said.

I raised my hands to try to calm them. "They're just visiting—they'll be gone soon."

Wobbler's withers twitched. "Hmph. One of them drove your sleigh yesterday."

The chutzpah of that made me laugh. "Because you two were recovering from fighting," I said. "If you can't control your tempers to the point that you end up injuring each other, I can't count on you to pull my sleigh."

"We wouldn't be fighting if Wobbler simply understood that Flouncy has made her choice about which of us she'd rather take to the Muzzle Nuzzle."

"Yes, she has." Wobbler lifted his head proudly. "The wise choice. Me."

"What gives you that idea?" Cannonball asked him.

"Because she told me so."

"That's not what she told *me*."

Wobbler looked incensed. "She couldn't have agreed to go with both of us."

Salty, overhearing us, shook his head. "You two have a lot to learn."

The two reindeer eyed each other, perplexed.

Luckily, I'd just prepared for this eventuality. I pulled out the questionnaire I'd drawn up during breakfast. "You two need to go at this more logically. Think less about attraction and more about compatibility."

Cannonball fixed his big eyes on me. "You mean, figure out which of us would get along with her better?"

"Exactly," I said. "You don't want to get trapped in a loveless reindeer relationship, do you?"

"No," they said in unison.

Wobbler tilted his head. "But how can you know in advance if it's true love?"

"I thought up a handy quiz to help you."

Salty, who'd taken the sheet of paper from me, scanned it with a frown. "There are a lot of questions here."

The reindeer moved to huddle around him, even though they couldn't read.

"When you're done, you'll have a better idea of who's actually more compatible with Flouncy," I said.

"But the Muzzle Nuzzle's tomorrow," Cannonball said.

"That's okay. Salty has my sleigh juiced up, and he can read the questionnaire to you. Take another day to nurse your bruises and to get your emotions under control. Flouncy's not the only reindeer in Santaland."

"That's true," Wobbler said. "There's plenty of moss on the tree."

Wobbler sighed. "But there's no moss quite like Flouncy."

I climbed onto the sleigh and left them staring over Salty's shoulder at the sheets of paper.

On the way to the Santaland Infirmary, I stopped by We Three Beans to pick up Juniper's favorite: a large eggnog latte with extra nutmeg. I bought plain eggnogs for the Candymints, guessing they would be there with Juniper.

Sure enough, when I arrived, they were keeping up their vigil at their son's bedside.

"He wriggled his foot," Mrs. Candymint told me as she accepted the eggnog.

From the excitement in her voice—and in the expressions of her husband and Juniper—I deduced that this foot wriggle was very good news. "Wonderful!"

"Doc Honeytree predicts that he'll come out of it today," Mrs. Candymint said.

Her husband added, "Smudge has always been strong."

Juniper pulled me out into the hall.

"Doc Honeytree said that Smudge *might* snap out of it today," she said. "The Candymints are just trying to keep their hopes up."

"There's no reason not to hope." It was what Juniper would have said, if she hadn't been eaten up with worry. "Doc Honeytree isn't one for painting overly rosy scenarios."

She paced restlessly. "I just worry that Smudge and I have left things too late. And that maybe I'm overestimating what his feelings are for me because I'm afraid of losing him."

"I saw his feelings for you in his eyes yesterday when he was concerned that *you* were in danger."

She stilled. "What did you see?"

"The same worry I see in your eyes now."

I could have swapped *love* for *worry*, but I wasn't sure it was my place to make declarations for Smudge. But weren't concern, caring, and worry closer to enduring love than all those love-at-first-sight breathless emotions that books and movies tells us are love? Love grew through life's tests. Maybe Juniper and Smudge's on-again, off-again relationship was more than just two elves vacillating to the irritation of all their friends. If things worked out and they ever did tie the knot, their relationship would be stronger for having their bond tested.

I promised Juniper to return and hurried to the constabulary.

Crinkles's eyes bulged when I appeared at the door. "Mrs. Claus! We weren't expecting you."

I smiled. "I was hoping to speak to Ivy. I didn't think I needed an appointment."

"No, no, of course you don't. Only . . ." His gaze cut sidewise.

Inside the cozy constabulary, the lawman had red candles lit and Dazzle Winterbright crooning "You Belong to Me" on the sound system. As usual, the sweet smell of baking wafted from the kitchen.

"Am I interrupting something?" I asked.

"No, no." He chuckled. "We're just trying to set the mood."

"For what?"

"Chocolate," he said, as if that should have been obvious. "Ollie's finishing up his entry for the night."

Given the other things happening right now, the Tournament of Chocolate seemed trivial.

"You do remember that there are two murders to solve."

"Two?"

"Sterling's murder, and the attack on Smudge."

"Oh." He looked relieved. "So just a murder and a half." He bobbed on his heels. "And the prime suspect's in custody."

"You've talked to her?"

"Of course."

"What did you find out?"

He shifted uncomfortably. "Well . . . without going into details too much, she has some creative ideas for standout chocolate presentation."

Great. "I meant did you question her about the murders."

"Oh—yes. She says she's innocent. Not sure what to think about *that*."

Without too much effort, I persuaded him to let me in to talk to Ivy. Crinkles led me to the bedroom that served as the prisoner's "cell." The room had two twin beds covered in thick quilts, woolen blankets, and extra pillows. Ivy perched on the side of the bed in her own clothes and fuzzy snowman slippers. She was even wearing makeup as usual—or at least her red lipstick. She hugged a pillow that had *Kindness Is Always In Style* written in needlepoint. I recognized it as a project Crinkles had worked on during his downtime.

"Hello, Ivy," I said.

As I'd walked in, I'd seen a flash of disappointment across her face, as if she'd expected a different visitor.

"Please tell me that Smudge didn't die overnight," she said.

I frowned. "No, he's still the same."

She crossed her arms. "Then I can't imagine why you're here."

Not a great start. I pointed to the twin bed opposite the one she was sitting on. "Do you mind if I sit for a moment?"

"Something tells me I don't really have a choice."

I sat down. "I talked to Flock."

Her eyes narrowed. "And?"

"He mentioned the money that you receive every month."

She scowled. "He had no right to tell you about that."

"He's worried about the business, and how it will survive."

"Okay, but if you think that money had anything to do with what happened to Smudge at the Mistletoe Tavern, you're wrong."

"I thought you didn't know who poisoned Smudge's drink."

"I don't."

"Then how can you know the money had nothing to do with it?"

"Because I've been receiving that money for years."

"Who sends it?" I asked.

She shook her head. "You just indicated that you thought the money and the murder are linked. If I name someone, you'll just decide they're the new prime suspect. Much as I don't relish staying in this room for very long, I'm not going to put anyone in the law's crosshairs just to get myself out of jail."

"Do you think it's from a secret admirer?"

She laughed. "You don't hear very well, do you?"

"I hear fine. I'm just hard to discourage."

Her lips twisted. "Of course it's not from a secret admirer. Did you ever see a guy do something and *not* take credit for it?"

"Yes." I'd witnessed Nick quietly helping elves for four years. Some of them probably didn't know that their fairy godmother was actually Santa.

"Well, I haven't. Especially not from guys who are trying to impress me. Smudge was different in that way." Her black bob, which she'd tried to push back against her ears, spilled over her cheek. "Probably too nice for me, if you want to know the truth."

"You're a lot calmer about him now than you were at the Caramels and Nuts contest."

"This week has been so horrible!" she lamented. "I flared up in the heat of the moment. Is that a crime?"

"You uttered threats," I reminded her.

"Empty ones."

I decided to press her on the earlier crime. "When did you last see Sterling Redwinkle?"

"He came into the store to order that stupid corsage."

"Why didn't you just say so days ago?"

"Because I was trying to save my reputation," she said. "You heard the elves in that bar last night. Poison Ivy, they called me. We decided it would be better to deny any connection to those cursed flowers. And anyway, *I* didn't make the flowers, I just arranged them. The Order of Elven Seamstresses brings me a bunch every week. I work them into Valentine's arrangements and other projects like Sterling's corsage—which, if you stop to think about it, could have killed me." She bit her lip as if a thought had just occurred to her. "In fact, if I had been pricked by that rose, I'd be dead now, not Sterling."

"You should have told us the truth straightaway."

"Why? Everyone suspected me anyway," she said. "You all thought I delivered that single rose to the Order with the poem, and I absolutely didn't."

"If we hadn't thought you were lying, Constable Crinkles might not have brought you into custody and you wouldn't be wasting your time here."

She hugged the decorative pillow a little more tightly. "I don't consider it a waste of time now."

"Don't you want to go home?"

"Not especially." Her lips flattened into a grim line. "You'll never convince me that anyone meant to poison Sterling. He was completely harmless. His only fault was being too tied to his mother's apron strings. But who would kill over that?"

I considered her question carefully. "Festa Redwinkle? I've only stepped foot inside the Redwinkle house a couple of times, but what I saw there seemed justification enough for sibling resentment. Mother Redwinkle worshipped her son and treated Festa like sloppy seconds."

For a moment Ivy looked as if she'd be willing to admit the possibility, but then she shook her head. "Festa might have felt jealous of Sterling, but then why would she have sent that Rose to the Order of Elven Seamstresses, or attempted to kill Smudge?"

"Maybe she wanted to make it look like someone else was guilty."

"That's right—me." She shook her head. "No matter how I turn it over in my mind, I figure that either someone just keeps killing the wrong person, or someone is trying to make me look guilty. Either way, I think I'm safer in here for the present."

I couldn't blame her for being focused on self-preservation. Constable Crinkles and Ollie might not be the sharpest at crime solving, but no one yet had breached the button locks of the constabulary's doors.

I stood. "Is there anything you need?"

"I'm being well taken care of, thanks." She sighed. "Best cinnamon rolls in town."

As I walked out of the cell, an elf I'd never seen before got up from the dining room table. Her salt-and-pepper hair was pulled back in a practical chignon, and she was dressed conservatively in a navy blue tunic and diamond-patterned scarf around her neck that matched her tights. Deep brown eyes looked up at me directly and she put out her hand. "Puddin' Bayberry," she said, introducing herself.

She had the grip of an arm wrestler. "April Claus," I said.

She let go of my hand and brushed past me to go into Ivy's room.

Crinkles shrugged apologetically at me and hurried to follow her.

Ollie emerged from the kitchen area wearing an apron that read *I Cook As Good As I Look*.

"Why is Puddin' Bayberry visiting Ivy?" I asked.

He pushed his cap back on his head. "I think she believes we should let Ivy go."

"Ivy doesn't want to be let go." I tilted my head. "Who hired Puddin'?"

"Not sure," Ollie said. "Flock, maybe?"

That seemed doubtful. Flock already felt financially pinched.

"It can't be family," Ollie said. "She doesn't have any."

Was that true? Ivy was an orphan, but that didn't mean she might not have family somewhere. Family who might feel ashamed to have let her grow up at the Santaland Home for Orphaned Elves. Who wouldn't want her to languish at the constabulary.

I left the constabulary to go get ready for my last night of chocolate judging. As I was walking out, I caught sight of a pale figure lurking in the shadows.

"Who's there?" I called out.

The sound of booties crunching in the snow around the corner of a building reached my ears.

On instinct, I hurried across the street and followed the sound.

An elf was speed-walking in front of me, but with my height advantage, I caught up with him quickly. When I was close enough, I put my hand on his shoulder and spun him around.

My hand dropped when I saw who it was.

Happy Greenberry's face was a mask of guilt.

I wondered if he had also been behind the sounds I'd heard yesterday night as I was walking to my sleigh from the Santaland Infirmary.

"Why are you stalking me?" I asked.

"I'm not. You just happened to be there when I was watching the building."

"So you admit that you were spying on the constabulary?"

"Not spying. Just watching."

Talk about a distinction without a difference. "Who were you watching?" I doubted it was Crinkles or Ollie.

He buried his hands in his pockets. "I'm worried about Ivy. We grew up together."

That's right. He was an orphan. "You both were at the Santaland Home for Orphaned Elves?"

He nodded. "We were around the same age—although she was a foundling who had been there her whole life, and I arrived when I was seven, after Granny Greenberry died."

The mention of his grandmother reminded me of the nougats he named after her—the ones I'd give second place in the contest. A frisson of lingering guilt rippled through me.

"Not that I'm claiming any special relationship with Ivy," he added. "The home wasn't all that big, but I bet she barely remembers me. I was never outgoing, and she was always beautiful and creative."

"You're creative. You make delicious chocolates."

"Only since I've been out on my own. Back in those days, they wouldn't have let us orphans loose in the kitchen. Things are different now, of course. I've heard that the Home for Orphaned Elves is a lot less regimented than it was in my time."

Poor Happy. I imagined him and Ivy growing up there. How strange it must have been to be dropped into that world as a grief-stricken seven-year-old.

Still, I couldn't help feeling just a little creeped out by the way he'd been standing outside the constabulary. "What were you expecting to see here tonight?"

"That they would let her go," he said. "Aren't they going to?"

"I'm not sure. I saw a counselor go in to speak to—" An idea occurred to me. "You hired Puddin' Bayberry, didn't you?"

Ollie had said that Ivy hadn't called Puddin', so someone must have called on Ivy's behalf.

Happy's eyes went as round as dessert plates. "Me? No!" He leaned closer. "Does Ivy need help paying for legal help?"

I shook my head. "I don't know. I doubt it. I just got the sense that someone had hired Puddin' for her, and since you were hanging around . . ."

He shook his head. "It wasn't me. I wish I had thought to offer, though. I don't know how much something like that would cost, but if she needs help, I'd do anything. I'd rob a bank if necessary."

"You're in love with her, aren't you?"

Even on a sidewalk lit only by dim streetlamps, I could see his face flush. "I've always loved her."

The rawness in his voice made my heart go out to him. "She's not a statue on a pedestal," I said. "Have you tried just talking to her, maybe asking her out?"

He looked terrified by that idea. "She's always involved with someone—Sterling, and then that new fellow . . ."

Those boyfriends seemed very unlucky.

I froze, suddenly seeing Happy in a whole new light. Could unrequited love have turned this shy elf into a killer? That seemed out of character for him. Then again, Juniper had told me that he'd gone wacky over late fees, and I myself had witnessed him blow his top after losing a chocolate contest.

Surprise, surprise . . .

"Were you at the Mistletoe Tavern last night?" I asked.

He shook his head. "I haven't been to the Mistletoe Tavern in years. I'm not much of a grog drinker."

"It's got nice atmosphere, though. And good acts perform there. The Swingin' Santas were playing."

I thought naming the wrong musical act might trip him up into contradicting me—"*Oh no, I saw for myself that it was Dazzle Winterbright*"—but he just shook his head. "I had to work."

"Where do you work?"

"*Elf World* magazine. Copyediting, mostly. But last night I was working on an article."

"You're a writer? You were just saying that you weren't creative!"

He shrugged modestly. "I just write little pieces and filler stuff, mostly. Quick profiles, listicles . . . Last month I wrote the quiz."

My jaw dropped. "The 'What's Your Sweetie Level?' quiz?"

He beamed. "Yes—that was my work."

I didn't know whether to laugh or cry. The elf who'd written the compatibility quiz for couples was a sad single elf who'd probably never belonged to a couple in his life. Juniper had been on the verge of using the results of the quiz as supporting evidence for why she and Sterling needed to call it quits. Even I had started comparing Nick and myself to bridge mix.

"That quiz has been very popular this month," he said. "My editor wants me to work up a feature for St. Patrick's Day next month. I'm thinking about a trivia quiz, so I've been doing a lot of research for that. Do you know where the first St. Patrick's Day parade took place?"

"Ireland?" I guessed.

"Wrong! The United States." He laughed.

The elf seemed to love his work.

"Did anyone see you at the office last night?" I asked.

"Oh sure," he said. "A few people are always wandering in and out of the office. And one elf, Dewy Stoutbeard, has been camping out on the floor of the copy room since his girlfriend kicked him out. He saw me working that night."

So he had an alibi. I was unaccountably glad. In spite of his short temper, Happy seemed like a good elf.

"I'd better go get ready for the contest," I said.

"I'll see you there."

For some reason, I was surprised. After two second-place finishes, I didn't expect him to try again. I had to give him credit for persistence.

I just hoped this evening didn't end in another heartbreak.

Chapter 19

Never in my life did I think I'd become completely sick of chocolate, but by the time I made it to the last table on the night of Brittles and Truffles, I was willing to admit that it was a possibility. My endless capacity for sugar consumption was reaching its limit. Still, I soldiered on.

What kept me going was that all the chocolates were so darn delicious. The confectioners of Santaland—both professional and amateur—did not disappoint. The only trouble was that I loved so many of them.

And there was Happy Greenberry again, standing behind a little plate of white chocolate lavender truffles. The choice surprised me, since some elves held that white chocolate was not real chocolate and didn't belong in the contest. I would have assumed that Happy would count himself in that number.

I took a tentative bite.

As on all the previous evenings, Happy's chocolates gave the taste buds reason to celebrate. In fact, mine were practically dancing along to the Swingin' Santas, that night's entertainment at Municipal Hall. They were playing "Twist and Shout," which had the entire crowd on the dance floor.

"Delicious," I told Happy.

"Thank you," he said, although his tone sounded as if he didn't quite believe it. Tonight, he wasn't going to get his hopes up.

I so wanted that crazy little elf to have a win. He deserved it.

Maybe I *was* biased.

I still had half a conference table worth of chocolates to go, and I held my breath as I bit into each new entry, almost praying that it would be disappointing. No one's offering was bad. But they were never as good as the white chocolate lavender truffles.

And then I reached Ollie's entry—the last one.

"Constable Crinkles isn't here," I said. "I guess Ivy is still at the constabulary?"

"He was still dealing with Puddin' Bayberry when I had to leave."

"That's good. Ivy seemed to want to stay awhile at the constabulary."

I inspected the card by his entry. *Ollie's Special Brittle! Luscious dark chocolate enrobes a square of crunchy almond-coconut brittle.*

Dark chocolate, almonds, and coconut. Ollie should have gone ahead and named his entry *Mrs. Claus Crack*, because those were practically my three favorite ingredients in the world.

Ollie grinned expectantly.

I looked down at my score sheet. I'd given the white chocolate lavender truffles a 9.5, which left room for another chocolate to squeak past it. I could have kicked myself. I wondered if anyone would notice if I went back and changed it.

I took a swig from the cup of hot lemon water I'd brought. And then I bit into Ollie's chocolate.

As I'd feared, Ollie's Special Brittle was a perfect blend of my three favorite ingredients. Each element seemed perfect, too: the dark chocolate was sharp but still smooth, and the brittle was buttery but still had a pleasing crunch. The coconut and almond flavors complemented each other in perfect balance.

Son of a nutcracker!

I closed my eyes, then lifted my pen. My taste buds had led me to an impasse, so I looked into my heart. I gave the constabulary's entry a 9.25.

Happy's eyes were as big as moons when I brought the blue ribbon to his spot. At first he was speechless as he took the ribbon. Then he swallowed and asked, "Are you sure?"

I nodded. "You deserve this."

The Swingin' Santas were playing "At Last," and it seemed like every couple in the room was taking the opportunity to have a slow dance with their sweetie. I skirted the dance floor, edging past the stray souls who weren't paired up.

"Hi, April!"

Dolly flagged me down, and I went over to join her and the wallflower contingent. She nodded to the dance floor. "Look at that."

Jake and Claire were draped over each other, slow dancing. My heart lifted to see them. They were so wrapped up in each other, they didn't seem to notice anything around them. I wasn't even sure they heard the music.

It was sweet that they wanted to spend their wedding eve here, together. I was glad we followed Claire's wishes and didn't plan her bachelorette party for tonight. Back when Juniper and I were trying to schedule her wedding week, Claire had insisted she didn't want to be one of those brides who partied all night and then spent her wedding day with a hangover.

Of course, the party last night had not been a rousing success. But what happened to Smudge wasn't Claire's fault.

"Did you know Claire's having a baby?"

I nodded.

"I guess I'm the last to know." She sighed. "I can't believe the wedding's tomorrow. I guess it will go on as planned, unless something new happens to stop it."

I gave her a hard stare. Even for her, that was a weird thing to say. *Nice wedding—shame if anything happened to it.* Surely she hadn't meant it as menacingly as it had come out.

"I'm just glad Claire and Jake worked everything out," I said.

"Oh, me too. I want Jake to be happy."

But I couldn't help noticing that as she said the words, her jaw looked tight enough to crush Brazil nuts.

"So do you think Juniper will still go to the wedding if Smudge isn't any better tomorrow?"

I hadn't really considered this question. Juniper had been by Smudge's side as much as she could be, only leaving the Infirmary to sleep. "I think so, but I bet Claire will understand if Juniper can't go."

"It would be a shame, after all the work she's put into the event. And she won't be able to wear her new dress."

"I don't think she'll care too much—and I don't think Claire will, either." I smiled at Dolly. "She has two spare bridesmaids, after all."

My phone vibrated. I pulled it out of my pocket and stared at the screen, amazed.

"What is it?" Dolly asked. She looked up at my face, then leaned closer to try to see the screen.

"It's Juniper," I said.

"Is something the matter with Smudge? Did he die?"

"Quite the opposite," I said. "He's regained consciousness."

There were probably too many of us, but given that it was a joyous occasion, Nurse Cinnamon allowed us all to squash into Smudge's room to talk to him. When I entered the room with Jake and Claire, the Candymints were right there at his side, as was Juniper.

With Mrs. Firlog's permission, we'd pinched several big balloons from Municipal Hall to brighten up Smudge's room.

Not that the room wasn't cheerful already. The smiles on Smudge's parents' faces were probably the equivalent of a thousand-watt light bulb.

I tied the balloons to a chair. "Hey, Smudge."

He smiled at me. He looked a little dazed. "Did you think you were going to get to play drum kit?"

I laughed. If he was able to make concert band percussion jokes, he was definitely on the road to recovery. "No, but if you didn't regain consciousness when you did, I was considering bringing in some crash cymbals to wake you up."

He laughed too, then winced. "Ow, my head." His eyes fixed on the ceiling and he swallowed. "I still don't understand what happened."

"Your grog was poisoned," I said.

He squinted at Juniper. "How?"

She looked uneasily around the room. "We're not quite sure, although Crinkles is keeping Ivy at the constabulary, just to be on the safe side."

Ivy thought it was the safe side for her, too.

"Wow, it's like a party in here!" Dolly announced from the doorway. She was carrying a tray loaded down with paper cups. "And I've brought the beverages."

She held the tray aloft on one palm like a waitress in an old-timey diner and scooted into the room. "I thought everyone might like some eggnog, so I got these from the vending machine." She looked at Claire. "But I know you probably aren't into eggnog while you're dealing with your morning sickness, so I brought you your favorite."

Claire's eyes brightened. "A ginger-lemon slushy from Snappy's?"

Dolly held it out to her. "I would have brought you a snow cone, but I didn't know how I would carry it *and* all these other drinks, too."

Claire reached for her slushy.

The wedding conversation Dolly and I had on the sidelines of the dance floor came back to me. *I guess it will go on as planned, unless something new happens to stop it.* Those words echoed through my head as I watched Claire take the slushy and bring the candy-striped straw to her lips.

"Claire, don't!" Without thinking, I batted the drink out of her hands. It rolled onto the floor, its lid unable to hold. Slushy oozed out onto Nurse Cinnamon's spic-and-span floors.

Dolly cried out in shock, as Claire gaped at me. Everyone in the room was staring, as a matter of fact.

"What was that about?" Dolly asked.

"I thought—"

I shut my mouth, suddenly unsure of myself.

Pro tip: If you're going to do something impulsive, stupid, or insulting—or a combination of all three—then it's best to have a reason. And an exit strategy.

"Something about that slushy didn't seem right," I said.

Dolly wasn't fooled. "Did you think that I was going to kill Claire? In a *hospital*?"

It sounded rather ludicrous.

I swallowed. "I'm sorry, I'm just so on edge."

Claire frowned at me, making me squirm. "That was rude, April."

That was the thanks I got for saving her life?

Hypothetically saving it, at least. I looked past her to Juniper for backup, but even she looked mortified by what I'd done.

Dolly wasn't mortified. She was hopping mad. "I thought we were friends!"

Just when I thought it couldn't get any worse, Nurse Cinnamon entered the room. She bent down to scoop up the slushy, half of which had dribbled out onto the floor. "Sugar water's not good for hardwoods," she declared. "Who did this?"

"April!" Dolly said. "She's trying to convince everyone I'm the Valentine poisoner."

I shook my head. "It was just instinct."

Dolly was nearly in tears now. "I've been trying my hardest to fit in, and this is the thanks I get."

"You have to admit you've said some weird things," I told her.

"I was probably just making conversation. I'm not from here."

I rolled my eyes. "I'm not from here, either, but I don't stand around talking about how jealous I am of other couples' happiness. The other night, you even mentioned the couples by name. Juniper and Sterling, Ivy and Smudge—both couples who've suffered tragedies this week. Why would you be envious of *that*?"

She shrugged helplessly. "I don't remember saying anything like that."

Now she was gaslighting me. "And this evening you as much as speculated that if something went wrong tonight, Jake and Claire might not be able to get married tomorrow."

"Well, isn't that just logical?" she asked.

"Sure. Especially if you intended to do something to nudge the 'something wrong' along."

Incensed, Dolly snatched the cup out of Nurse Cinnamon's hands. The sides of the paper cup glistened with sugar water.

What was she going to do with that—throw it at me?

I braced for impact, but it turned out that Dolly didn't have aggression in mind. She was more interested in vindication. She lifted the cup, stuck the straw into her mouth, and sucked up the remnants of the slushy until the contents were all gone and the straw started making gurgling sounds. Then she handed the cup to me. I took it—my hand instantly feeling sticky.

"There!" she said. "You can send that to Algid Honeytree for analysis, or you can stand there and watch me to see if I keel over from thallium poisoning." Her lips flattened. "Or you can just take my word for it. I'm not the poisoner."

"I'm sorry," I said.

"Sorry?" she squeaked, weeping for real now. "I've never been so insulted. What must you have thought of me all along? To imagine I'd do anything so terrible!"

Claire crossed the room, took my arm, and steered me out into the hallway. She left Jake to try to smooth down his cousin's ruffled feathers.

In the corridor, Claire shook her head at me. "Have you taken leave of your senses?"

I couldn't quite let go of my defensiveness. "She really did say all those weird things I mentioned."

"Because she's *weird*. You know that. She comes from a place where people have to spend their lives dodging polar bears and abominable snow monsters. Social niceties and chitchat aren't really drummed into kids up there."

Everything she said was true. I'd acted impulsively, and wrongly. Stupidly, too, because now I was going to have to endure an entire wedding as part of a bridesmaid trio with an elf I'd accused of being a homicidal maniac.

Talk about awkward.

"I really am sorry, Claire. I hope I haven't ruined the wedding."

She laughed. "If the wedding is a bust, I have no one to blame but myself. I've been so out of it." She sank down onto one of the benches, and I joined her.

"Never fear—Pamela has *not* been out of it. In fact, if you'd been a no-show, I think she was prepared to walk down the aisle herself." I added under my breath, "She certainly has the dress for it."

Claire sent me a questioning look.

"You'll have to see it to believe it," I said.

"I guess I'll see it soon." She clasped her hands together and sucked in a breath, as if she couldn't quite believe it. "Pamela called me today and gave me the whole rundown for tomorrow. Apparently we're going to have breakfast at the castle and do a brief rehearsal, and then Sparkle's coming to do our hair, and Blanchette and Snowbell will arrive with all the dresses, and then we're going to take pictures, and then, finally, Jake and I get married."

"And then five hundred and forty-three people will sit down to an intimate dinner."

She sighed. "Your mother-in-law is something else."

"She certainly is," I agreed.

As we were both contemplating the North Pole marvel that was Pamela Claus, Nick arrived. I jumped up to hug him—I'd called him from Municipal Hall to give him the news about Smudge, but I hadn't expected him to get here so fast.

"I flew," he said. "Is Smudge still doing well?"

"Yes, but I've been exiled from the room on account of being an impulsive idiot."

As Claire and I were rehashing the slushy incident, the double doors at the end of the hall pushed opened, and two orderly elves wheeled a gurney down the hall toward us. We all stood up straighter. It had been a busy night for Santaland EMS elves.

Nurse Cinnamon bustled behind the gurney, with a crimson wool uniform cloak from the Order of Elven Seamstresses draped over her arm.

I stepped forward. "Who is this?"

"One of the elves who works for Madame Neige," she said. "Poor thing threw herself off the roof."

I looked into the elf's face. It was Snowbell. Her eyes were closed and her skin looked waxen.

Doc Honeytree appeared, and followed the gurney into the nearest room. Claire, Nick, and I all waited in the hallway for him to examine her. Nurse Cinnamon closed the door and the sounds of paddles being used on her chest could be heard. The loud, percussive thumps made my heart sink.

"That's what they use to restart your heart, right?" Claire asked.

Nick nodded, and we stood silent.

The doors at the end of the corridor swung open again. This time, instead of hospital workers, two elves from the Order of Elven Seamstresses headed our way in their long red cloaks. In front was Blanchette, followed by Button. Behind both of them strode Puddin' Bayberry, the counselor-arbitrator.

What was *she* doing here?

The sensible heels of Puddin's navy blue booties clacking down the hallway toward us now seemed to be the only sound in the hospital. Somehow, that was more ominous than any emergency equipment.

When the trio was close enough, I nodded toward the door where Snowbell had been taken. "Doc Honeytree's with her now."

Blanchette and Button glanced at the closed door, then back at me.

"Did you see her?" Blanchette asked.

We all nodded gravely.

And then the door opened and Doc came out, his face drawn and almost as pale as Snowbell's had been. Seeing the trio that had just come in, he addressed his remarks to Blanchette.

"I'm sorry. Snowbell didn't make it."

Chapter 20

"She jumped from the cupola," Blanchette explained.

We were back on the hallway benches. I wasn't sure that there was a logical reason for any of us to be there now, but no one seemed to want to be anywhere else—except Puddin' Bayberry, who'd whipped out her phone the moment Doc Honeytree had announced Snowbell's death. Puddin' had disappeared around the corner and hadn't yet returned.

"Suicide?" Claire asked.

Button nodded. Her eyes were swollen and red. "Poor Snowbell. She took Sterling Redwinkle's death very hard."

I remembered seeing her down in Hades, working the gigantic old press. I'd thought she seemed anxious.

"Did Snowbell know Sterling?" I asked. "Personally, I mean?"

Button bit her lip. "Not that I know of. Of course, we all knew *of* him. He was awfully handsome. Maybe she had a crush?"

"She was very sensitive," Blanchette said.

I had just berated myself for letting my imagination run amok when it came to Dolly Frost. But I couldn't stop thinking about Nurse Cinnamon walking in with that red cloak draped over her arm.

When Bumble the snowman had told me that he'd seen a female elf in a red coat, could he really have seen Snowbell in her red cloak?

Nick touched my knee to get my attention. "I'm going to have a few words with Doc."

I nodded, then cleared my throat. "I never knew Snowbell very well. Did she get out very much?" I directed the question at Blanchette and Button, but I could feel Claire's curious gaze on me.

"We're not prisoners," Blanchette said. "Elves at the Order are free to leave if they're not scheduled to work."

"So Snowbell could have gone out at night."

"Of course," Blanchette said. "Just as I went out to the Tavern last night when you invited me."

I nodded. "Do the elves of the Order have to sign out?"

Button blinked. "You mean, like we're in a dormitory?"

"Something like that."

"Madame Neige assumes we are all adults," Blanchette said carefully. "Even the youngest among us. But the truth is, the elves of the Order of Elven Seamstresses treat our lives there as a vocation. It's not exactly a convent, but the level of devotion to the life of the sartorial and fabric arts is analogous."

I looked up at Jake, who had joined us. He could see what I was doing and gave me a nod.

In for a penny . . .

I took a deep breath. "The night before Sterling Redwinkle was poisoned, he was seen meeting with a female elf in the street across from Flock and Ivy's."

Blanchette frowned. "Ivy, surely?"

"The witness says no," Jake said, careful not to use Bumble's name, or even to let on that the witness in question was a snowman. "The witness knows Ivy very well."

I was starting to feel as if this could be a breakthrough. If Snowbell had some sort of relationship with Sterling, that would make a few puzzle pieces slot into place. She obviously had experience making flowers at the Order of Elven Seamstresses—she'd just cut her finger on one when I was trying on my dress for the first time and knew they could break skin. Snowbell also could have been out of the room just before Sterling came in. She'd told me that she'd been in a dressing room at that time, but I had no corroboration of her claim.

While Sterling was in the foyer helping Dolly look for her purse, Snowbell might have had just enough time to grab the corsage box off the foyer table and switch his for a corsage laced with poison.

And how would Snowbell have known that he was bringing a corsage? Because she "just happened" to bump into him on the street across from Flock and Ivy's the evening before. He might have even revealed his plan for a surprise proposal.

"These questions . . ." Button's eyes narrowed. "It sounds almost as if you think poor Snowbell had something to do with Sterling Redwinkle's poisoning."

"You said she seemed very upset by his death," Jake said.

"Upset enough to jump off a building," Claire added.

I concluded, "Maybe what she was really feeling was guilt."

"No!"

Blanchette's face was as red as a Christmas ball. "Poor Snowbell has only just now been pronounced dead, and you're slandering her. An innocent elf with no one to stand up for her."

I flinched a little at the criticism.

"She obviously has you," Jake said.

"And me," Button added. "My friend Snowbell was no murderer. Poison Sterling Redwinkle? Why would she do that?"

"Why are most crimes committed?" I asked. "Love—or hate. Or love that's turned to hate."

Blanchette shook her head. "If she had a relationship with Sterling, this is the first I've ever heard of it."

"Me too," Button chimed. "It's just not true."

Blanchette added, "Do you think there are *two* poisoners on the loose in Santaland?"

I shifted, then admitted, "I don't know. The modus operandi was slightly different in the two cases."

"It was poison," Blanchette said. "Everyone knows who the prime suspect is."

Button scowled. "Poison Ivy."

Blanchette and Button got to their feet. Their anger at us was palpable. "Madame Neige will not be happy when I tell her that one of her elves was spoken of in this way," Blanchette said.

"And she just died." Tears spilled down Button's face.

The two of them marched down the corridor, leaving the hospital the same way they'd come in.

Jake, Claire, and I exchanged uncomfortable glances.

"Maybe I should have waited to make accusations against Snowbell," I said.

Jake shook his head. "Your line of thinking made sense. And there's an elf at the constabulary in custody. If Snowbell's guilt can exonerate her, we can't just let that go."

"True." I thought through my Snowbell-as-murderess scenario. So much seemed to fit, I was embarrassed not to have contemplated her as a suspect before. But there was a reason for that, wasn't there? "The last time I spoke to Snowbell, she didn't seem grief-stricken or guilty to me. She seemed nervous."

I frowned, trying to remember her manner as she worked the giant press. "Maybe she'd been afraid of being caught . . ."

It took a few moments for it to sink in that I was the only one still involved in this conversation.

Jake and Claire had locked eyes and were absorbed in each other. Neither of them had probably wanted to spend the night before their wedding at the Santaland Infirmary.

Claire stood. "Ready to go home?"

He nodded. "We should probably take Dolly with us."

They fetched Dolly out of Smudge's room. She scooted past me, red-faced and resentful, on the way out.

Definitely not my best night, diplomacy-wise.

Puddin' Bayberry came winging around the corner and flopped down on the bench next to me. "What a mess. That poor little elf—luckily she doesn't seem to have had much in the way of family."

"That's lucky?"

"Fewer people to worry about complaining to the Order of Elven Seamstresses about not putting a safety barrier around that cupola."

"Oh—you mean lucky for Madame Neige's liability insurance premiums."

Although, come to think of it, I'd never heard of liability insurance in Santaland . . .

She blinked, obviously realizing that her remark had sounded callous. "And fewer people to mourn the tragedy," she added. "So sad."

"Blanchette and Button seemed very upset about her passing. They're not family, but they genuinely seem to care."

"I'm sure everybody over at the Order of Elven Seamstresses is mourning poor Snowball."

"Snowbell," I corrected.

"I just got off the phone with Madame Neige. She's very upset."

Not upset enough to come here in person. "So you represent Madame Neige?"

Puddin' nodded and reached into her handbag for her card. "If anyone at the castle ever needs help, I handle all sorts of issues at reasonable rates—wills, estates, adoptions, arbitration . . ."

I stared at her card, which was plain black lettering against a white background. No-nonsense, just like Puddin'. "For some reason, when you came in, I thought it was in connection with Ivy."

She frowned at me. "Ivy? Is she here?"

"Of course not. She's at the constabulary."

Puddin' was on her feet in one bound. "How can that be? I just got her *out* of custody."

"How?" I asked.

She snorted. "It's not hard to sway Constable Crinkles. All I usually have to do is bring him a few cupcakes, cite a little bit of the Santaland Civil Code, and remind him that Judge Merrybutton and my dad used to go ice fishing together."

"But I spoke to Ivy before you did," I said. "She didn't want to leave the constabulary."

She rolled her eyes at that. "I know. I had to talk her out of that attitude. The evidence against her is circumstantial, and elves are already up in arms against her. That horrible name—Poison Ivy! And the longer she stays in that jail, the longer a whisper campaign against her—not to mention her business—will have to build."

All sorts of ideas were bouncing around my brain now. "You're the one who puts the money through Ivy's door every month, aren't you?"

She blinked. "Why are you asking me that?"

"Ivy's partner was telling me about her benefactor. It's Madame Neige, isn't it?"

"That's not something I'm at liberty to discuss."

"Why would Madame Neige take an interest in a florist who grew up as an orphan?"

"I'm *really* not at liberty to discuss this."

She didn't have to. I think I understood why. Madame Neige's past had always been mysterious, and something she never mentioned. The fact that she might have a child out of wedlock and had given it up as a foundling to the Santaland Home for Orphaned Elves would explain some of her reluctance to talk about her past.

"It's funny," I mused. "If you'd asked me to name someone who might be Madame Neige's daughter, I would have guessed Blanchette. They're so alike."

"Blanchette has been with Madame Neige since she was a young apprentice," Puddin' said. "She practically is like a daughter. In fact, Madame Neige's will gives Blanchette equal standing with Madame's natural daughter—who I'm *not* saying is Ivy, you understand."

"Do you have a long-standing business relationship with Madame Neige?" I tapped the card she'd given me. "I've been thinking of having a new will drawn up, but I'm wondering if it would be necessary."

Sensing a business nibble from Castle Kringle, she assured me, "Believe me, if it's on your mind, it's probably time to rewrite that old will. I've worked on Madame's estate for years. In fact, I drew up a new will for her very recently."

"Good to know." I transferred the card to my handbag. "Thank you."

"Thank *you*! And if there are other people at the castle who could use my services, I hope you'll recommend me."

I smiled. Actually, I would recommend they find legal help that was a little better at guarding confidential information.

Puddin' walked away, pleased at having done a good evening's work.

Too bad Jake wasn't still here. I wondered what he would make of Madame Neige's connection to Ivy. Maybe it was Madame Neige who'd told Ivy to tear out the page linking Flock and Ivy's to the delivery of the corsage. She had been at the florist that day before I went there.

I looked at my phone, tempted to call Jake. But no, he probably had other things on his mind now.

When Nick didn't come back, I stood and looked in on Juniper and Smudge. She was still at his bedside, holding his hand. The Candymints were leaning shoulder to shoulder on the couch, asleep.

"I'm going home," I said. "I'll see you for Claire's big day tomorrow, right?"

Juniper looked at Smudge. "Even if Doc Honeytree doesn't release me, you should go for Claire and Jake," he told her.

Juniper was clearly torn, but I could tell she wanted to go. Finally, she smiled and nodded at me. "I'll be there."

"Don't forget we're starting early. Breakfast at . . ." I frowned. Actually, I didn't know.

Juniper laughed. "Nine. Good thing I *am* going."

I smiled. "Jingles tells me where to go, and when."

I left them and found Nick coming down the hallway toward me. "Where have you been?" I asked.

"I talked to Doc Honeytree about helping with Snowbell's funeral arrangements. Poor thing—I think she was all alone in the world."

I remembered Blanchette and Button. "Not entirely."

Nick hugged me to him. "Ready to go home?"

This time I joined him in his sleigh for the ride home—the second-best sleigh, pulled by a team of four. As the reindeer jangled their way up the snow path up Sugarplum Mountain, Nick and I huddled together with a lap robe around us. We passed the chateaus of Kringle Heights and I looked over at the littler cottages of Christmastown and the surrounding valley, all lit in pink and red for the holiday. I couldn't help thinking about all the secrets behind each door: people falling in love, suffering unrequited love, pining for beloved lost children, or just clinging to the love of found family like the elves at the Order of Elven Seamstresses.

February was bitter cold, but beautiful, with newly fallen snow nearly every day. The fresh whiteness reflected the moonlight, making the world seem as if it were glowing. As we watched the lights of our castle home grow closer, I couldn't help noticing that the sky was clear and still. I hoped it would hold for Claire's wedding day. Valentine's Day.

I took Nick's arm. "I predict that tomorrow will be a perfect, unforgettable day."

As it turned out, I was half right.

Perfect? Not quite.

But definitely unforgettable.

Chapter 21

"We're still a harp short," Jingles announced to me as we descended the staircase on the way to the wedding party breakfast. "But Flit assures us he can get it here in time."

He was wearing his best dress tunic in the green and red colors of Castle Kringle, and his cap had bright gold polished jingle bells. All but one of the bells had been muted, which was a good thing. Jingles was so keyed up for today, the last thing he needed was more bells. He would be jangling with every breath.

"Just pace yourself," he advised me, as if he himself weren't completely hopped up. "The Dowager Mrs. Claus and I have the entire day mapped out. It's going to run as smoothly as resurfaced ice."

"I'll just think of you as the day's Zamboni," I told him.

The comparison actually seemed to please him.

I was one of the first down to the breakfast table that had been set up in the intimate family dining room. Even though it was set for the wedding party, Pamela had left nothing to chance. Each place setting had a name written on it. I was in my usual spot, and I couldn't help noticing that Dolly's place card was next to mine. After Slushy-gate, this would never do.

"We need to change this," I told Jingles.

I looked around the table and made a quick calculation. "We can switch her and Christopher." Which meant Dolly would be seated next to Pamela. That would work.

Jingles took Christopher's card and I picked up Dolly's. Then I got distracted by a little gift sitting on Tiffany's plate. It was wrapped in pink paper with a red bow. "What's that?" I asked Jingles.

"Flit brought it early this morning. I think it's from Burl Silver-tree."

"That's so sweet."

"Must have been a successful date," Jingles said. "Although maybe we should reserve judgment until we see what exactly's in the little box."

I sighed. "It's the thought, isn't it?"

Then I noticed that many of the places had little gifts. A spray of flowers bloomed in the middle of Pamela's plate at the head of the table, and Juniper's also had a posy set by her water glass. A jewelry box rested on Claire's plate.

I suddenly felt like the forgotten Valentine. The most conspicuously barren places were mine and Dolly's.

"Has Nick been through this morning?" I asked.

"I think so," Jingles said. "He had to leave early to go to town for the Tournament of Chocolate final."

So . . . no little Valentine surprise would be forthcoming. It was silly to feel disappointed. It was going to be such a busy day, he probably figured that anything he gave me would be lost in the shuffle.

Or perhaps he just hadn't bothered. That was okay, too. I'd loved our midnight sleigh ride last night more than I could possibly love any gift. Moments like that trumped jewelry boxes.

Actually, the fact that he *didn't* give me some trinket or quick-to-wilt bouquet just showed how rock solid we were.

Christopher breezed in and dropped a red card by my place.

I snapped it up like a frog snatching a fly. "Oh—thank you!"

Christopher scowled. "It's just one of those dumb Valentine cards. Mother made me give one to everybody."

"Oh." I lay the card back down. "Well, that was thoughtful."

A hubbub sounded at the doorway as Jingles led in Juniper, Dolly, and Claire.

"Gracious gumdrops!" Juniper said, her eyes bright. "This table is gorgeous!"

"All credit goes to Pamela and Jingles," I said.

As if I'd conjured her just by speaking her name, Pamela appeared in the doorway, regal in her best silk royal blue dress, complete with a gold circlet in her hair.

"How nice! People are arriving on time."

I couldn't take my eyes off her. Her decision not to wear her old wedding dress today came as a relief, but it puzzled me, too. "You look beautiful, Pamela," I said.

She cleared her throat. "Thank you. I decided the other dress was better saved for some other time. My blue seemed more suitable to the occasion—and to my position as hostess."

The feeling in her voice made me understand how hard it had been for her to put that dress, and her memories, away. But I shouldn't have been surprised. Pamela Claus always rose to the occasion.

Christopher, who was still distributing his cards, huffed in frustration. "What happened? I thought I was sitting next to you, Grandma."

She frowned. "I did, too. What happened to your place card?"

Dolly had begun to circle the table looking for hers, too.

I had them both in my hand. Jingles looked over at me. *Get out of this one,* the look in his eye said.

I slipped the place cards into my pocket.

"I'll just sit here anyway, Grandma," Christopher said, dropping into the chair.

Pamela looked over at Dolly. "Dolly, you're supposed to be next to April."

At that moment, Dolly's eyes met mine and I could swear she knew what I'd been up to. Or maybe it was only my guilty conscience speaking.

"Where's Jake?" I asked.

"I told him it's bad luck to see the bride before the ceremony," Claire said.

Pamela looked startled. "But how are we going to take wedding pictures? I thought we could do a few official portraits before the ceremony."

"We could start a new tradition," Juniper said. "It's only unlucky two hours before the wedding ceremony or earlier."

I was smiling at that when my phone vibrated in my pocket. I dug for it, hoping for a texted heart or sweet message from Nick. All of the other people I regularly texted with were present in the room. I flipped open the cover and looked down. I frowned.

The message was written in all caps, so at first I wasn't sure if it was spam or an emergency. It was definitely the latter.

HELP! IVY IS IN THE SANTALAND INFIRMARY. ELFICIDE SUSPECTED. I THINK SHE'S DYING. PLEASE COME. —FLOCK

I must have let out a gasp. When I looked up, everybody was staring at me.

"Who's your message from?" Juniper asked.

"Flock."

Pamela let out a moan of dread. "It's the bouquets, isn't it? I *knew* we should have had those picked up yesterday."

Lucia sloped into the breakfast room, followed by Quasar. The two of them wore matching white mufflers with red hearts knitted into the pattern. "What's the matter?" Lucia asked.

"The message from Flock isn't about flowers," I said. "It's about Ivy. Flock says Ivy's in the Infirmary. It sounds like someone tried to kill her."

"How?" Claire asked.

"I don't know. I'll have to go see for myself."

Pamela's braying followed me as I headed for the door. "You can't go to town now! We've got a whole morning and afternoon planned. The wedding!"

As if I could possibly have forgotten the wedding.

I glanced at Claire, apologizing to her with a look. "Don't worry. I'll be back in plenty of time."

While I ran to grab my things, I called and asked Salty to bring a sleigh around to the portico. "Any sleigh with some fast reindeer," I said.

It was just a hunch, but this already had all the earmarks of a day that might call for flying.

When I went outside to catch my ride, I found my sleigh waiting for me with Cannonball and Wobbler in double harness. The sight of the two of them stopped me in my tracks.

"I assumed you two would be off to the Muzzle Nuzzle."

They both kept their heads up and exchanged a glance that was notable for its lack of animosity. "We've decided to skip it," Cannonball said.

Looking into their faces, I noted that the various bruises and cuts they'd given each other were starting to heal. It appeared that the rift between them had settled down, too.

I hesitated to bring up the name in case it was a sore spot with them, but my curiosity was too strong. "What about Flouncy?"

"We took the quiz you gave us," Wobbler explained. "Turns out Flouncy wasn't a good fit for either of us. Flouncy and I only scored at the 'Bag of Hay' level."

In my reindeer-centric version of the "What's Your Sweetie Level?" quiz, I'd adapted the scoring levels to reflect reindeer treat preferences.

"Me too," Cannonball said. "But then Salty noticed that both of our responses were very compatible with each other."

Wobbler nodded. "Together, we're the 'Full Pan of Lichen Brownies.'"

"That's great," I said.

"Besides," Cannonball added, "Flouncy decided to go to the Muzzle Nuzzle with a reindeer named Swifty."

Wobbler muttered, "When it comes to love, some reindeer have no sense at all."

I was happy to have my guys back, and getting along.

"I need to get to the Santaland Infirmary," I told them. "Pronto."

"Hop in!" Cannonball said.

I did, and picked up the reins. Wobbler, especially, appreciated formality in a sleigh driver, so I took a deep breath and called out, "On, Wobbler! On, Cannonball!"

The reindeer lunged forward and took off at a smooth double-time trot. In spite of my worry over what I might find at the Infirmary, it was exhilarating to have the team back together.

We made fast time into Christmastown. At the Santaland Infirmary, I jumped out and ran inside. Smudge was still in his room, but he was asleep, so I just waved at the Candymints and headed out to ask Nurse Cinnamon which room was Ivy's.

Before I reached the nurse's desk, Flock poked his head out of a room and flagged me down. I hurried over.

To my surprise, Happy Greenberry stood next to the bed, his hands in his tunic pockets.

Farther back, in the corner, stood Madame Neige, white-faced and still. I knew why she was here, of course, but it was still a little jarring to see her. She was rarely spotted outside her dominion.

How had she known to come here? She read the question in my eyes. "Dr. Honeytree summoned me," she explained.

Doc, who had been at the birth of nearly every elf in Santaland for the past fifty years. He would have witnessed Ivy's birth, too.

"I heard about it at the Municipal Hall," Happy said, since we were sharing. "I'd just set out my lavender truffles when I heard someone mention that Ivy had been taken by ambulance sleigh to the Infirmary. Contest or no contest, I dropped everything and rushed over."

He looked down at the figure on the bed, his eyes filling.

Ivy was lying in the bed beneath a downy quilt. For a moment I worried she was dead, but then I detected the faintest rise and fall of her chest. Her face surprised me—it was mottled with red, and a thin, angry welt angrily circled her neck. It made it look like she'd been strangled with something.

"It wasn't thallium?" I asked.

Everyone seemed surprised by the question. "Why would you ask that?" Happy asked.

"I'd just assumed she was poisoned—that this was the same modus operandi as Sterling's murder, and the attempt on Smudge."

Flock shook his head. "I found her when I arrived at the shop. It looked like suicide. She even left a note."

A second suicide, on the same night as Snowbell's? I hesitated to ask this while Ivy's mother was standing right there, but I had to know. "What makes you think that she attempted to kill herself?"

"Suffocation. She was lying on the floor when I found her. I couldn't believe it! For one thing, I thought she was still at the constabulary."

I cut a glance over at Madame Neige. She'd sent Puddin' Bayberry to get Ivy out of custody. Ivy would have been better off staying put. The anguish on her face told me she regretted her decision.

"And why would she lie on the ground?" Flock wondered. "But there she was next to a fiddle leaf fig. There was a plastic bag over her head and secured around her neck with green florist wire."

That would account for the red welt.

"Tell Mrs. Claus about the note," Happy told Flock.

He picked the paper off a table and handed it to me. *Fingerprints,* I thought, inwardly shaking my head. If this paper ended up being the clue in a murder case, we were contaminating the evidence. Still, I was too curious not to take it and read it.

The words were printed childishly in blue ink. *I can't go on after what I've done. I'm sorry.*

I hated to say it, but that seemed fairly straightforward to me. Ivy committed the murders and felt so much guilt—or perhaps just felt such unhappiness at being known as Poison Ivy—that she didn't want to keep living.

Straightforward, and yet all my nerves were jangling. If Ivy had killed Sterling and tried to kill Smudge, why would Snowbell have thrown herself off the cupola? Could Snowbell have been having an affair with Sterling and killed herself because of unrequited love? I guess that was somewhat plausible . . .

Or maybe Snowbell's death had nothing to do with any of this.

Ivy's killing Sterling would be the quickest distance between two points. Except that she had no real motive, did she? Ivy had said it herself. She'd moved on.

"That note's not right," Flock declared, shaking his head. "The longer I think about it, the more wrong it seems."

"You don't believe Ivy could be a killer?"

"Oh, I can imagine her killing someone," he said. "I've seen her in a rage. But I *really* can't imagine her apologizing."

"Me neither," Happy chimed in.

"I've been her partner for nearly half a decade," Flock continued. "I've seen her blow up lots of times—at me, at customers, at elves who drop litter on the sidewalk. But those outbursts were never followed by an apology." He thrust his hand out toward the note. "And now her last words—the ones she wanted to leave for posterity—are 'I'm sorry'?" He thumped the paper with his hand. "Well, *I'm* sorry, but that just not the Ivy I knew."

Madame Neige remained a hovering presence in the back corner. She resembled a sharp old crow. It couldn't have been easy to stand by in silence as elves berate your secret daughter for being an unapologetic hothead, especially when she appeared to barely be hanging onto life.

"I'm also not sure about that writing," Flock said.

Happy leaned in to examine the note. "At the Home for Orphaned Elves, we were all taught to write in very tidy cursive."

"She would've had to write it with her left hand, and why would anyone bother doing that?"

I scanned the note again, frowning. When it finally dawned what was bothering me, I felt a fool. I hated to contradict the others—or at least two of them. I was pretty sure that Madame Neige would have noticed the same detail I did. "That ink is the same color as the ink in the poison-pen note that was delivered to the Order a few days ago," I said. "The one with the poem."

Surprise, Surprise. So maybe despite all her protests Ivy *did* write it.

I hazarded a glance at Madame Neige, but she seemed to be focused inwardly. Was she sifting through her memory for signposts she might have missed that Ivy was seriously disturbed and capable of murder? Not that she would have been present in her life frequently enough to witness those signposts.

Or was she blaming herself for giving up her baby and depriving Ivy of a mother's love?

Madame Neige didn't strike me as a squishy maternal type, though. Even now she was so worried about keeping the secret of Ivy's birth from the public that she couldn't make herself approach what might be her daughter's deathbed.

Step forward and claim her, I wanted to yell at her. Ivy was so like her! How could she have spent years giving her to an institution to raise, and then shoving money through her door, and acting like a business colleague instead of a real mother?

Doc Honeytree came in, along with his nephew. Algid nodded to us all, but seemed surprised to see me there. "I thought the castle's hosting a big wedding today."

"We are." The others were probably finishing their breakfast now. Maybe Sparkle had arrived and was setting herself up to fix everyone's hair. "The ceremony's not till the afternoon."

Nick would be officiating at the wedding, and he was downtown right now, too, at Municipal Hall. I wanted to tell Happy that *he* should be at the Tournament of Chocolate finals, but chocolate seemed insignificant next to what had happened to Ivy.

Doc directed Algid to look at the back of Ivy's head.

"Oh my," Algid said, peering at Ivy's skull through his thick glasses.

"What is it?" I asked.

Algid turned Ivy's head so that it was resting at a more natural angle on the pillow, then looked at all of us. "This was not suicide."

"I knew it!" Happy said.

"How can you tell?" I asked.

"There's blunt-force trauma to the skull," Algid said. "And it doesn't seem consistent with a fall."

"She's bound to have a concussion," Doc said, "and for a little while, at least, she would have been completely unconscious."

"And in that little while, whoever it was who wanted to kill Ivy put the bag over her head and tied it tightly with wire around her neck," Algid explained. "By the time Ivy started to come to, she would have been running out of oxygen and passed out again."

"That's terrible," I said.

"That's murder—or attempted murder."

I looked at Flock, wondering. Would he have a motive for killing Ivy? Her reputation as Poison Ivy was hurting their business now. On the other hand, the monthly deliveries of cash from Madame Neige had probably kept their bills paid. That would certainly dry up if Ivy died.

That was an important *if*. I turned to the doctor. "What are the chances that Ivy will pull out of this?"

"The injury looks bad," he said gravely. "Very bad."

My heart sank.

Happy let out a sob. "Poor Ivy!"

"Now, now." Doc shook his head. "There are few certainties in medicine, Mr. Greenberry. Ivy was oxygen deprived, so we'll need to watch her. And we need to make sure there's no bleeding beneath her skull. But if we give her oxygen and rest and treat her concussion carefully, I don't know why we shouldn't expect a full recovery."

"That's excellent news." I looked over to Madame Neige to see how this optimistic prognosis had struck her, but the back corner where she'd been standing was now empty.

I glanced at Flock, then Happy. "What happened to Madame Neige?"

"She left while the doctor was talking," Happy said. "Face like a thundercloud, fists at her sides. Really angry." He frowned. "I don't know why she was here to begin with."

It seemed surprising that Madame Neige decided to leave. If she was furious, would she be furious *at* someone? Did she know who did this? Maybe there was something in that note that had jangled some bells for her.

"Did she leave before Doc explained that Ivy will probably live?"

Flock cast his mind back. "Actually, I think she left after Doc said the injury looked bad."

This was not good. I reached for my hat and smashed it on my head. Then I grabbed Happy Greenberry's arm. "You're coming with me," I said.

He gulped, looking as if he might dig in his heels. "Why? Where are you going?"

"The Order of Elven Seamstresses," I said. "But *you're* going to go win yourself a trophy."

Chapter 22

Happy was astonished at how fast I'd whisked him out of the hospital and over to the Municipal Hall.

"This doesn't feel right," he lamented. "I'm so worried about Ivy."

"Fine—worry about her while you're winning the Tournament of Chocolate."

"I might not," he said.

"I think you will." I knew my husband's tastebuds. Lavender white chocolate was right up his alley. "Anyway, Flock is with Ivy and I've given him instructions to keep us updated."

The elf still hesitated to get off the sleigh. "Do you think Flock is in love with Ivy?"

"No. He's in love with having a business to run." I gave him a nudge. "Go—or you're going to miss the judging."

Finally, he hopped down. My arms tensed with the reins again, ready to drive the team up the first rise of the mountain to the Order of Elven Seamstresses. "Can you do me a favor?"

He turned, eager to oblige. "Of course."

"Tell Nick where I'm going. Also tell him that I think Madame Neige has it all figured out."

He repeated the instructions aloud.

"Now go—and good luck!" I called out.

"Good luck to you, too, Mrs. Claus."

I hoped I wouldn't need it.

I had such a fire lit under me to catch up to Madame Neige before she could seek vengeance for a child she mistakenly thought was going to die, that I forgot that the rest of the world wouldn't feel the same urgency.

We caught a little wedding traffic poking their way up the snowpath. It was so frustrating. The wedding itself didn't begin for hours yet.

Luckily, the reindeer knew what to do. I hate to fly, but sometimes you just have to. Who doesn't want to leapfrog their way out of a traffic jam?

Button was back at her post at the Order's door, which was a little surprising to me. She'd been at the hospital late last night, and from the sad, drawn expression on her pale face, I doubt she'd slept much. More likely she'd probably spent most of the night crying and thinking about her friend.

Nevertheless, she'd been trained well. She wasn't about to let me through without an appointment.

"Did Madame Neige just come back from town?" I asked.

"Yes, ma'am."

"I really need to talk to her—it's urgent." When Button still didn't appear inclined to let me through, I added, "I just saw Madame Neige at the hospital. I'm sure she'll see me."

"Was she there about Snowbell?"

I shook my head. I wasn't at liberty to reveal any of Madame Neige's secrets. Her relationship with Ivy was their business alone.

"Please," I said. "This could be a matter of life and death. Just show me to her office."

"She's not in her office," Button said. "She went down to Hades."

I drew back. "What's she doing down there?" Madame Neige seemed like the type of elf who would send others down to that steam bath.

"I guess she needed to talk to Blanchette about something."

"Blanchette is in Hades?"

"Actually, we're supposed to call it the pressing room." She bit her lip. "Snowbell was good with the press, and she and Blanchette were supposed give the wedding clothes a final press today and go to the castle to help you all around one o'clock." She sniffed and brought out a handkerchief. "Snowbell was really looking forward to that."

"I'm sorry, Button. I really am. I just want to prevent another tragedy from occurring here today." When she still hesitated I blurted out, "And for what it's worth, I don't think Snowbell jumped from that cupola. I think she was pushed."

Her mouth dropped open. I could tell she wanted to ask me more, but I think she also—finally—understood my urgency. She stepped aside.

"Thanks. I know the way."

I ran for the door and barreled down the steps, steeling myself against the furnace blast of heat as I descended. I wasn't prepared for what I saw when I stepped onto the basement landing and turned toward the press room, however.

I had expected a confrontation. I had even braced myself for violence. I never imagined that Madame Neige would apparently sneak up on Blanchette unawares with an iron coal shovel, clunk her on the head, and tie her hands to the handle of the giant press.

When I arrived, Blanchette was stuck to the high handle, practically balancing on her tippy-toes. It looked incredibly uncomfortable—like something out of the Spanish Inquisition—especially with Madame Neige menacing her with that coal shovel. But the worst part of her ordeal had to be the heat. Steam hissed and billowed out of the machine, and at some point Blanchette's right cheek had already collided with the red-hot metal. An angry burn blazed across her cheek.

That press, if closed, was big enough to squish a whole person. Blanchette was just one strong whack with the coal shovel and a pull of that lever from being a Blanchette panini.

And I couldn't help noticing what Blanchette had been working on when Madame Neige had found her. A white dress with ruffles lay across the press's hot surface, cooking.

Blanchette whimpered pathetically when she saw me.

"Madame Neige—stop!" I said. "You're making a terrible mistake."

"It's not a mistake that Blanchette has waged a campaign of terror this week to frame Ivy." In her anger or her distraction, Madame Neige's French accent had almost entirely disappeared. "All of the flowers coming with the Flock and Ivy mark. It didn't make sense to me at first. Even if Ivy *wanted* to kill someone, she wouldn't be so stupid as to do that. And she would never have written that terrible poem.

"I began to suspect that the culprit was someone in our own population of seamstress elves. Here we make the flowers—and as Ivy said, anyone could get their hands on a florist box. Flock and Ivy is one of the only florists in town. It wasn't until I saw that suicide note this morning with that poorly written address in the deep blue ink that I finally understood."

I shook my head. "So Sterling died, and Smudge almost died, just to frame Ivy?"

Blanchette was weeping now. "I was always loyal to you," she said, tears spilling down her ruined cheek. "I came here as a teenager. You said I was like your daughter." She sobbed. "You told me that I would have the business—but then you changed it. What did I do?"

"Nothing." Madame Neige brandished the shovel just below Blanchette's jawline. "I loved you *like* a daughter, but Ivy *is* my daughter. And I realized the little I give her each month was not enough to assuage my conscience for giving her up." Madame Neige inhaled a ragged breath. "Now all that's left is for me to avenge her death with yours."

She gripped the shovel handle with two hands and twisted from the waist, like Babe Ruth preparing to knock one out of the park.

"No!" I hurled myself across the room to wrest the coal shovel from the old elf's hands. "You don't have to avenge Ivy's death, Madame Neige. Ivy's still alive. You left the Infirmary before Doc Honeytree told us that if she responds well to treatment, Ivy will make a full recovery."

Maybe that was an optimistic spin on what Doc had actually said, but I wanted to get Madame Neige's attention and to reach her conscience.

It worked. She stopped midswing.

But there was one thing I wanted to know, and I wanted to hear it from Blanchette's lips, before she had time to fabricate a lie. "Did Snowbell really jump?"

Hate blazed from her eyes. "Why should I tell you?"

"Because I just saved your life!"

"Saved it for what? Exile in a freezing wilderness?"

"Yes," I said. "Would you have preferred the alternative?"

She glanced at the press, perhaps imagining what could have happened if I hadn't interceded. When she spoke again, her voice was ragged with defeat. "Snowbell saw me switch the corsages in the foyer. I thought I could keep her quiet with threats. But when Smudge drank the poison, she warned me that she was going to call the authorities."

And that, I assumed, was the end.

Then a banshee wail shrieked behind me. Button flew into the room, grabbed the shovel handle, and took a swing at Blanchette. She hit the press instead, creating a terrible *clang* that echoed throughout the basement. She tossed the shovel aside and jumped on Blanchette. The upper joint of the press started to descend.

I piled onto Button's back, trying to peel her off Blanchette.

The trouble was, in the tangle of arms and legs, I was in danger, too. A few times my arm felt a shock of heat. And a sizzling sound followed by a sickly smell confused me until I saw my own hair trapped in the mechanism.

Unfortunately, Blanchette seemed to have a little life in her yet, and in a horrifying moment, her elbow jutted out, then cracked me in the jaw. I spun around, losing my balance, and headed straight for the press's hot flat-iron surface.

Mrs. Claus panini, I thought with dread.

And then, suddenly, I was being lifted. Nick had me by the back of my coat and pulled me free of the press just in time.

Relieved, I threw my arms around him. The words that came out were not the ones in my heart.

"She killed Sterling!" I yelled, as if there was any chance of Blanchette fleeing and escaping justice. "And Snowbell."

She lay in a heap on the ground, moaning in pain from her various bruises and burns—and the prospect of a lifetime of punishment in the terrifying, frozen north.

Constable Crinkles stepped into the fray, helping Button and Madame Neige off the ground. The two elves clung together, glaring at Blanchette. For a moment I worried that the violence might start up all over again, but in the blink of an eye, Madame Neige turned her back on the elf she'd trained up to be almost a second daughter.

"You are a good elf, Button," she said, dusting off Button's tunic. "Wasted on the door, I think. I will need a good hand in the coming weeks. Report to my office tomorrow."

"I beg your pardon, Madame," Button said.

For a moment, Madame Neige stiffened. She wasn't used to being contradicted.

"What about today?" Button nodded toward the press, where Claire's wedding dress was still cooking.

Madame Neige took in the broiled gown and nodded in understanding, and appreciation. "I leave the wedding in your hands to solve as you wish." She straightened proudly, as if she hadn't just tortured one of their own. "I have more important business today."

A flash of panic showed in Button's eyes then. A wedding to prepare clothes for all on her own, and the custom wedding dress crisped up like breakfast bacon? It was a lot to take on. "Where will you be, Madame?"

"At the hospital with Ivy." Her shoulders straightened. "My daughter."

Chapter 23

"I have good news and bad news," I announced when I was finally able to join the wedding party. Pamela had set us up in a spare room down the hall from Nick's and my bedroom on the second floor, so I'd had to thread my way through a castle crammed with elves and people in wedding finery. Needless to say, after my time in Hades, I wasn't looking my best.

As we'd left the Order of Elven Seamstresses, Nick had assured me that I'd clean up fine, but from the way Pamela, Claire, Juniper, Dolly, and Sparkle the hairdresser all gawped at me in horror, I understood that he was just being tactful.

"What happened to you?" Juniper exclaimed.

Lucia strode in to the room, curious. "Is that you, April? When I saw you from afar, I thought Imelda the ice witch had been invited to the party."

I sent her a withering stare.

In her pink Three French Hens smock, Sparkle approached me, looking mournfully at my hair. "What happened?"

"I got a little singed."

"It looks like you've been through a brawl," Pamela said. "In a volcano."

I told them everything that had happened since I'd left them at breakfast. For most of the story, the group was slack-jawed with surprise. The reason for the murders, the heartlessness of Blanchette, the family secrets . . . There would be no shortage of things for the guests at this wedding to talk about.

"You're lucky you didn't get hurt!" Dolly said.

Juniper shot her a sharp look. "What are you talking about? Look at her face. She got hit and burned."

"I mean like *really* hurt," Dolly said. "As in dead."

"I do feel lucky," I confessed. I would never forget the relief I felt when Nick had plucked me away from the hot press.

Pamela shook her head. "I'm glad so many of these problems got cleared up this morning," she said, "but I would have thought you'd be a teensy bit more careful, April, knowing how much preparation has gone into today. You're going to look peculiar."

"I'm not the only one, unfortunately." I eyed Claire. "Should I start with the bad news?"

Behind me, Button strode in, carrying Claire's crispy wedding dress. It was unrecognizable except for a few brown ruffles still clinging to it on the bias.

Her jaw dropped, and she ran up to it. When she touched the material, it was so brittle it made ripping sound. "What am I going to do?"

"That's the good news. Madame Neige sent over several ready-to-wear samples in your size."

Pamela sucked in a breath. "They won't even be necessary. Why wear ready-made when you can have an heirloom?"

Claire blinked at her until realization dawned. "Do you mean *your* wedding dress?"

"It's all ready to go," Pamela said. "Fit for a princess."

"You two aren't quite the same size," Lucia remarked.

Button stepped forward. "I'm a whiz at last-minute alterations."

"It would make me so happy to see it on another bride," Pamela insisted.

And it did make Pamela happy. When Claire appeared in the dress and twirled once to get used to the big skirts and train, my mother-in-law sighed happily. "My dear, you look almost as radiant as Lady Di—or me."

Despite the change in Claire's gown, the bridesmaids' dresses still looked perfect—Blanchette had already finished pressing those before Madame Neige had descended on her. Juniper and Dolly looked beautiful, and Dolly even found it easier to stomach being in proximity to me now that I was battle scarred. She seemed to look at my bruised jaw and singed hair as just retribution for having falsely accused her.

Sparkle remained in despair over my hair. "Maybe we should just cut it short," she suggested.

I was willing, but again Pamela, in her best blue silk, was able to come to the rescue. "Nonsense—I can fix her up in a jiffy."

Within seconds, she had my hair wound into a perfect ballet bun. She even gave me her circlet to wear. I hazarded a glance in the mirror and was shocked by my transformation. After Sparkle sprayed my bangs out of the way and did some serious work with pins, I looked like a real Mrs. Claus. I stood up straighter.

The sound of seven harps warming up floated up from below. Pamela had been correct. It *was* an unforgettable sound.

Claire held her stomach with one hand, then outstretched her other arm and snapped her fingers. Dolly produced a Snappy's slushy. "Keep them coming," she instructed us.

Lucia, who had changed into what passed for wedding finery—clean pants—ducked her head in. "It's showtime."

"I can't believe this is it!" Claire hugged me. "I hope Jake and I will be as happy as you and Nick are."

"Me too," I said, tearing up.

"Aw, that's so sweet," Dolly said.

"And mostly," Claire continued, "I hope I can make it through the ceremony and the dinner without having to do a hundred-yard dash to the washroom."

After the last toasts were made, and the caterers were Hoovering up the mess created by a day-long house party, and Jake and Claire had flown off to honeymoon in a cabin on Angel Lake, Nick and I escorted Juniper into Christmastown to visit Smudge at the infirmary.

The patient was doing better, and was able to enjoy the big slab of wedding cake we brought him.

"I'm sorry I missed Claire and Jake's big day." He peered curiously at my face. "What happened to you?"

"So much." On the way in, I'd looked in on Madame Neige, who was keeping a vigil at Ivy's bedside, along with Happy Greenberry. A large winner's trophy filled with flowers sat next to the water pitcher on Ivy's side table. Happy told me that Ivy was recovering well, and was just sleeping at the moment.

"I'm sorry I missed the excitement," Smudge said. "And the wedding."

"Claire looked so beautiful." Juniper sighed. "I *love* weddings."

"Maybe there will be another one soon," Smudge said.

Juniper smiled at him, and took his hand.

And with that, Nick and I retreated.

We'd driven in the large, second-best sleigh. For some reason Nick decided our trip required six reindeer tonight, including Cannonball and Wobbler. A huge tarp lay over some of the cargo area. I put my hands on my hips. "What *is* all this stuff?"

Nick smiled. "It's your Valentine's Day present."

I tilted my head. "You didn't need to buy me anything. You saved my life."

He shrugged wryly. "If I'd known I was going to be doing any lifesaving, I might have spared myself the trouble."

I laughed.

"Aren't you going to look?" he asked, his voice impatient.

Cautiously, I pulled the tarp back a bit. My largest suitcase was there, tied down with bungee cord. "What the—?"

"Jingles helped me decide what to pack. I thought we could do something spontaneous tonight, like fly to Paris. I've been studying the most scenic routes all week."

So that was what he'd been up to with those maps. I'd assumed the work he'd been buried in pertained to his annual Christmas delivery route.

"Or if you'd rather go to Vienna, Rome, or Tahiti . . ." He smiled at me. "The world is yours."

Tears sprang to my eyes. How long had he been plotting and planning this surprise for me? And I had been worrying that the romance was gone.

He gave me a hand up into the passenger side of the sleigh, and followed that with a lingering kiss. "So where will it be?" he asked me.

I gave it a moment's thought.

"Let's start with Paris," I said, "and figure it out from there."

Santa's sleigh travel. It wasn't just for Christmas anymore.

I leaned back as Nick hopped in next to me. Being Nick, he stopped to put a warm lap robe over me before we started, and carefully tucked me in. He was practical like that, even when he was being spontaneous and impractical.

And I wouldn't have it any other way.